Saratoga, Hot

Hortense Calisher

SARATOGA, HOT

Doubleday & Company, Inc.
Garden City, New York
1985

Library of Congress Cataloging in Publication Data
Calisher, Hortense.
Saratoga, hot.
I. Title.
PS3553.A4S87   1985   813'.54
ISBN: 385-19975-9
Library of Congress Card Number 84-24695

Contents

Some short works are close to the novel in spirit. They seem to try for more than the short moments of a life. They try for the life.

Saratoga, Hot

Gargantua

T HAT WAS ITS NAME, Gargantua, the mammoth sea lion or gorilla whose long bellow could be heard from time to time over the morning and evening rooftops of haphazard, beaten-down but sporty old Eighth Avenue, through the window of the hospital room where my mother was slowly recovering from the operation which hadn't killed her, the pleurisy which almost had, and the low blood count for which she was required to eat slice after slice of liver daily—that being almost all they could prescribe for anemia back in those days. Not long ago, only last spring, happening to be down in that neighborhood, what did I find myself walking past but the old Polyclinic Hospital, still wedged in all the clangor and gas of downtown, grimier than ever of façade, but still, in spite of all the new high-rise riverbank hospitals like this one, a going concern. And down there too, not far, was a Madison Square Garden with its spring circus. There they were, the two arenas, one old, one a new version but still together, a sign perhaps that there's more continuity to New York—and perhaps, in the world—than the antiquarians give it credit for.

Anyway, I heard the beast well enough myself, the first

time on one of my daily visits to her in my suddenly
changed and changing character—from December's birthday girl, spotty, harebrained and sixteen, to January's high
school graduate, to March's idler-at-home waiting around
for college in the fall, sloppy enough in mind and emotion
and gear, but nevertheless, whether pushed to it from
within or without, also the newly dutiful daughter to be
expected by death-brushed mother and, for the moment,
headless household. I was right there to hear it, that long,
dark brown sound, just as I was giving her my daily marketing report, my knees hunched together under the
jumperskirt and blouse smartened in vain toward what she
hoped from me and had never yet got of me, scruffy article
that I was, for all one so new to the shop, but still—shag-
haired daughter-of-the-house. It was true that she had to
draw my attention to the sound, even in that quieter era of
untrafficked streets, but though at that time the general
cacophony was more likely to be mostly mine, in those
days I was quite able to tell a real sound from the others.
Later on, as more of her visitors heard it, it became my
mother's main run-on joke, brought out in the spritely way
sick people often adopt in hospital, to whip up the flagging
spirits at their own soirees. And still later on, just at the end
of her stay, she even reported that she had caught a glimpse
of the beast, even describing it in her own way, with a
certain lovely frivolity that I was unable to understand at
the time, and never gave her proper credit for. She never
said precisely what the creature was, even though it's quite
possible that, with this same earthbound frivolity so common to our sex, she knew.

But just now, just *then,* she said, "There! There, didn't I tell
you! Noon must be its feeding time, for then it always—.
But this is the first time you got here by noon."

I held my breath, with the precautionary habit of almost
a lifetime—which worked pretty well when I could remem-

ber it: if I could only remember that to argue an offensive truth was to enlarge both the truth and the offense. It was true that I slept forever in the mornings. The shopping account was yesterday's; today's—for tomorrow's agenda— was still to be done.

Lying back on the pillow to which she was kept—for they rarely let them up for weeks after an illness, in those days—her profile, so worn, so hatedly beautiful, carried with it a smile, not of pleasure, more of satisfaction, and as her chestnut braids slipped back into sculpture, she had the look of a mother superior in her long, single sarcophagus, at the very moment the rending noise of resurrection is heard. "Listen! There, didn't I say?"

Now that I listened, I heard it, of course, yet could still figure why it had gone by me unnoticed, for it was very like one of those long, biblical noises the city emits now and then from its boats or its funnels—or from the bellows of that central furnace which must exist in such a city, but can never be found.

"What is it?" I said.

"Gargantua." She said it gaily.

"But what *is* it. What kind of animal."

"Some say an enormous ape, others a sea lion, bigger than ever found before. But nobody around here's actually been over there." She shook her head over me. "The posters must be up all over the place—and you were always so crazy about the circus. How do you ever get about in the world—!"

The sound came again. It was almost like the roaring nausea of the seals in the park, magnified many times over; yet it could be that timbre I had read about, which the great apes of the forest were said to drum from their own chests —it could have been either.

"Gahd!" I said. "Gah-hd!" This was a leftover and forbidden habit from high school, one that I myself was bored with and looked forward to college to rid me of—which it did, giving me the expletive "lousy!" instead.

"Must you?" My mother was looking at me in the only way she ever seemed to, at two spots just above my temples, where all this future of mine could apparently be seen, already horning on the head. "The word is 'God.' " She hit it neatly somewhere between "Gawd" and "Gud."

Just then a nurse came in, carrying a tray in that high-breasted smart-ankled way the young ones do. "Fe-eeding time!" she sang out, and in answer my mother—whom I had never heard do so—giggled. (It's a peculiar thrall, isn't it, the one that comes over us women in hospital? Slap the buttocks-oh, and a high-born lady becomes a baby or any of several other things she's been hiding; the little grand-mother from Seal Harbor shakes out a leg or a laugh like a chorus girl's.)

"*She* heard it, Miss Stokirk!" said my mother. "But I think you're too late for it again."

"Ah, it knows better than to make a fuss on *my* shift." She set down the tray without a real look at me. "You'll help her with this, eh."

"It's just like a child," said my mother. "Never will perform when you want it to. Like *you*. My daughter, Miss Stokirk."

I bent my eyes submissively under the only-child's burden—its own legend. Every year of my life, and most of the parts of my body, decent or not, hung by some tale always ready either for me or the general assembly; if I had good teeth, for instance, it was because I'd been kept nine months at the breast—during every one of which, with only my hard little gums to do it with, I'd bit my mother daily.

But the virtue of nurses is that they have no time. And they never really look at the family. If Miss Stokirk had, she might well have given me the look I was so used to when under the mother-wing—how come such a gentle

dame of the silk and the fleur-de-lis had been fobbed off
with such coarse merino? She would have seen large eyes
like the mother's green ones, but of a brown that sunk
them to woebegone, the same high bridge to the nose, but
ending in a pudged square—if either of these, plus the in-
consequential rest, could be seen under that bag of hair
wound incompetently straight across the forehead and
round again, all its seams frayed. The hair, waist length
when down, was being saved for the day it might ripple its
Venus-waves boyward, over a bathing suit—though we
were a mountain-summering family and spent perhaps one
day a year at the beach. Or, scarcely acknowledged to itself
in the midnight mirror, it was in waiting for the way it
might look to somebody at night.

But my mother and I were left to look at the tray together, on it a ring of foods in the yellow-white hospital
spectrum, at their center a plate with two plumped-up
slices of liver. In the small, single hospital room with the
silence sifting by on rubber-shod feet in the corridor, there
was an unwonted peace, and between my mother and me,
while I helped her with her custards-and-mashed and other
messes, an uneasy communion. Spring was at the window,
a great brawling poster, the sunlight thin in the air but
shining black on the low, tarred roofs that stretched toward
the Garden and past it to some larger circus beyond. As I
humped over, cutting up the liver which she always left to
the last like a penance—"I can't eat the other stuff after"—I
felt my flesh stretching finally away from the child-ease of
never being looked at square. I wanted her to look at me
square, not to tell me who I was—for with the strength of a
ninth wave I thought I knew that—but to see me both for
what I was and what I wasn't yet: a ragged creature but
ready to be magnificent, the universe ready to grow right
out of my stomach, just as I had grown out of hers. But that
was the simpler part of it. Love has its variations, ninety-

nine times more than the Hindu. I thought I hated her, yet I wanted her to tell me how to be just like her.

"Have the pan hot but salted," she said. "So it won't stick. Sizzle the slice on one side then the other, just enough to turn it gray, the inside just not raw. Flame off, soon as the blood juice comes. That's the way I have to have it. Remember now; you may have to cook it for me." Every day she said this, and every day I nodded, the wads on my temples shifting like pot-holders, and watched that narrow, silken coif of hers, its perfect madonna parting. As the crown of her head bent daintily over its preoccupation, it was still years away from a crone's, and I, lumped over mine, was years away from that crown—if either of us glimpsed a generative resemblance-to-come in all of our various selves there, it wasn't I.

But neighbor, what of Gargantua? Listen.

The trouble between us then was that in our three-pronged household my mother was the thing: with my father forever at his necessary disappearing act out to all the business coasts, she was as much the core and blood juice of our lives as that piece of liver on her plate was temporarily hers. My father was a strong enough man both to want it and to keep it that way; she and he each came from long-range families—the kind that could pack a living room with four generations, across whose rippling decades it could be seen that the mothers were always like her, and the fathers —no matter how kindly they warmed down from their self-assured altitude—all like him. Meanwhile, in the daily sphere that was all hers it seemed to me that short of the deaths and illnesses which belonged to Gud, my mother could make almost anything happen, and often did. What of my seventh year, during those two brief months when a prematurely born brother couldn't be saved from dying, when she had turned me into "Sister" without a qualm?—

even inside my own skin it hadn't felt the same. In a time
of disaster she usually decreed something. Right now—
though my father might deny it to the brink of apoplexy—
we were poor. The maid of years' standing had been dis-
missed, or nearly—shanghaied to one of our sisters-in-law.
A fellow had been engaged to slop mops about, more in
accordance with our new station. Against the idea of Easter
outfits for anyone, only the weather now frilling the parks
was not severe. At home, from which, now that she was
improving, my father had dared a trip away, the air, already
blighted by the lack of her chestnut-green presence, slowly
tarnished with the tea things, under the dark rain of pov-
erty insensibly falling. All that domestic network of
butcher, vintner and other special suppliers—in whose
center our ménage normally sat like a fat gourmet spider—
had been stopped. For the first time a member of the family
shopped at the A & P. For this purpose I had been supplied
with an extraordinary contraption, a nest of five hard-
clasped black leather change-purses, each two cells of
which shared a common heart wall. We were poor. It had
been decreed. And I was now the daughter of this house.

"Want to try a little?" My mother's voice was oddly seductive, almost as if she was offering me, as in the long ago,
a piece of herself. I took a bite; it tasted plain, primal, a
meat to be eaten without sauce. We watched each other
while I chewed. I couldn't know that my thickish mane,
roughened as it was and even dirty, had the naïve, brown
sheen to it that can never be duplicated by later pomades.
But I already knew what my new body was—not yet sliced
by the surgeon, or borne into by men, or soapworn by time.
I was beginning to carry it high and swinging, as if it were
something wonderful to have come by, and maybe it was,
and maybe my mother thought so too. Maybe she could
even smell it, not unwashed but strong with its oils of in-
between. In her room, I smelled only her, paper-delicate
with soap, weakness and mystery—all the dark perfumes

of strength tried. This was all the quarrel between us, but
maybe my mother herself did not know this. Her eyes were
the first to lower. I was staring so hard I wasn't even aware,
wondering whether or not she would help me in my battle
to be her, whether I could trust her to. Perhaps neither of us
knew.

We both spoke at the same moment.

"I ought to go."

"You better go now."

I stood up.

"And *do* something, will you," she said, "about that
hair."

I waited until I got to the door before I answered. "I can't
be you."

I managed to sound defiant. So perhaps she never knew
the truth.

"I don't want you to be that," she said, faint from her
pillow. She didn't look at me. "I don't want things to happen to you."

"*I* do!" I cried out, suddenly happy, all my cacophony
vibrating up to me, from the rooftops of all the seasons to
come.

She turned on her pillow. "Such *things,"* she said. *"Such*
things. Well . . . maybe we'll both get our wish."

I stood rooted there, straining to understand this. I
couldn't—or why I chose this moment to concede something. "Maybe I'll go to a beauty parlor," I said slowly. She
had never been able to get me to; I was afraid that between
them they would cut my hair. "I'll take a little money from
each of the purses," I said. "So it won't be noticed."

Her eyes crinkled over this, but she nodded. "And
take—" She stopped.

I waited for what I knew she was going to say. Take
somebody with you to tell the man what to do, since I can't
—and you certainly can't be trusted to. But I was alone on
my own now. I waited.

Her own smile must have been strange to her. I remember just how she struggled with it. Then she nodded. "Take care."

Outside the room, I heard her sigh aloud, the words obscured by a sudden cry from that unknown in the Garden. But I had already heard them. "Gahd!" was what she had said. "Gah-hd."

Back in our neighborhood, at the shopping, I myself did what was fairly strange. Until my father should return on the weekend, there was no one at home to provide for except me and the dog. I bought us both a pound of liver, sliced. And that night, along with a can of the stewed tomatoes which for months had been my current fancy, we shared it for dinner. I was no cook, but I had a recipe. Flame off, when the blood juice comes. While we ate, the dog sat at my feet, a mongrel blend both of himself and us; long of nose, eye and ear, he might have been a member of the family, on my father's side. But the day I had brought him home, a tiny pup who skidded toward *her* on the waxed floor, then piddled, deplored himself to her, and awaited his doom, it had been she who had knelt to take each of his front paws in two of her fingers and sing with him, as she had used to sing in handfast with me once: *"Es ist kein Fuchs; Es ist kein Haas; Donnerwetter, was ist Das!"*, then in her light English rendering: "It isn't a fox; it isn't a hare: for pity's sake, what *have* we here!"

The wild moments of serious people are the ones to watch, and women, once you get past the egret feathers of their brains, are most serious. While we chewed, the dog and I, I thought of that. She had decreed him, as she may have done me. I chewed on mindlessly, thinking of it. The next day I bought us only three quarters of a pound, but otherwise it was the same every evening. I had no idea why I was doing this. At my side, the dog ate share for share what I did, but without apparent imagery; he was only a dog.

Can you tell me what I was doing? You, maskface over there on the bed opposite mine?

(Ah, she's asleep, my semiprivate neighbor; perhaps I've sent her there with my talking. Fantastic what we will tell one another, under the peculiar thrall that comes over us in hospital. Asleep or not, where both death and life are, as here, one goes on talking. In my mother's day, privacy, if one could pay for it, was totally favored over such democracy; but one must remember that this left her alone with Gargantua.)

So, my semiprivate friend—whom I met only the day before yesterday when I "came in," as they say here—what was I doing, back there at my blood-suppers, what was I trying to be? Once, years later, I looked up the meaning of the word transubstantiation: "The change, by and at the consecration of the elements in the Eucharist, of the substance of the bread and wine into the body and blood"— but that's too awesome, that belongs to the Church. This was much simpler and nearer the jungle—a family matter.

For several mornings I told her nothing. My evenings had drugged me in more ways than one, and the days too; who doesn't remember that first period in life when one is left on one's own, that exploratory dream? I came late to the Polyclinic, gave my report in exchange for whatever recipe or reproof floated to her far gaze that morning, and listened or not to the interrupted, cautionary tale from the Garden. Then, on the day before my father was to return, as I sat looking out her window, at whose sill the fine weather was still holding as if foolishly trying to keep up with the eternal sameness of the hospital, I heard the words "salt . . . sizzle . . . flame" and, turning, said almost absently, "I know. I've done it. That's why there was so much meat on the market list. I've had it every single night."

"You *have?*" She half raised herself. A faint color of rose came to her cheek, and not from diet. She was a woman of reserve, as must now be clear—and I, though I didn't know it yet, her true heir—but this was one of the few times in our life together that I could be dizzyingly sure I had pleased. "You did it so that when I come home . . . so that you . . ." she said.

Wasn't this why I had done it, in part? Head bent, I nod-ded.

But in the matter of secrets, I was still in between, no match for her. Her nose breathed in sharply—what scent? —and her eyes and mouth, though still quirking, narrowed. "You're *rehearsing!*" she said.

At that, I raised my head. I shrugged, not awkwardly, and—since she considered shrugs vulgar—not imitation. She said nothing more, and I saw that I had confused her, not as the chick can sometimes confuse an adult, but as the grown confuse the grown. She had lost her pure version of me. I was opaque.

I got up to go before she said to. For I had something more to do; I had—as she might have said herself in one of her frivols—another iron in the fire, a curling iron.

Early next morning I was up, tied my big new head in a basket—with what I had gone out to have done to it the afternoon before, it felt new, was enormous, and the only scarf big enough to keep it from the wind was a lattice-patterned muffler of my father's—and set off with it, on my usual journey. Tonic early mornings infuse the sluggard with righteousness, especially in the teens; bumping along on the bus, carrying my head like a tariff to the tax office, I recalled other spry mornings of my youth—the years, say, from four to ten—as if these were the childhood of a church heroine, and, inhaling deeply, told myself that I was back on the track now, ready to grow, grow, in a straight line. The universe, or rather, the local egg-candling center that was my portion of it, of course had other plans. There comes a time when the schmaltz of the teens has to turn into something else, sinister, joyous or sad, or just ordinary left-right. This turn has nothing to do with the tragedies inherent in our so fancy flesh; these can make their entry at any time. An attitude toward them is what is ultimately required of us. I count that day as the first on which satire, or the satiric spirit, entered my life—and my mother was its agent. I was lucky—or perhaps not, as you may think—for in our country this does not happen so early, or even often, to girls.

Whether or not the luck, when I walked down the gray, slick corridor along which her room was the last-on-the-right but one, everything was the same as yesterday—when is the practical eternity of a hospital not the same? The nurses were trotting by, handmaidens of that eternity. As the elevator opened and closed on a flashbulb shot of a swathed figure on a cot going "up" or coming "down," an orderly passed, yawning, pushing a wagon on which one might surely drop any appendage, a leg say, or even an organ more secret, and have it swept into one of his covered utensils without comment, like a crumb. The corridor always wore the same demeanor, a fact more chilling than its marble. No matter when, no matter who, and apparently no matter—as now—what noise. For the single noise that now was belling and rebounding there was enormous, hoarse, but with a daunting steadiness, the voice of a narwhal or a behemoth—or any out of that bestiary of metaphors which my inflamed mind's ear was so ready for—and it seemed to be coming from the last-room-on-the-right but one. I ran forward, then stopped just short of the door, lacking the courage to peer in. Gargantua had entered it, somehow. By the window, my mind's eye took it to be, his great limbs—if he had them—having made short league of the roofs between us and the Garden. Either my mother was clasped, lily white in spite of all that liver, in the great growl-arms of the gorilla; or else—if Gargantua was a sea lion—then I would see a leviathan of that vaudeville tribe one could have no fears of, a long blubber stretching upward from the dark brine of his flipper-waddle, his face whiskering at the ceiling, for her amusement. Already I had some perception of her character.

She was alone of course, lying in profile in her mother-superior position, hands clasped. If I hadn't had in mind that prior picture of her amusement, I might have missed a slight curl of it, between nostril and lip. The noise, as I realized now, was bearing in from a register over her head, from the room next to hers, the last-room-on-the-right, bar none. And as I recognized too, it was a human voice, but an almost Gregorian chant of one, past groaning and on the way to music, like the multiple, polyclinic voice of the hospital itself.

"What is it!" I burst out.

"You?" She rose from long, quiet thoughts, I could see that. "Whatever are you doing here so early?" Good acts solo never gained me any credit with her; gross natural reform was what was required. She and I gazed at each other moodily, across this delicate imbalance in our relationship. "And what's that you have?—why that's your father's Sulka muffler!" She half rose in bed, and already I knew the progress of her vision—from me to other family magpies to outside pillagers, all of us on a field day with the family effects.

But I was saved by the vox humana next door.

"O Lord," it said. Then came a pause, in definite tempo, then, on a great misty swell, "O Lord, let not mmmmm-*y* will . . . but thhhh--*ine* . . . be done." After a silence all the intervals were repeated regular as a water wheel. "O Lord," I understood it to say, "Let not *my* will . . . but THINE . . . be done."

My mother gave the headshake which resigns itself away from the important to the trivial. "She came down last night. And ever since she began to wake up. I don't know where she gets the energy. Ever since about four."

I had been around there long enough to know what

"coming down" meant; I had seen my mother when she came down. In those days I guess they came down immediately after the operation—there mustn't have been a recovery room.

(Nowadays, the way the folder they gave us says, "afterwards the patient spends some hours in the recovery room, attended by a corps specially trained in post-operative techniques." I myself have been in one several times; the worst is if you wake up there from only a light anesthesia. Then you can hear above your head every prattle-rattle between the nurses and the male technicians, talk as light as a glass of water with the sun in it, yet you yourself lie tongue-stopped, face down in the stream. The groans you hear may or may not be your own. And I don't know that people are so different now, when they come down. Their faces are the same pure wax, as if embalmed but still owning such entrails as have been left to them, and they are faces which have reached conclusions.)

"Is she praying—really?"

"What've you got under there, curlers?" my mother answered. Then she folded herself absently, as one does for an anecdote. Her stories, even when they had real people in them, always came out folklore. "Fresh over from Ireland, they say. A single girl, though not all that young. A domestic, I should imagine. That's the way it would be. She had a fibroid, nothing bad. They told her that. But they say she'd been going to the cathedral to pray for weeks beforehand. And this is the result of it." All the time, she was speaking through the steady waves of it. And now I saw again that faint curve, between nostril and lip. "For now listen, do you *hear* what she's saying?"

I gabbled it. "OLordletnotmywillbutthinebedone."

"Listen!" said my mother, with a grind to it. "When are you ever going to start listening and looking at the world around you!"

I listened more carefully and then I heard what the next

room was really saying. "O Lord," it said. "Let not *thy* will
. . . but MINE . . . be done."

Three things then happened simultaneously. My mother
and I burst out laughing—together. From the Garden, Gargantua began his morning calling, still a hard, strong call
but smaller-seeming, coming as it were reduced through all
our own jungle braying. And my father entered the room.

He didn't belong there, we felt that at once, not in the
cozy nest we had all made for ourselves—the two of us, the
unknown Irish girl, and Gargantua. He didn't belong there
any more than he belongs in this story, where he will only
briefly appear. This is a *woman's* story. So we looked at him
with the narrow eyes women use on their circumnavigating
men returned. The men . . . somewhere of course they
have their own Gargantua, but that is another wing of the
hospital. Yet we loved him, our third prong—and knew that
he had come to save us.

He was a middle-size man, neat of foot, sharp of cravat,
long on sympathy, and, from an inbred tradition that repose was decorum, short-tempered as hell over any breach
of it. To this, life had added the hotel traveler's image of
himself as the focus of rivers of hot-and-cold service always at the ready, whether or not used. As we know,
neighbor, women have less trust in this service, being
nearer the source. But my father came in twinkling as a
Mercury winged in from trains that were still as plush as
divas and as soaringly named, the Twentieth Century, the
Golden Arrow. "Snowbound in Toronto!" he cried, bent to
kiss her, and then stood very still, in bedlam. After a moment, his own voice came incisive through it. He inclined
an ear to her explanations, then he spoke again. He was a
man who had no God-troubles, at least as to the accent the
deity may be invoked in, or in the company of what other
words. Then he left us.

I don't know that we said anything to each other while
we waited for him. She may have looked curiously at my

head, but didn't speak of it. As to what I was thinking all
that long while he was gone, I draw a blank. I can hear the
steady chant of some woman in the next room . . . but
. . . I draw a blank.

(Or . . . am I blanking in. *Surely* this bed is moving . . .
and there are voices. But I can move nothing; arms, tongue,
eyes, all are pinioned; I am a blank in a cage. Mother, I am
—help me. Father . . . is in another wing . . .) Ah, here
he comes back.

"You're going home!" he said to her. "Out of this. Tomorrow." While he bent over her, telling her how it had
been arranged, and she stared up at him, I was lost to them.
I suppose the scarf slipped from my head when I leaned
forward to listen to them, to the world around me. The
doctor had been talked to, he said, and the head supervisor.
Orders had been given and were being carried out everywhere. A nurse would return home with us. The maid, res-
cued, was even now on her way there, with instructions to
reinstate every ruby comfort as of yore. All aunts and other
family females were on the phone, retingling our entire domestic network; tomorrow, on my mother's return, the cor-
ridors of the castle would be lined with them—I heard her
sigh. And I thought—perhaps with her?—how swiftly the
world around one could change.

"Canada's beautiful, this time of year." My father
stretched grandly, account given, task done. "Wish you
could've been with me." Though she never had been
known to go on a business trip with him, on his returns he
always said this. "Fine people, too, a sight to see them
stamping in out of the snow in their furs, into the lounge.
And what furs—I brought you a muff. Big fur shakos too,
they wear, men and women both." He turned genially to
me, rubbing his hands out of that cold. He stared a bit.
"What's that thing on *your* head, child?"

I had had trouble telling them at the shop what I wanted
—just as she could have warned me. What I had seen myself in was a crown of braids, though somehow not braided,
my hair being too thick for it. But no, it was not to be
thinned, or cut. Finally, an old man sitting in the back of
the shop in his fedora, hands on the ball of his cane, had
come forward—he was the owner's father. He knew just
what to do, and plinking and twirling the iron they had
fished out from somewhere, he had done it. At home, in the
kitchen, we had a piece of French ovenware, light brown
china with a braided and rippled border. This dish, used for
the rare soufflé or winy chicken, my casqued head, in a
reverse way, now resembled—a head en casserole. I already
knew this. All last night, not knowing how to dismantle, I
had doubtfully preserved it on the pillow, in my nose a
singed smell of burned devil.

What could I say to him? I said it. "Hair."

My mother's shriek overrode his expression—she had a
lusty shriek in time of need. Her hand covered her mouth
for some moments, but she was finally able to withdraw it.
"How it brings things back!" she said. "Where did you ever
. . . a *marcel!*"

In the sudden silence . . . how have all those noises
stopped, except a small one, like the hum of an elevator?
. . . I could hear the spring growing at the window. A
nurse entered with a tray, stepping off her revolving stage.
My father said gaily, "We'll be off now. I'm going to take
this young lady to lunch. Afterwards, maybe we'll go
across the street, to the circus. We'll find out for you what
that specimen over there is."

"Just lunch, thanks." I would have tossed my head, if
able. "I don't know why people can't see that I haven't
cared a hoot about the circus in at least three years."

The three prongs of the family now regarded one another, my mother's expression not quite decipherable even
now, my father's more readable; I suspect he sees a resem-

blance between the other two. And, from my first proud
distance, I am seeing them. But it's my mother who speaks,
not looking at us, but out the window. What has brought
her to it, at last? Is it the presence of the nurse, against
whom we must all be united? Or is it that my mother, who
can look about her without turning her head, sees that once
again we are rich. It has been decreed. "Well, then," she
says, "better take her shopping."

And now I can see the dénouement, clear to the end. My
father is making the large gestures which coming expendi-
tures always induce in him; he says he will get the sales-
clerk to help us. My mother does not answer this. In the
end we are to do quite well by ourselves by buying the
most expensive, since he avers the best will wear me better
—and I don't tell him that this is not why a woman wears
it. I distinctly remember the blue Ducharne silk with the
wool capelet, and the smocked bronze silk for extra. I can
see it all now, including the look with which my mother
despatched us. It had to be a look that would last, for I
didn't see it then—and it has lasted. She turned from the
window and gave me it. "Take care."

There's one more picture, though even that is not the
end. When we came to get her the next morning—I along
only because I was wearing the blue—she was already
dressed, sitting in a wheelchair by the window. When I saw
her in clothes again, the slim toque above the tawny,
S-shaped bun, all of her with an air as if she could be
drawn through a ring, and if so would be the same before
and after, I understood the futility of adornment—and that
I must spend a lifetime as one of the adorned. She said
nothing but a nod when she saw me in my duds, but she
might have done worse—one must remember that she too
in her way was still growing, though who she was trying to
be is not yet known. The room next door was quiet now—
she saw me mark that.

"The circus is gone too," she said. "Yesterday must have

been the last day. I happened to be awake at dawn, and I saw them leave."

Gazing out with her, I fancied that the hoardings already had a tattered look, past the season, but the rooftops were the same, and are yet—they've not failed me.

And just before we left, she beckoned me to lean down to be whispered to. "I saw him! I saw Gargantua leaving!"

"You didn't!" I too whispered. "What did he look like?"

Her eyes veiled. "He was in a cage, of course . . . and at that distance. And it was barely dawn."

(Here comes the dénouement, or almost, and I find I cannot touch, cannot quite *touch* it—can one ever? Or is it merely that my arm is spellbound; I cannot move it. But the bed, at least the bed is no longer moving. And there is no Gargantua here—this is a high-rise hospital.

When I "came in" as they say, a day early, I lay that whole day watching the river spread below us from this ninth-floor height, watching how the sun walks north on it in a bar of gold, until that blue and always vernal moment when the bar leaps up and in one dazzle is transubstantiated into the whole disk of the sun. I could see for myself that there was no beast here—and besides I know this area well, this is the old neighborhood. Down below is the parking lot for this place, for Harkness Pavilion, but it used to be the parade grounds for the Institute for the Deaf, in front of whose fence I often played under my nursemaid's eye. Even in those days, with the mutes drilling behind us in their gray uniforms, all of them children too, there was no Gargantua here. Nor is there now, down there where the light is shed on the serried car tops like a thirty-year snow. This is a pavilion, not an arena.)

"But you must have seen something!" I said. "Mother. Or why do you mention it at all?"

Yes, I was her true heir. For I knew even then, even when she slanged me the way one does an exasperating pup one

loves, but which will never make best of show—*Donnerwet-*
ter, was ist das!—that she never claimed anything personally
for what she did know; even her humor, if humor it was,
was folklore. She was a person, I know now, who had an
accurate sense of the tragedy of events, but her vocabulary
was inadequate to it, like that of us all. And I knew even
then that *I* was not her tragedy.

"Bend down," she said. "Bend down and I'll whisper it."

("No, don't move your arm, Mrs. Mmmm, can you hear me?

Why yes, you're the young nurse who said last night you
would be my special. I can't answer you but I can hear you.

You're down now, Mrs. Mmmmm, you've had your . . . it's all over.
Careful of your arm now, it's strapped to a board, but that's nothing,
that's just for the intravenous. You're down now and you're fine. Can
you hear me, Mrs. Mmmm?

The voice that breathes o'er Eden, how sweet and unan-
swerable. So, I'm "down.")

I bent down, neighbor, and she whispered it, her eyes
merry. "I guess I've been here too long," she said. "But I
swear to you, darling. It looked like nothing so much as an
enormous old slice of liver."

So we'll never know, I said to her, back then, what Gargantua really is—and she didn't answer. And I didn't much
care, for she had said "darling." And we went home to be
rich.

But I'm downstairs now—are you still across the room
there, neighbor?—and I do know. Everything gets sorted
out here by the surgeons with their thin-skinned fingers. I
even know why, sometimes, I serve a certain old dull meal
to the children. An old meal, old compulsion, can be like a
dark, intermediary day that reminds one this is the way it
is, was—this is the way it all goes on. And what I'm really
saying to them is "Yes, I know, I'm your old slanger, I'm the

scourge, but *listen. Look about you in the world!"* They have got it out of me at last, the surgeons. This is a good hospital.

So, listen, neighbor, and I'll finish the story of how my mother told me who Gargantua was, how she tells me now. Though it's harder than it used to be, to tell the real voices from the others. "The beast that haunts us, the nameless," she says, "why, it's nothing but an old slice of liver. Or, while I say it is, in this merry-dark way whose lilt you hear yet—it *is* only that. How many years it has taken you to learn, bright as you are, but I have finally taught you. There are things I can't decree away from you—*such things,* my darling. But while I say it is only that, I hold back the beast."

Wake up, Mrs. Mmmmm, ah, she's a hard one to wake.

It's because I've been here, or a part of me, all the time, nurse; my mother and I have been here together all this time. Forgive us for groaning. We are Gargantua.

Better lie back, Mrs. Mmmmm.

Ah, nurse, it's just that I want to see if my neighbor is over there, my random roommate. I want to tell her something. Ah yes, she's here, we're all here with whoever's next door; neighbor and I, and my mother and I as we once were, and as we are. What shall I say to all of us, here in our cozy nest, to all our selves?

Neighbor! Neighbor, the people one lives with and loves can be like cornucopias in the mind; even after they are dead we can abstract their riches, one by one. So this is a happy story. We all, with the help of a bit of satire, make our stories come right in the end. O Lord . . . not thy will . . . but ours . . . be done.

And now I lay me down to wake. Help me, Mother. For now—for now I am you.

Real Impudence

"**Y** ES, WE'VE DONE VERY WELL, Aunt and Denny and me—" Doreen says. "Considering."

Her violet mirror-glasses jump on her nose. Her hair had once been carrot. Denny, her hairdresser son, gladly keeps it that way, pleased that she hasn't requested a matching violet instead. Not that Doreen's would have been anywhere near that washing-powder blue thought genteel here for gray hair. "Considering that we came to the States."

There are those who feel that Doreen's glasses, which cannot not be seen through, cloud her judgment.

The young minister of what the creature known as Aunt calls "that raunchy church around the corner" is not one of them. He balances a teacup and takes another of Aunt's melting scones from what she calls her muffin-stand, also made with her own hands.

Like everything that comes from them it is extraordinary. Six dinner plates, graduating up to the smallest, have been glued to dinner forks which serve as caryatids, in turn embedded in what appear to be lumps of cannel coal, and are. These have come from the basement of the rectory, though not via him. The sitting room rages with what she terms

her fancywork—which the people who go mad for it and
are able to wrest a piece of it from Doreen—at a price—are
finding does work perfectly, whatever its function.

The scone goes down like a poultice for all the sins of
cookery the minister's gullet is subjected to in other houses.
"Oh, but you didn't just come to the States," he says. "You
came to Greenwich Village. 'And that has made all the difference.' Or is it: *And oh, the difference to me?*"

He is fond of poetry, but vague. Before the ministry he
had been an actor.

"Browning?" Doreen says. "Or Wordsworth too, probably." She isn't educated, but her long, black-silk legs have
carried her into a great deal of very allusive male company,
for whose remarks in any field she has, as she says "Tap-
dancer's recall. Comes from the feet, really."

Aunt makes a noise—the one which reminds the minister
of the geek in the traveling circus he had first run away to.
Aunt has other noises, but this is her jack-of-all-trades one.

"What did she say?" he says.

"She said ' 'Tisn't Soho here,' " Doreen's son, Denny, answers, entering. "Meaning London's. Not that we ever lived
there. But she's been in a 'tisn'ty mood ever since your cake
sale."

"I know." The sale alone isn't why the minister is here.
The house reminds him of one of those BBC television
hours where everybody at the pub has too much character.
He can't keep away from it.

"So is Doreen, 'tisn'ty. Though nobody knows why."
Denny's chestnut hair hangs to his ears in one go, to his
shoulders in another, fraying all the way down his center
back. One of the operators in his all-girl, four-chair barbershop downstairs does it for him.

He is said to be involved with all four girls, which is
false. He usually runs to two, kept on as fine a balance,
Doreen says, as the cheese-scales at Balducci's. There will
be an endearing tonsure on Denny's crown someday, but

the minister suspects Denny will leave it there and go on to some other role, which is the way he finds his livelihoods.

At the moment Denny does the hair of rock stars only, most of them English, for whom the downstairs shop—furnished with a collection of barber's gear which Doreen has told the minister "the V. and A. wouldn't mind having," is a home away from home. The Victoria and Albert Museum, she'd explained.

The minister has never been abroad, owing to his livelihood. Doreen and her son are so comfortably changey about theirs, they can't ever understand the fixity of his. They have a general scorn for the fixity of things, especially where it occurs in the States.

Aunt gives another of her wheezes. She too has come to her latest earning power by accident, and in layers rather like Denny's hair. Or perhaps the waves of creation which overtake her come on magnetized by her bulk. She can speak well enough but the minister has learned that only rage moves her up from wheezes, which are due less to asthma than to a laziness toward all except that handicraft which the galleries around here are beginning to take for art. As the cake sale at the church has made clear.

"What did you say, Auntie?" A term he knows provokes her.

"Aunt is my name, handsome."

Nobody at the church knows whose aunt she actually is. She however knows the word that can send him back to being a seminarian.

"She was furious they couldn't eat the cakes," Doreen said. "The people who bought them." She turns to Aunt. "You know jolly well we gave that gallery all rights in exchange for the percentage." She turns to the minister. "Half to the church. And you were in the parish house when they came and sprayed the cakes." She is always turning in that lovely, eely way, Doreen; she has a gift for it.

"They said the spray wouldn't be as lasting as if Aunt

had made the cakes first off out of some special material, but was good enough for them to be sold as art." He says "art" like the holy word it is, to a church commanding these poet-and-painter-haunted blocks. "We have that wonderful braided bread of hers you framed, in the kitchen at the rectory. Grace Kung says it's an inspiration." It was through Grace, who cooked for minister and his senior, that Aunt had procured the cannel-coal lumps, in exchange for a recipe for a shepherd's pie he can still happily taste.

"Aunt says, in an emergency you could break the frame; the bread still could be et." Doreen turns to Aunt. "But that's not her real complaint, is it, love? She says she should never have set herself to do the cathedrals of England, even though she had hearty encouragement at the time."

Aunt glares stage front, but this is a dig at Denny, for being the philistine of the family. But Denny has gone.

"She says, minister, that even in an eighteen-egg recipe, St. Paul's is not suitable for art. But what her trouble really is—isn't it, duck?—is that she's reached a new stage of development." Doreen's bright green silk roils with enthusiasm.

The minister doesn't doubt Doreen has designs on him, marriage not the question. Fortunately he is about to marry a wonderful nurse from St. Luke's Hospital. But Doreen is still the prettiest forty-five-year-old devotee of Mammon you could ever yearn to have a walk-out with. Her word for it.

"Aunt—tell minister."

Doreen always addresses him so. Possibly it is a London habit, all the Trotters, gathered from whatever corners of Britain, being so much from there. Though he has long suspected that Doreen herself might be from the Colonies, or even—from an episode where she seemed to have been a 1960s bride of a member of the American forces at Wimbledon, that she is an American. God help him, he has even at times suspicioned that none of the Trotters—Aunt's surname, by which they are generally known—are related at all.

Aunt makes her noise, a low growl-purr this time, like one of those enormously competent street cats his house-keeper, Mrs. Kung, refuses to take in. Not waiting for inter-pretation, she leans over her many tightly buttoned, con-centric rolls of fat to put a white hand on one of the lumps of cannel coal. For a person of her shape she has a long neck, reminding the minister of his grandmother's Buddha incense burner, on which a wired head nodded. Though Aunt hasn't many nods to her, she can be an explicit mime. Slowly she circles the hand, her right one, on the coal lump, then holds up her palm. Her fingers are like five white sau-sages of equal length, yet the minister has no doubt that in Aunt's studio, which is the kitchen, they move as deftly as her felt-booted feet do under her smock. The palm is now black. "Quick, Doreen, lend me your slip."

Doreen squirms, even blushes. They are all so fair-skinned, even Dennis, though Aunt at times has Dennis dye her hair raven. "Aunt, I'm not wearing one."

"Paper, then. Summat of that you wrapped the cakes."

She is breathing hard, and most certainly in English, but he wouldn't have been surprised to hear her give a Bacchic yell.

The paper is brought—a large white sheet and one of manila brown. She places the white one on the floor and bends to it, not wheezing a bit. Alternating between coal and paper, holding one corner of it with a foot, she roams it in washerwoman swipes.

"Oh—finger painting," the minister says, disappointed.

She raises a burning look at him, stubs her fingertips one by one on the coal, dots the paper all over so swiftly she might be playing piano, then finishes with a crackling rou-lade from the heel of her hand, and rolls the paper into a tube. She then attacks the brown sheet, but after a minute

shakes her head, looking down. "Uh. Uh-uh . . . Ahaha!"
She grunts.

It is like a trade demonstration of being seized by inspiration, but somehow he believes in it, even when she goes at the paper with her boots. He can see why. The paper is tougher, darker, and a bigger square; it needs those grinding strokes. Such a prize Aunt would be, teaching the children's group at church what the deeper decorative impulses are.

Now she's considering again, hands hanging, face so pink he fears for her. "Chocolate bits?" she mutters. Shakes her head. "No more food. Too dangerous." She heaves an asthmatic sigh of farewell. Rocking on her own fulcrum, she peers the room. He marvels at how well he can surmise what she is after—a substance to collage; she might easily teach adults. Now she is eyeing the sheared-lamb lining of his galoshes; she even feels it with her thumb, smirking up at him.

"Finger paint," she says deep and scornful. Then with a cry she seizes the scissors and string Doreen has brought too. A series of slashes flash triumphant across paper. He can feel their harsh slant. She is tempted by the string, even making a few fast fisherman's knots with it, then lays it chastely down. She is done. Rolling up her second canvas like the other, she hands it to Doreen.

"She's been doing abstract," Doreen whispers, "she's already done forty of them. We do thank you for the coal."

Is he to let himself out now, or stay? He and Doreen never can tell, until Aunt says.

"Tea," Aunt wheezes suddenly. She has settled back. "And bring the cheese straws." In repose her eyes and mouth are as round as a person's can be. Aunt likes good-looking young men as much as any woman, Doreen has informed him, in the hushed way she drops these scraps, imparting the lore of a deity. Aunt does, the minister thinks, especially if the worshiper doesn't mind licking his lips. His senior has had no luck with her.

"You and Aunt *are* getting on," Doreen said. "We've never had so much conversation here before."

On his way out Doreen slides an envelope into his hand, at the same time whispering: "The gallery will want the full parish-house basement next, they say. If you could open those sliding doors, as you do for the musical comedies? And in about five weeks?" He hopes she isn't giving him the cake-sale tithe in cash; the gallery should have sent him it direct.

Outside he sees that one of Denny's rock groups has arrived. They come to the barber shop from all over the world in lurid vans, painted with mountain scenes that dip ten-gallon western hats toward the environment, or awhirl with sci-fi moons, or covered with scrawled mottoes so in-tramural you would have to attend the concert to catch on. Denny has told him that what with dance and visual added, the groups are now mixes of any sort. Rock is really on its way out, Denny says, even if his old friends in the business still think that rockers are what they still are.

The vans shouldn't be parked here, but none of the street's householders, which include the poor rich and the endowed poor, retired poets and publishers, grande-dame dancers, working artists and dilettante businessmen, would protest. The vans help keep them in the forefront of what they in part live here for. Most of them support the church too, if less for God than for neighborly sentiment. Denny here does not attend the church but gives him his confidence—as much, the minister feels, as Denny can give any-one.

The church, by day a Quakerish crackerbox on stilts, on a foggy night like this a noble, doll-size Parthenon, serves an ethic so suited to these human-scale houses that he can scarcely bear to leave, though his nurse fiancée assures him that her hospital serves the same ends and has in addition a garden close. Church attendance in general is poor, but de-mands on the house calls high.

Down the street, the minister regularly visits a hermit who calls himself a "paraplegic of desire," which Jung could not have said more nattily or truly. On other side-streets farther afield, a much scruffier crowd besieges the church for productions of their happenings in verse, song, or drama—for one of which it has been requested that the parish rooms, which can indeed be opened to form one large space, be flooded to make ice.

Much is refused, but the warmth down here, not all of it churchly, persists. The trustee who gives the winter's coal, the cannel being for the staff fireplace only, does attend, hoping not to be too fat a rich man for the eye of the needle. A part of the gallery's tithe will go to feed a writer-girl who sports a load of spaghetti hair. It would help if she could eat it, instead of only topping it with her beret while she writes. The truly sick go to St. Vincent's, where among the intercommed Hail Marys the minister puts in a weekly half day hunting his own communicants.

All down the street the garbage cans line the stoops. They are the wrinkled gray fauna of this place—brought up from the areaways or the back gardens, or simply left there the week through. A sour-sweet smell comes from their maws. The sky above is brindled, and not stationary. He watches a woman lead out her dog and clean up after it with a little pan and brush. It's all moving, the minister thinks. What am I still lonely for?

In back of him, behind the barbershop's blinds, there is a golden light; shadows move on the blinds. The new crowd of rockers would be smoking whatever they had brought; Denny is known not to provide. If the minister were inside, they would offer it. Some groups swashbuckle the place, taking it over; others stand about with bony, remote foreheads held very still, as if inching through nonmusical time. They miss their gear, which is always being sent on.

Standing against the Trotters' iron railing, the minister tries out both attitudes; he is still an actor. The envelope drops, maybe a warning not to pretend, as he too often does, that he upholds the theater of everybody he knows. And what is his gear? Picking up the envelope, he weighs it —if it is an assignation from Doreen what will he do?—and opens it under the light from the blinds. The clouds are still moving. It is a recipe for plum duff.

Inside Denny's, the four barber's chairs gleam from neat's-foot oil on their brown Spanish leather, and jeweler's rouge on their chrome armrests. The chairs are Edwardian and come from Bath. He had brought them over from the London shop in a freighter, where he could go down in the hold to watch them easing over the waves in their satisfied way. It is ritual here to admire them, but this group is not doing so. Two of the four men have gone off to Denny's sauna in the garden; the girls have gone off with his own girls to their quarters, which are not in the house.

The pair left are gooning restlessly about the shop, picking their feet up and putting them down again like horses in stalls. Denny thinks he knows what that means, though they are not a set he has met before. Spin-offs from the Hot Gossips—not from that group proper but from the craze for it, they call themselves Real Impudence, a name he approves of and has therefore booked on impulse, the way he does everything, although the network of phonings and drop-ins that he lives in, plus scrawled notes from his regulars or hints from managers met around town, usually provide all needed references.

This crowd, though, are more dancers than rockers. Just to look at them makes him feel history. The early groups he had serviced in Liverpool, Edinburgh, and Glasgow, then London, had most of them been made up of reedy men, come to music out of slumdoors, not interested in true nourishment. That could keep them looking young for a long while. As they aged yet flourished, putting clerkly gold-rims on their pointy noses and mandarin hairs at their mouth corners, they had begun to look like sophisticated mice, come to the fairytale ballroom in their own coaches. Yes, rock was all slight men when it started and that was why amplification had been needed; he wondered no one had noticed this. They'd bathed in it as they had in wealth.

Next had come the rag-heads—great mops of simulated carelessness like his own. This was when, after teaching school at a crammer's, and after a spell of his own at the drums, he had opened his shop, and prospered. Even now the style isn't altogether gone, but he can see it being estimated in the eyes of these—what should he call them? They do not intend to be merely his first-night guests, with a lot of music-making and the girls coming in. He watches the pair wander the implement-stocked shop, the corners for the strops, the moustache cups, the beard rakes, and the straight razors, inspecting each. Customers are what they mean to be, and he knows for what.

Cropped as the pair's heads are, they aren't skinheads, those politically shaven bulletheads during whose reign over there he'd had to turn from barbering to the general agentry he does now. Skinheads hadn't ever been rockers, but the bands of the time had briefly adopted that toughie style, the heads oiled and the bodies too, shining down to the bellies when they tore off their skimp shirts, showing torsos not quite ready for David Hockney, but still pinker and fleshier than rock had seen before—products of the welfare state.

After them, punk rock had nearly skidded the art back to the weedy again, and even to the runt. But people had had enough of them almost as soon as begun. Their makeup was too near the clown, for one thing. For another, they hadn't the right style of violence. Went at it like mimes, they had, in mascara and green hair, when the public wanted it lean, monotone and sinister. A couple of shabby murders hadn't helped.

This pair are skull-boys, the newest of the new. He can't

help being proud of his country's leadership. Though almost as tall as basketball players, they have none of that pituitary-giant looseness. They are each tightly of a piece, and all of it leads from that skull, running fish-smooth into the neck. One of the pair is black, the other white; the same goes for the other men and the girls. Silver jumpsuits show all the group's measurements as identical, just as their woman manager, in here yesterday ahead of them, had bragged. A choreographer, she had created them.

The bridge of her nose had made a long shallow dive from between her brows to its pert tip. As with all those nose jobs, your eye kept taking the dive, which made you uneasy, wondering how honest the person was in other directions. Instructing him on the group's hair, she said: "Close to the bone, yes, the girls too, but not, God, cropped. Like fine fur. Or velvet nap." And the hairline was to be natural, only exaggerated. "None of your widow's peaks in front or ducktail backs. Satanic, but natural."

Her own hair was a Chelsea tangle he wouldn't want to get his hands in. "Our entire group is heterosexual." She gave him a cool look.

So was he, but he saw fit not to mention it. He had gone to a good grammar school, on a scholarship, where he had had his standards solidified if not raised—for he had never been ashamed of them. That woman was what his favorite stepfather, a retired docker who now bred lab hamsters, would have pointed out as one of those Oxbridge chippies with no standards to begin with, who now and then barged into the dad's local at Wapping Old Stairs. But she did make Denny homesick. "We'll all have a party tomorrow night," he'd promised her.

Which is tonight. The group would open tomorrow. He isn't worried about tonight's party, not after some of the groups he's been keeper to, slashers even, with no blood left to run. But he is itchy. He would like to know for sure why—before Doreen has to tell him.

"All your gear in, boys?" They haven't yet asked about it. The stage manager has phoned—are those drums all of it, those few traps and snares? And something called a gamelan?

"Tha-at's all," the boy nearer Denny says, shifting his feet. "We're mostly standing up in it."

Denny sees with amazement that the boy is wearing a fawn-colored sandal on one foot, but has a really glorious snakeskin boot, inlaid with turquoises, on the other. The other boy wears one each of the same. It is a long time since Denny has been amazed. And yes, the two say, it is the same for all the group.

"Hadn't you caught us on your TV, last month?" the white one says. He is examining Denny's collection of ivory-handled straight razors.

"Of course." They wouldn't be here, otherwise. But the footwork had been so fast he hadn't noticed the boots. "You were wonderful."

This is obligatory, but they had been, their whirling stomps all smooth, with the underneath jolts passing on to the audience like electric shock. Their rhythm was all threat. So that even on TV, whenever they came forward, hostile and beautiful, you cringed back. Oh, they were the new silver all right, buying you what you wanted.

These two were called Pure and Blackie, for obvious reasons; he didn't know yet about the girls. "Thought you might have more sound, coming later."

"More sound?" Blackie says, arching his neck. "No, man. The lady says keep it minimal. It goes with us."

It had. Guerrilla-style yelps from the men, a low, almost maternal growling from the girls; the music itself might even have come from a record. The live accompanists you never saw. He had blamed that on the cameras. "A record!" he says now.

Pure, the one holding the razor, only smiles. He has pulled the long, narrow blade from its case, a beauty with a mermaid carved on it. "Thought these were gear for joints. Man, your customs officer washed us over as if we were gold dust. Couldn't believe we don't carry anything."

"Here—let me close that," Denny says. "It's very sharp." He smiles back at them. "I could shave you men with it." Though they are boys, they will prefer not to be called that. He had once had that vanguard slouch himself. He gets them each into a chair.

"Dennis, man," Blackie says, "your gear is super. Isn't it, Simon?" He catches Denny's eye. "That's why she had the idea to call him Pure. My own real name is Oliver." He fondles the chair arm. "Super. And we're looking forward to your party. In fact, we could use a little of it now."

Denny flexes his scissors, which are four-inchers, Damascene. He had better keep a joke ahead. "Think I'll cut your hair alternately." He nips at Blackie, then at Pure. "Maybe because of those shoes."

They laugh. "Denny, you are just as we heard." No, the shoes are custom-made, they tell him, not just two pairs divided. "Though she lets people think that," Simon says. "She's very good at that sort of thing, actually. Made our costumes at home as well, until we no longer needed the sincerity."

He recognizes their opportunism, the fresh breeze of it. Clipping at one, then the other, when he has got them used to his rhythm, for though it no longer depends on drums, he has never lost it, he says carefully: "Party, yes. And welcome. The girls should soon be along. And the drink. But as for the other—gear, I don't carry anything here either, you see. No joints, nothing . . . Watch it."

He got his scissors out in time, glad it hadn't been the razor. Both heads had jerked. In laughter.

"Den-*ny*. We're *dance*-rock."

He finishes in silence all round, not bringing out the back mirror when he is done. Let these two check the job on each other. They know their own heads, they do.

"How he has got the style of it!" they say, nodding like fortune-tellers in his chairs. "Bang on!" they politely say.

"On the house." He can't help being pleased.

"Lo-ving," Blackie says. "Lo-o-*ving.*"

Denny knows what that means. He and his kind used to say "Beau-tiful." He knows the life they lead, the madly traveling energies, vanities. But what has happened to the noise? And other—gear? "You really don't, then? *Use* anything?"

No. But not for health reasons. It is simply the new thing.

"A new crowd, you mean." Well, hadn't he expected it?

While he cleans up, it doesn't help that although he has wound down the chairs, both boys are so tall they must be able to see his bald spot.

Maybe it's still different in the States, they say, lounging.

He isn't the States. Or is he, by now? Look at him, owning a house.

"So rock is over," he says. If it was over back there it soon would be altogether; they set the trends. Or something beyond any of them does—the same rhythm that had slackened Doreen's flow of husbands and put him out of step, and now has contrarily spun Aunt up and up like a gritty old top.

"No, rock's not over," Pure says.

Blackie is the brash one. "It's us."

They leap up and bomb around the room in that kind of prayer-arms-up that is a dancer's whistling.

Once the girls swarm in, making their fluffy talk and wearing those snake heads he had shorn to specification this morning, he can think better, as he always does when people are flickering about. He brings out the drink, noticing how little they all take.

He is that way himself, even though for as long as he can remember he and Doreen, and then Aunt with them, had lived the communal life. Even in the early days people came and went; some clung, like those white balls to wool in the experiment for static electricity, and some dropped off and out. After the grammar school, and with Doreen off with a husband in the Argentine and Aunt with her, it was this need of people which had pushed him first to the crammer's, where he'd found he was little more than a dining-hall attendant and nanny for the younger ones, and then to the drums, to which he came right out of the audience.

Hard rock, they called that world now, but between friends it had been as soft as anywhere. What else was a group but a guerrilla action against that other secret wave which sent people zooming up, and then cracked them down? First Doreen had supported their three, then he had, and now most likely Aunt would be their mainstay. After a while you came to see that it has nothing to do with livelihood—and after another while, that you have to move on for it.

The girls are all over the chairs now, which he always enjoys watching. Neither of his two would come away from New York with him, but what he and Doreen and Aunt are will always attract, though it doesn't do to be smug. Perhaps he'll try the Argentine, this time? Though Doreen no longer corresponds over there, he has half-a-dozen names for a start. This house will market like a shot. Sell the chairs, too; they are only England.

The two boys whose names he doesn't yet know come toward him, sleek from their bath, the other pair following. Funny, how modestly they all move, in private. The new style. But those red eyes and drawn mouths want something, all the same.

"Where is the party?" They all close in on him, the girls too. Their silver suits are darker down the back of their legs, lighter toward the front. It does give them an eerie look of always moving forward. "I have *got* to have something," a girl says. She has taken a strop down from the wall, sliding it along her waist like a belt. "Look at me. Nothing since noon."

So it is all a fraud then. Once he had been beaten up here. But he has never had to call the police. "I don't," Denny gets out, "stock anything."

Blackie's hand on his shoulder. Pure's breath in his ear. "Food, Denny Trotter. Dancers have got to have fo-ood."

"Yeh, yeh, yeh," their girls echo, stomping toward him, their hands out in mock.

He isn't the sort to put his arms around people. But it is a loving moment. His own girls watch. Girls can smell change.

His smile gathers them all up. For the new era's march to the kitchen. They know what they have to have. So does he. "Come meet Aunt."

Later, toward four in the morning, upstairs in the second bedroom, Aunt and Doreen are raking over the immediate past—the party—with occasional forays farther back. Denny has always had the master bedroom, being the man. Doreen occupies the third best, but on nights like this she likes to fall asleep on Aunt's featherbed, with Aunt being as she can be at these times, perfectly outspoken.

The fourth bedroom, kept in Doreen's best Irish linen for her chance houseguest, has been unmussed for some time, though not for want of applicants. And though Doreen is what Aunt calls "ready," which means Doreen has had her divorce.

"I took down those sateen valances in there this morning," Aunt said. "They wouldn't be to minister's taste. Or they won't be until he knows you better. And why wasn't he at the party; I put a note in with the receipt for the plum duff? I'll tell you. *You* took the note out again, didn't you."

Doreen lies on the feathers dreamily, twisting her ankles.

"When you say 'minister,' he melts. Worse than for my scones." No answer. "And when I asked for the lend of your slip, did you see his face?" Again no answer. Even so, Aunt always knows when she is being too cute, just before she thoroughly sickens you. Or as soon. "Doreen. You are ready, aren't you?"

"Call it that."

"Five years," Aunt said. "Looking for a man you didn't want."

"We had to find him. I don't fancy those mental divorces."

"Stuck you in the Argentine. On a hacienda with three sheep. You don't call that mental?"

Doreen is building castles with her hands. She has that tendency.

"Meanwhile, I've been doing my family duty, girl. Been up to St. Luke's."

"Oh, Aunt."

"I do have a perfectly good bad knee, you know. Though I had to give a false neighborhood address before they'd have a look." Aunt leaned forward. "She's a nurse in the clinic there. His fiancey. Doreen—you'll have to work hard."

"Pretty, eh?"

Doreen seems half asleep but Aunt knows better. Doreen is dreaming of somebody. But who? "He does like a pretty face," she says. "And body. She'd make twice of you."

"He'll need it." Doreen sits up. "Give it up, Auntie, please. Minister is too innocent for us."

Most are, Aunt's look says—but why say it? She goes to the electric grill which is her lifeline up here. "Cuppa?"

"Ta."

Aunt snaps the ice chest shut. Small and choice like all her arrangements, and installed by her own hands, it had been a wall safe once. People who see it are mad to have one but she will not repeat. Denny, downstairs, has the only other one. She brings the teapot to her chair, which is realistically large. Her weight cannot sit on the side of a bed. Pouring the milk in, she speaks to the cups. "I might do a portrait of minister then, very suitably. In porcelayne enamel." She keeps her eyelids hooded. "The Beanery says I'm ready for such. Teacher says it."

The Beanery is the art-devoted settlement house which has discovered her, though Beanery is certainly not its name.

"Portraits," Doreen says, half to herself. They all know what that can mean. Teacher himself had called her and Denny in at the time of the first gallery proposal, to warn them where Aunt's constant need for embellishment might well lead artistically. Gratefully they had seen what Aunt saw in him—besides the art, of course. He'd understood at once that they would both consider themselves led.

Portraits, mind. And landscape yet to come. Doreen tucks in her ankles, clasping them. Even without a man she is still limber. Aunt's room has no curtains. They can see the sky, getting light now. The room is hushed. They might be listening to the cups only. They stay that way until they hear the clangor of the garbage detail.

Then Doreen lifts herself in one graceful turn to the window. Aunt is already there. They watch. The garbagemen are thick-handed, with arms that make it from shoulder to bin in one gouty curve. The light coming up over east rosies their faces.

"People are more porcelayne than not," Aunt says, "even the garbage detail."

There is no reason to linger, yet no reason not. Their tea is in them. The street is blank, easy to measure.

"Denny already wants out," Doreen says. Aunt moves, but only to pick at some white bird dung and pebbles on the sill. "Out from here, Aunt. Not from us." The two women breathe more calmly. The sunrise is a success.

"Where should that be this time, do you think, Aunt?"

"Don't hope for England," Aunt says. "After portraits, I

mean to rise to the nude. And the nude one does only in France."

"Ah."

But one can hear Doreen is disappointed.

And downstairs, the doorbell rings.

Aunt makes the noise she always does at the onset of strangers.

"Some of the party, no doubt," Doreen says. "Coming back for breakfast. When it's a good party, they do that."

Aunt makes the shrugging sound which means Give them what's left in the emergency larder—the presence of two here being in part why house and shop had attracted, five years back. Fourteen years ago, when she and Doreen had first got together, pressed for the cause of her noises she had replied, "I'm shy." In those days they had been easier to interpret.

"What I don't understand," Doreen says, getting up, "is why your noises have got worse with the fancywork."

She was out the door when Aunt answered, in dignified words. "Self-portraits, teacher says. I'm to do me own creamy body."

Closing the door, she disrobed in front of the mirror, regarding it. Noting for the first time that there were no curtains, she went upstairs and got the valances.

So now we have the whole picture, of how minister did or did not get together with Doreen. For when she opened the downstairs door, it was the garbage detail, asking to ring for an ambulance. They'd found minister lying in the areaway, where he'd been mugged for having no money on him, only a recipe. He wasn't too concussed to demand to be taken upstairs instead, which he was, to the spare bedroom.

After some days, his fiancée nurse came herself to care for him, but she was very annoyed.

"He likes us for the poetry in us," Doreen explained.

But the nurse continued so annoyed that she latched onto Denny instead, whose two girls had meanwhile latched onto the new group, making off in one of the vans. "It's all a question of knowing who to latch onto," Denny said.

The minister, gradually less concussed, watches his fate. From such a well-lighted bed it is almost a pleasure. The British can be too cute for words, which is why they tell such good tales for children. He has been too innocent for the Village; now he is not. One day, when the Trotters have all landed in England again, which he is sure they will, he will visit them, if only to be able to say he too has been to the V. and A.

Meanwhile Aunt, deserting the kitchen, labors in her room. The valances have not been a wise move; they make too much of a frame, the mirror being where it is to reflect them, and her figure within.

It will soon be said in art's annals—and may already have been—that Aunt Trotter has the primitive's kinship with similes from nature. That should be of small use to one in a bedroom, but Aunt's powers are never bound by the usual. No matter how she disposes herself according to all the rules of composition, or shifts distance between canvas and mirror, or holds a pencil out plumb, the image there, so much more than a nude should be, still seems to her scarcely a self-portrait, looking back at her, in its concentrically folding layers of the fairest complexion, like nothing so much as a great white waxy beehive.

So, in that picture whose auction will ultimately buy the Trotters a villa in Aix-en-Provence, a hotel in Menton, and an endlessly accommodating warren in Hampstead—that picture in which Aunt is said to have come into her own—although you will see everyone else there, and *all moving,* from the flying double wedding of Denny and the minister's nurse, and Doreen and the monumentally armed head of the garbage detail, with minister reduced to smaller scale than the others though he officiated, and clinging to the church's portico in wavering farewell—and while at the reception after (in the picture's lower right-hand corner) the nurse vainly hides her stomach under a children's book, Grace Kung brings in the flame-pointed plum duff, rockers' vans cram from curbside to the lighted shopfront inside which all this is going on—and above it all a lone windowsill rides a forever brindling sky—what you will *not* see—is Aunt.

The Library

THOUGH HE WAS GOING to see her at the morgue, not her funeral, and it was already a hot New York June, he couldn't keep himself from putting on a dark suit. Trembling, he put on a tie as well so that he might wear the stickpin she'd given him when she left off living with him. She'd known he never wore them. It had been a sign of leaving.

At the last minute, frowsting among the neat closet bags she'd instituted during her time here, he pulled out the gray silk jacket she and Emery had sent him from Paris for him to receive last year's honor in—and flung off the dark one. He couldn't find the stickpin.

As he dressed, he felt some of the confusions of women, those which she had always embodied for him. When they were living in Paris themselves, he'd watched her dress for her mother's funeral, and almost make herself late for the London plane while she hung over the gold watch fob with the mother's locket on it. "Shall I wear it? It was her favorite." Handed to her, the youngest of six, when the mother ran away from them.

What she was trying to decide of course was whether she

had loved her mother or not—nothing she had ever been
able to settle during the mother's long life. Whether she
must now assume her mother's flesh. She'd stood there, a
Brunhilde of a woman with a face constantly mollified by
laughter or rue, quite aware of the indecorum of this delay.
"Such ghastly frivolity," he heard her mutter. "My curse."
But her final decisions were always decorous. Held against
her svelte six-foot black, the gold ornament, small but brilliantly worked, was startling. "How can it? Look so
louche?" No, she wouldn't wear it. In the shaky hydraulic
lift of the old house on the Ile where they'd been lucky
enough to have an absentee's two-year sublet, he'd held
her in his arms. She'd always had to have a man tall
enough. "You loved her," he said.

Impossible that anyone should have to identify her—that
she should ever need identification. Only the gross state of
New York, or a city too improvidently supplied with suddenly dead persons of statuesque mind, heart and manners,
would require it.

"You were married to her once, weren't you?" a man at
the club had asked him just recently, but though he hadn't
been he never denied it, feeling she wouldn't want him to.
She'd never minded conventions except when confronted
by them. Or had never observed conventions, but never
wanted to flaunt that fact either. While always, down at
the bottom of that modest schoolgirl's locket of a heart
inhabiting breasts by Renoir, she'd envied certain women
of smart, scarecrow figure and even skinnier emotions—the
women who could be louche. He'd been surprised once, to
find the word in his English dictionary, though escaped
from its French aura: (F. *louche* squinting, L. *luscus* one-eyed)
Not straightforward, oblique.

"I was in love with her when she and you three men
were all there together," this same man had said. "From
afar. I wasn't a Rhodes scholar."

Emery from moneyed St. Louis, Mahlon from rural West

Virginia, and he himself from a Rhode Island heritage somewhere between—three tall Americans digging in the Ashmolean Library for Oxford gold. He and Emery would in time find their share and repolish it for posterity. She, the local girl, who'd still been Anglo-Irish enough to leave that university to go dig among her ancestors, would send up a gilt shower of books whose carat content was nowadays still felt to be indeterminate. Too original.

He himself had done better. History was never that original, if you stuck to the facts.

Mahlon, leaving for Ireland with her, only to be left by her in turn, had defected home to Harvard Law, and eventually to being among other things the lawyer for all of them.

"She could never quite decide whether to *love* a man or to *be* one," this man said. "Don't you agree?"

And he himself had answered, "I rather think *she* told you that."

Four generations of the women on her mother's side— from her great-great grandmother on down, she'd told them all early, had stayed married long enough to have the declining but still enormous families of their day: fourteen, ten and eight respectively, down to her own mother, who'd had only the six. Each had then repudiated the husband, in those days having had only one.

She'd reversed the process or modified it, having no live children of that opulent but hesitant body of hers—but a family of husbands. Which all her lovers had been, if without benefit of clergy. As each had also continued to be family, even after she had finally married one of them.

"Will you go?" Emery'd said yesterday afternoon, on the phone from Paris. "Identify her? It seems somebody has to. They won't release the body, unless. I would like it to be you. She would."

He could see the green of that garden on the Île St. Louis

from which Emery must be phoning, on the extension phone out there, wrangled from the telephone company by himself when Emery's tenant there, but still a rickety connection. Emery, returning once again from a bout with the home branch of that business a scholar should never have inherited but somehow did wonders with, had been their absentee landlord. And his good friend. Her lovers often occurred in chain style that way. It was natural. Similar men responded similarly to such a woman, and she to them.

But that time the mode of it had been different. The house he and she had sublet, Emery's, was linked with a whole web of life he didn't represent. Not money only, but a lot of it. Not merely the social web which expensive Paris could extend—but that too. "I've loved men—" she told him at last—and told Emery. "I'll only marry a life."

It seemed that she had had to. "The state of her heart—" Emery said now on the phone. "Well—her life always depended on it."

As he listened to Emery's voice, the big, oak-bordered, crescent-shaped window centered opposite him in the whitewashed wall of his own flat had seemed to expand and grow even more framelike, as it hadn't done since she'd left. The window, of a shape now and then seen in the former servants' quarters which sometimes nestled under the eaves of these old apartment houses in the West Fifties, had been important to them not merely for what they saw from it but for what it had shown of them. All the while the great half-moon chiaroscuro of the world looked in on them, their own two lives—optically glazed and varied with company, or peached in careless nude—had answered back. Meanwhile, homing in at them from heights far above their own twelfth floor or looking up from unknown levels below, people must now and then have reminded themselves, "There's a personal drama going on there."

Now, with the late sun piercing the dim corner where he

crouched hand to ear, and the attic roof lines peaked with light, he could be in some parish church dedicated to the end of that drama. "We make too much of that window," she'd sometimes say, hand on his shoulder. "It's what people like us do when we have too small a view." And then had gone on to make much of it.

"Emery—where—?"

He'd been about to ask all the questions when the Paris connection broke. While he hung up and waited, he had time to revisit that lustral garden of theirs, as he had last year. He saw again familiar white perennials, amber sparks which had been to him new. "Étienne calls those 'lion-spit,' " she said of the gardener—languidly for the way she usually reported Étienne. He'd attributed this to the new peignoir, much like the one in which he used to tell her she resembled Renoir's portrait of the young actress Tilla Durieux. Emery was meanwhile once again thanking him for the convenience of the phone, which still sat in the center of the round glass table, now and then cheeping to itself like a bird looking at its own image.

"She should have married you," Emery said, quite kindly. An outsider might find it improbable he wasn't being nasty, but he wasn't. That was the kind of man she liked—and he himself was only another of them.

"She always has higher opinions of people than they have of themselves," he'd answered. "Of course, goddesses do. Leaving us gods to do the other thing." So he'd again paid her one of the divided compliments she loathed.

"No, Emery—" she'd said then, "I'd rather be married to you. You don't make too much of my being a woman." Yet she must have married him for precisely that.

Emery could afford to be as silent on that score as on others, having Paris and the garden—as well as the deep amiability of a provincial American who'd tried everything and liked much of it.

"She'd have said the same to me about you, Emery," he'd
told him. "And you'd have received the letters."

She always corresponded pithily with whoever was absent, solid one-pagers which might have been perfumed or
had one of her hairs in them, for the way they brought her
through his door.

"I'm living the life of a well-placed cocotte" one had
read. "Have you ever known a woman who had weekly
appointments at the couturier? You do now. Emery sometimes goes with me. To keep me in breath. On the other
hand, when we hop over to London—if you can call flying
the car over with us a hop—we stay in a bedsitter near the
St. Catherine's Dock and pretend to be young. No use. Emery won't let me bike."

In the most recent letter there was also an unwonted ref-
erence to the Ashmolean. "Remember those stone heads
outside it?"

Those sculpted severed heads—the three friends had
asked, bumping into her the first week of term-time—were
they of kings, and broken off in Cromwell's time, or classi-
cal? We're Americans—they'd chorused—and haven't had
time to look it up.

"Does it matter?" she'd said, taking in the three of them.
"That's how it'll be. How it is for everybody. A head on a
pike. Isn't it the same in the U.S.?" All she hoped was that
the pike would turn out to be one of her own making, she'd
said when she knew them better. "Just let the pike be my
own." She was twenty-two at the time.

"Well, it has been," she wrote in that last letter. "Head
not always to be trusted. But the shaft's mine, all right."
She was coming to Atlanta to a conference, she'd added.
Emery thought she oughtn't, not in the June heat. "If
you're going to be in New York," she wrote, "I could fly up
afterwards." He'd answered everything but that. He hadn't
always felt the same as she about heads and pikes, but he
did now.

So he hadn't heard what the letter might really have been saying. No bikes. No heat. Save the breath. "Women—" he said to her too late and still offending her—"trust men to read between the lines more than they do." Over his shoulder she answered him. "Emery would have. Did."

A light mist, scarcely a rain, had broken up that last threesome in the garden.

"Why does London get all the reputation for this mineral-water kind of climate? Paris's just as bad." Emery's only grumble was the weather; in London he'd have touted perhaps Puget Sound, as having a better mist. He made them move inside. The other two—he and she—kept silent, suddenly a twosome. As all three knew, they would have stayed outside.

When they were at dinner, Étienne brought her the evening's flower, a kind of orange lily. A swart branch of a man, he hoarded speech as he did his blooms, and watched his mistress as if she were one of them. The flower always matched her dress. Nodding to the visitor, his former employer, he waited, shoulders squared. She always spoke for him. "Étienne's just come back from the convent," she said in French. "He saw Marthe take her final vows." Marthe, Étienne's daughter, had had a longer than usual novitiate, the officially given reason being that she was perhaps too worrisomely good for her age. No doubt the canny nuns had wanted to be sure that Marthe's call was all her own. She'd picked a cloistered order.

That had given him the grizzles when he lived there, and still did. She was a handsome half-Breton girl, as big-boned as her mistress. In the kitchen he'd sometimes come upon them sitting opposite each other at the deal table, often turning to look at him with the same strange kitchen rue.

"So Marthe finally became—just good enough?"

The other two, both lapsed Catholics, stared at him. He even smelled that incense, still joining the two of them. Or was it the flower, moving gently in her hand? "Étienne's very happy," she said, in French. Étienne, serving stiffly, straightened even more. Ceremony clung to simpler folk for days after. It invested them. Étienne spoke up. "Now, I'll know. I'll always know where she is." His tone was matter-of-fact.

His mistress raised the flower to her nose. Whenever she was wanting to be off and vagrant, the caged pupils of her eyes darted left-right, right-left, but this time one couldn't be sure. She'd stuck the lily between her breasts. Her eyes were bent on it.

"And how's Mahlon?" Emery said.

About the same time she'd come here to live with Emery, Mahlon had finally married, choosing the latest of his young girls. A fine enough young woman, with the pink nostrils of a good filly, she was however considered by some of his friends to be highstrung or withdrawn because she wouldn't live in New York, wanting Mahlon to give up his practice here, and the pied-à-terre he kept for it, in order to join her and the children, now five, three and one, on the Cape. Certainly the wife's eyes had filled up, the one time Mahlon mentioned it.

"He's moving to the Cape."

Watching her tableau with the flower, he played his old game of choosing a painter for her. To be fair, the tableau wasn't hers but his. The cheeks were almost too cerise now, though still not from rouge. There were new lineaments. Not Klimt any longer though, or any painter whose main devotion was to women. He couldn't decide who.

When he and Emery chanced to look up from the carving of the cook's bronze-armored duck, she was gone from the table. Emery blanched. She always vanished in this style. But Emery went after her, as he himself had never done.

This time she hadn't gone far. Over Emery's shoulder he saw her, in that kitchen with a woman in it which he himself hadn't been able to afford for her permanently—sitting across from the swollen-eyed cook, Étienne's wife, in her familiar spread-knee'd way. She needed the touch of another woman in the house, she'd said, not so much for their services as for their common situation.

Peering up, she saw him in his gift jacket with his new honor in its lapel. As he'd so often warned her, his distinctions earned him just about enough to keep him at earning them. That was why he merited them, she always replied; she wouldn't have him any different. She hadn't yet commented on the fit of the jacket.

Now she and the cook had a swift exchange on it which he couldn't quite catch. Or on him. *"Oui,* a button is *autre chose* from a ribbon," she told cook. She smiled up at him. "Wish I'd seen you get it."

Emery, who had a ribbon in his own buttonhole for certain services to France, not all of these involving money, said nothing. She'd seen it put on him.

Rising slowly, she'd linked arms with both of them, and so abreast they'd marched back into the dining room. She was happiest when all of them were in their places. Sooner or later, she always came back.

"She was found early this morning, your time," Emery said, coming on the line again, not from the garden this time. His voice had an indoor sound, more like him. It wouldn't be coming from that built-in desk, jutting from the boiserie in the sitting room, which had so amused her in his own time; that was still hers. Emery would be at that great desk in the hall which he himself had used—"the captain's desk," they'd called it, though there was nothing seafaring about that *terra firma* of a house. Or about Emery. "They got to me around three. Dinnertime here. Luckily, I was here."

"Who?"

"The police."

"But you said—wasn't it her heart?"

Silence. Emery must be nodding.

"A—massive attack."

Silence. On both their parts.

"You must have noticed her color, last time," Emery said almost irritably.

"Yes, I noticed it."

Silence. On both their parts.

"Mahlon had dinner with her—last night. At the club." The connection was now so good that Emery might be in the room, carrying his face as he always did, forward of the rest of him. Though nothing would be got from it. "He's— in the middle of moving. Apparently he flew to the Cape very early the next morning. *This* morning." Emery paused to cough. "He phoned *me,* from there. They must have found his address in her wallet. The police."

That figures. He didn't say it.

"We've both been trying to reach you all afternoon. Where *were* you?"

It was typical of them all, he supposed, that Emery felt free to ask. Where had he been, where had he a right to be, if not with her, or handy to her, when she died? Just as typically, he would now never ask Emery why he wasn't going to fly over himself.

"I was at Muffy's graduation. I just got back."

As the first of their trio to marry, late and brief as it had been, he was still pretty old to have this one chick of seventeen. All the sibling-crowded day he'd felt it, Muffy too. The junior parents had had little to say to him. Mahlon would have a lot of such graduations ahead of him.

"There was nothing from her on the message-taker; I've just checked it. She didn't let me know she was here." Over the phone a lie can be heard, but this wasn't quite. "Of course, Em. I'll go at once." He took a deep breath. He'd never known her to stay in a hotel. "Where do I go?"

While he waited he noted that his window had returned to its normal scope—that narrow slice of outlook often to be found at the top of not-too-plush older buildings of the West Fifties. "Emery. You still there?"

"I'm here," Emery said. "I'll wait here. She's at the morgue."

Sundays the morgue opens at one. All Saturday night he waited up. It wasn't a wake. Wakes were populous, and orated the known facts. He didn't yet have those. He was sitting up with her, as Emery was. He wasn't sure of Mahlon. But during the course of that night such a treasury was accumulating in his own breast that he began to understand why Emery hadn't come. They were similar men. The window did not again expand. At 6 A.M. he dressed.

He sat tightly in the swaying bus, through whose open windows summer wooed. Anybody would know this air for a Sunday's, and him for a tryster, as she used to call them: young women with their mouths quirked around love errands, young men humming to the landscape. Or even the spruced-up putative half of a couple like themselves.

"Papers say hot" everyone in the city, in the bus, was saying, though from experience they knew this already. He couldn't help smiling. Buses were his kind of solitary, even when he had been with her. Cabs always jangled him. One had to assume a personality for them even briefly, and then was left on the pavement with it, as the door banged. "How you love people—from a distance," she said, was saying. "The populace. You never get enough of them." Traveling where he was going, it was still true. Only convention accused him, with its dark suit. That storehouse of repose, widening but no gap, was still in his breast.

Downtown medical New York had been altogether cleansed since he'd used to come on call to Bellevue, to spring a colleague who always signed himself in on the fourth day of a drunk. The looneybins and charnelhouses were now bright prophylactic buildings which went on for blocks. The morgue had a trust company's façade, dedicated to a past medical examiner in gilt and sky blue.

Inside the lobby a police sergeant sat behind a long, bare, polished desk, facing a ring of empty chairs. He gave his name, glimpsed a shift in the courtly black face, and saw he must give hers. Yes, that was the hierarchy here. "About forty-five minutes, sir. Please have a seat."

He sat opposite the desk. To the sergeant's right there was a dim mahogany recess leading somewhere. To his own right there was another. The high brown wall which lofted behind the sergeant was bare also. He was slow to catch on to what was being striven for here. He'd expected hospital white.

In the farthest corner, on two chairs apart, a young man and woman, Puerto Ricans by the look of them, brother and sister maybe, sat in ethnic sullenness. Or dignity. Perhaps a second brother had been shot. In his own corner he hung his head for assigning them the violences here. The snobbery of history had begun.

Shortly a woman entered. Tall and elegant though not young, she too might have made her concessions between weather and circumstance, in soft black but with an open-throated white shirt and a tan slouch of patterned hat which half hid her face. She gave the name of the dead at once. "From The Hague. I don't know why the hotel should send him—here. He spoke at the UN only two days ago—everyone knows who he—is." She stopped short, with a clenching-in. The sergeant paused, explaining gently then that the hotel had had no option. His manner was remarkable—not too much of it. But the job mustn't have cynicized him. Perhaps he was a natural minister. "My brother-in-law—" the lady said, mollified. "I didn't want my sister to—." They exchanged looks now, the sergeant nodding. She took her seat, concentrating on her rings. These were good. But her story was over.

He stood up, restless. "Anyplace to get something to read?"

"Maybe the gift shop. At the hospital."

"How far?"

"Long block down."

He checked his watch. "What's yours say?"

"One-twenty."

So did his. "Be back at one forty-five, right?"

"About." All the sergeant's words echoed. Perhaps the man knew that.

At the door he turned back. "Which way?"

The man's patience was stately, endless. "Turn right."

The gift shop had a few paperbacks no visitor would conceivably want to read or give—but hospitals had low opinions of visitors. Or did over here.

He remembered visiting her when she was in for surgery —appendix—in the hospital in London, near where she'd had her first lodgings after university. In the lift there, two convalescents in homey wrappers snuggled bottles of wine just bought for them in the shop below. "Cheaper here," their glowing relatives said. Upstairs, as her three friends neared her bedside—Mahlon just over the water with his new law degree, Emery and himself in from their own first lodgings in Chelsea and Pimlico, she'd held a finger to her lips. Nurse was just instructing the old lady in the next bed. "Now, Mrs. B. After the op, your cats may be brought to visit. But mind you, only one at a time."

He walked back from the gift shop slowly, pacing himself. One thirty-five. On her thirty-fifth birthday, in New York—Emery being in from his adopted France for a first gander at the business inherited, and he and Mahlon newly established in bachelor flats not too far from her new Central Park South sublet (his being cheaply west of it and Mahlon's professionally east of it)—she'd cooked dinner for them. Or rather had lavishly ordered it in, presiding from a rented sofa much too small for her long bones, in

the first of the peignoirs. Abortion suspected, but not
stated. The appendectomy was mentioned, since they were
all three once again gathered around her, eating their tray
suppers, as they'd once or twice done courtesy of that long-
ago London hospital. Though of course the suppers—
sprouts and mince versus beef Wellington—weren't comparable. "American doctors always admire my neat Hampstead scar though. Appears they did me rather well," she
said amusedly. "It is rather neat, isn't it."

And like two fools, he and Emery had both nodded.
Mahlon, finished with his plate, hadn't looked up. He'd
been busy balancing her bills and British-American income
taxes, for by then she'd begun her habit of subletting quarters too charming for her earnings and blaming this on her
standards, since no lovers ever went with them. It was Emery who stood up, knocking over his champagne.

But he'd brought plenty. Though he would remain dark-
haired to the present day, he was even then filling out to be
a grandee. "Why are all your satisfactions so visible?" she
would sometimes moan at Emery.

He himself had already been graying, well on his way to
her predicted: "You'll be the silvery one, and of course still
the handsomest," which had annoyed him then, though
nowadays Muffy was pleased.

For Mahlon's wild shock of hair and easy body habits,
oddly topped by eye-crinkles of more than statutory wis-
dom, she would never predict.

But that time, Emery had been nasty, sweeping out an
arm to include all three of them. "All your cats," Emery had
said.

The rest of the way back to the morgue, his shoulder
hugged the building wall, feeling a conformation which
was trying to tell him something. Turning, he stared back
through the glare he'd traversed. The pavements were an
institutional mottle, broad and capable. Behind him, the
morgue's wall was blank for two, maybe three stories up.

He envisioned that basement civilization, depot to the arc-lit floors above. Which surely would be white.

Inside, the sergeant shook his head. Not yet.

He sat down in the same chair. "Nothing at the shop."

"Like a look at the *Times?*"

There lay the thick, unbroached packet, smelling of lazy Sundays layered with newsprint like a Braque. Was the city always this kind to the populace? "Yours? Or I mean—is it provided?"

"Mine."

Too much kindness, would it break into his storehouse? "I'll have the first section, thanks." Surely that would be enough. He leafed through it for politeness, carefully keeping the creases, and after a few minutes handed it back. The sergeant was not surprised.

At this moment the woman in the concealing hat came out of the recess to the sergeant's left, patting herself as women do. So that was what was on that side. She sat down two seats beyond him, as was proper. He was next in line.

An entourage of three women pressed through the main door. He sat back, feeling the rhythms here.

"—forty-five minutes. Minimum."

This the leader of the party, angular and powerful in a high African turban, wasn't about to accept. "These two have come all the way from North Carolina. They have to catch an afternoon bus back. Only bus that goes." The two others gazed up at her, their urban authority. Two dumpy little folk in headcloths, the elder one twisting her hands.

The sergeant leaned forward. "Well, now, I'll tell you." Whether he had been chosen for the job because of his own character, or had become job-molded, its rhythm had taken him in hand. Though the three before him were black too he was no more deferent, no less. The rhythms here went beyond race. He raised one hand, pointing upward. Rested it on the desk again. "Not to mock—this is a library."

Those two from Carolina, they understood right away. What in spite of his walk he himself hadn't confronted yet. Why you wait.

Even the leader backed off, her biggity stance sagging. "There anyplace they could get a, maybe a cuppa—?"

"The hospital coffee shop. Turn right."

He himself was in the Ashmolean's stacks—where all the thousands of books waited to come down, some to be chosen, some not—when her name was pronounced.

The recess to the left led to a small alcove, where a young woman took graceful charge of him. She had a spidery tininess of waist and limb, long neatly flowing crimped hair and a sweet voice. He was grateful to her at once for sparing him from babbling the absurd details of a life, of his connection with it. A printed form was set before him, with the slightest flourish. Copy of the death certificate it must be. What he knew of the facts was correct—her name, profession and home residence. The date of the death—yesterday. The time of death was new to him: 4:30 A.M. The address she'd been brought here from was not. His eye was transfixed by both, and after that by the familiar signature which had signed her in here. He wasn't really surprised.

Mahlon's pied-à-terre—he'd been in it only once, one night, years ago, when Mahlon and he, caught in a cloudburst handily near the place, had on his own suggestion ducked in. At the time it was merely Mahlon's bachelor flat. He'd never been invited there before, and never wanted to go back. There Mahlon must keep that inner sprawl of life which a successful lawyer wouldn't show, or not one who'd briefed himself out of the slum-alps of Appalachia.

He himself had seen only one other domestic disorder so profound. Her own parental home in Oxfordshire, where they'd all stopped for tea once during a bike trip when they first knew her, had had this same mad inversion of comfort, though on a larger scale. In her family's case, as she'd forewarned them on the doorstep, it came from "a mating of Irish landpoor with British academic fug."

There had been one fastness—her father's biologicals. Otherwise, half the objects in that household, from stray ladders to the odd envelope, were plainly still migrating toward long-gone destinations, while others were as clearly set down in discernible anti-paths of owner use, with both sides happily compounding. The only apparent steadies being kettle on hob, milk jug on carpet and huge biscuit box, near it a deserted broomhandle on which hung a tennis skirt—her mother had been a noted player—dried almost to parchment. The house had had an Irish name.

"Loughskilly!" he'd exclaimed, standing dripping inside Mahlon's door. There'd been no particular mark of woman there, nor of either sex really, only that almost masterful hodgepodge of—yes—like minds. By stretching, he could have stuck his inside-out umbrella into the milk jug.

Mahlon hadn't answered. He never did. So in time he'd receded before the frontal presence of himself and Emery, with our ribbons and our buttons and our too habitable houses. Mahlon had always been the least tall of the triumvirate. But here now was his generous signature, as present to them all on dozens of their own documents. At four-thirty yesterday morning, after dinner at a club which closed at a prim hour, her lawyer and last witness had signed her out of his house—as attested to by an officer of that precinct—and in here.

Surely he himself had a right to know—how. And Emery.

The girl was waiting—how well she waited!

"The family—will want to know the circumstances." He was family, and being nasty at it. Similar men.

The girl answered without checking any medical report he could see; did she prepare herself beforehand for each circumstance? "She was found face up, in bed." Her eye

was steady on him, still modest, but she folded her hands
and stood up now. It was time.

He'd expected an elevator, which would take him to one
of the high forensic floors. There, between marble slab and
arc-light, they two would meet.

Instead, he was moved only a few feet on, into what
must be a central recess beyond the wall back of the sergeant's desk. The recess itself was totally dark. Stunned, he
saw why. Museums did the same.

The window was waist-level, framed in double bands of
chrome and of heavy plate glass, clear as air. The space
behind the glass was larger than any coffin, smaller than
any room. She lay on a table, or shelf, level with the lower
band of chrome, and about a foot behind it. Perhaps it was
a platform, on which she descended or rose into this painful light. In the shadows to his left the girl attendant re-
mained, just visible enough. It was a tableau.

She lay on her right arm and hip, the nude forearm pro-
jecting. From under the armpits down and over the swell of
left hip and upper thigh, she was wrapped. The left leg also
projected, the foot most nakedly. The wrappings: white
linen, or not linen. Now—the face.

He felt the shame of those who may look their fill. The
lips were parted, showing the teeth, in what he knew
wasn't a smile. Yet it could be. The eyes were partly open—
so that their color might be recognized? He recognized
them, averting his own to that high-ceremented hip. On his
doctor's desk there was an ivory Chinese lady from a period when the patient, modestly clothed or even concealed,
tapped out the locus of ailment on such a surrogate. In her
own pose there was now that chiselment, even to the vul-
nerable foot—a draping from some hand behind. There
they were, those new lineaments. He could assign her an
artist now, if not name him. One in whose work lingered
that coming mortality which solved the affairs of both
women and men.

But it was her complexion that dazzled him. He'd never seen any but the tannined or emaciated older dead, never anyone dead in his or her prime. Or at the prime of that? Studying her with the lore of their own shuttered afternoons, or verging, crescent dawns, he was sure. Caught in the massive act, of both living at the height and dying of it, her limbs were lifted in assumption, and tinted with that capillary rush.

Bending his head aside so that the window was only a bas-relief, he made the smallest cross he could and turned away.

The girl had waited, not pressing him. Probably she had to speak, if softly. "Is she—your person?"

He did redden. But no harm was meant. The girl was only one of the lesser handmaidens, not here to provide asps, only to hang onto the facts, while each arrival passed his own legend through the actual skein of knowing. He was here to identify her.

To Emery: the body. To Mahlon: to have her always in the middle of moving. To himself: the grand tableau.

Marveling at that lifelong apportionment, he nodded, and went to sign her out.

The girl gently now extracted her pen from his hand. "Excuse me, but—"

Yes he must move on now. Here's where the rhythm speeds up.

"—Excuse me, but what decoration is that?"

He looked down at the button in his lapel. It came with a jacket, more or less. "An award. For—a history."

An envelope was tucked in his hand.

On his way out he stopped at the desk, reminding himself he was to inquire after her effects. Her address book especially, Emery'd said.

"Disposal," the sergeant said, "yes." The two women from Carolina and their duenna entering just then, the sergeant held out his left hand, forefinger up, nodding to

them. It was time. So holding, he bowed to the inquiry on
his right. "Only to a blood relative, sir. As part of the estate."

She is her own estate, he wanted to cry, or no one's. But
the sergeant would already know that, and the girl inside
also. Long since, their jobs would have instructed them.

"Thank you. Her lawyer will handle it."

As he hesitated outside the lobby door, the woman
whose turn had followed his came out of it and stood near,
sobbing hard into a handkerchief. After a minute he ap-
proached her. "Can I get you a cab?"

"Please." She blew her nose. "That girl. I was all right
until then. She admired my hat. Wanted to know—where I
got it. It broke me up." She had a nibbling stage diction and
a long-chinned, familiar profile. He saw who she was. Or
had been, for his generation. So they liked to have their
stars here too—why not? Or hoped for them. "Perhaps—
she knew you."

She colored, acknowledging. "Uh-uh, though. She did it
out of pure kindness. That's what got to me. She did it for
me."

There seemed to be no cabs. He considered the bus, for
both of them. Just then a cab did draw up. He held the door
for its passengers to exit, a hobbling old couple, then
helped her into it. For a moment she considered—whether
to offer him a ride. Then a second cab drew along, dropped
a load he didn't see, and hung waiting. Her cab's window
was down. She leaned over it. "He should have died at my
house. I wanted him to." She pulled down the hat. He
waved both cabs on, envelope in hand. Nothing concluded,
though one pretended it. Nothing was original. She'd be
about sixty now, the same age as him and his friends.

He opened the envelope, in it the certificate, a copy. Also
an ink-scribbled, spidery note. "There was no autopsy.
People like to know."

Oh, but there was.

He's beginning to hurt from it. This city's too kind to its populace. Even here one may watch how that Ashmolean current rolls in, rolling out again. Even on a Sunday. But here the storehouse wall behind him is blank. The heads on their pikes are not too long displayed. To one another. We are borrowed, we are returned, this is our estate. Love us for it. Who can love us enough for it? We are all lent.

Not to mock.

But this is a city which can't escape its own windows. He waits on his particular level, knowing well enough what it sees of him.

He's a silvery man, buttoned too. Standing at a window. He will stare without shame now at that foot with its eternally waxed arch. At the wrapped breasts. At the slitted, ambiguous eyes. The tryst will be endless. Though she is not breathing. Though she is not smiling. Though beneath all he can see that fixed ocher, as of yesterday's lily. She will always know where he is. He is waiting to be identified.

And she? She is learning to love him from a distance. Watching him, she seems to rise and float in a rosiness just beyond the needs of life, louche beyond the dues of death —flushed with all the labors of the heart.

The Sound Track

THE STORY of Shiltie Edwards and Millie White is too well-known not to repeat. It's the kind even a subtle person will tell, in certain restaurants.

This one isn't the Polo Lounge, but on a snowy day with cabs scarce, on Park Avenue not Beverly Hills, worlds overlap. This is the one where that famous bead-curtain window-wall ripples the hours like newsprint, upstaging all customers. Whose regulars swarm in every noon anyway, to have a new try. There's also a Picasso you can fall into like down a moon crater; it won't take backtalk from any chef. This is the place where real art came back to restaurants. Our table though is from out of town and more full-blooded.

"This the place where the book trade comes to eat only burgers?" the head man at it says. "Or that something with grapes?" Number One never talks business over foreign food.

His Number Two and Number Three are doing it for him.

"Of course they wanted Shiltie Edwards for the part, who wouldn't," Number Two says. "Sandor flew here him-

self to see him. In that apartment of theirs. Shiltie sits there,
Sandor says, having his little snort of coke. But polite. Offering it. He was always a mannerly little guy."

"He don't act, in private life," Number Three says.
"That's how good *he* is."

"Come on. Anyway, he says no to the part, for six or
eight reasons. Which means the usual one. Nothing doing,
unless there's a part for Millie too. Which Sandor is supposed to broach like on his own. Which that stubborn
Hunky won't do."

"This place was designed by a Hungarian," the head man
says. As a blue-eyed white man with a shock of white hair
all his own and not one clubby trace of Semite or even
black or yellow in him, he can't afford a racial slur. Or any
physical one. He will not even use the word "bald." But he
has joined the conversation. That is, he is permitting it.

"Well, twenty years it already is for her. Since she cut
Boojum's Party," Number Three says. "The teen-age disc of
all time," he adds. A Number Three always says too much.

"My kids had that disc every part of the house." Number
Two always talks kids to Number One.

"A hard act to follow—" Three says. "Yourself."

"So you're a kid can sing a sexy fifteen at thirteen and
please everybody. No knockers yet, even a head bow like
Rebecca of Sunnybrook Farm. So at fifteen you can still
pretend thirteen, so at sixteen even—on the road."

"On the road. That was a mistake. Any star."

"So the teenagers in St. Louis, they know that? Come on,
Three. With a disc still in the millions? And the studio,
they didn't push her? Okay—so at sixteen."

"Still a smart cookie. She went on to college too, right
along with her audience."

"That's what my kids liked. The smartness showing
through. That was always her quality. So they could like
identify." Two gives a fatherly cough. "So then. So then, all
of a sudden you're eighteen—you *are* sexy. You're like ev-

erybody else. So what can you do? You go along with it."
His voice has dropped to a whisper. "And you're like everybody else."

"She wasn't that bad. That early chain-saw voice." Three
is their music man.

"She's never bad, what's that got to do with it? When
even today *Boojum* still sells."

"Your image gets stuck with an audience, you can't compete with it."

"No way. My kids treasure that record—the original. Begun the babies on it. They went normal into marriage, both
mine. My eldest the same age as Millie. Thirty-four."

Three is counting up. "So Millie was fourteen really—
when she was thirteen?"

"Fine little trouper," the head man said.

They wait for him. But he says no more.

Three begins the next round. "Shiltie, he was lucky.
Never to be a child star."

"They were kids next door, you know. Somewhere in
Jersey. He and Millie."

"What do you mean, 'somewhere'? Short Hills. Her father was the banker there. His father had a record company, New York. And Shiltie, he made her cut that disc.
There's a twist."

"So then, *they* went normal." Two's voice is soft. "By
then, Shiltie is an actor, Off-Broadway. Doing a little job
called *Tents.*"

"Not 'Off.' Off-off."

"Off off-off, so okay. You know anybody ever catch him,
that play? My kids did. They lived here New York their
mother then, followed the theater. They say the whole
Shiltie Edwards image was already there—the nostalgia bit,
the rubber knees. And like already not a lead; he's too small
for it. Like—*shhh*—a character actor. At twenty-four. And
he knows what he is. When an actor knows what he is, and

the audience goes along with it? Yeah. And at twenty-four."

"Not so young, for one of those kind," Three says. "And when you're twenty-eight. But then you make just one film bit, with your head on the boobs a major star. And the next morning—well, you know the story."

The story is too well-known not to repeat. Though from here on the two voices go so fast we almost can't distinguish them.

"So the head of we know what studio calls every producer into the viewing room, says 'Gentlemen—I'm not going to mention names. But I'm wanting you all to look at this."

"And after seeing that bit, a bit that takes a very sharp eye, every guy in the room says 'Hakim—'—oh boy, does Hakim Goulouris know how to stay on top—" Three makes a swallowing sound. Yes, it's surely Three. " 'Hakim—' they say, 'is the name you're not going to mention Charlie Chaplin, or isn't it?' "

A pleased silence.

"Some guessed Woody; I heard a few." Is this himself, Number One? It is. But always modest, this is all he will concede. Let the others pick up on it.

They do.

"And they were all of them wrong."

"Except Hakim, here. Except you, Number One."

"Shiltie turned out to be—Shiltie."

"Not a comic only. Not only a comic lover."

"A lead. A two-hundred-million-dollar five-foot-four all-by-himself-in-a-room rubber-faced—lead."

"Shiltie walks a very thin line. But the audience can follow him."

"And when he's with a woman, an older woman especially—dynamite. How old's he now?"

"Thirty-three. Thirty-four last year."

"He does the reminiscence bit better than anybody. He was doing it that day."

They must be being served now. It doesn't take long.

"Those boobs—" Number Three says, with his mouth full. "Hakim—what was her name? Those were major boobs."

Three slipped badly there, with Number One. Music men are not in on everything. He is now Number Four.

"So these are the famous steakburgers," the head man—Hakim Goulouris by adoption, Quincy Appleby by birth, Hank to women stars only—says. "Well, give me an avocado at the Lounge."

Farther up Park in a newish building, on the lowest floor of a triplex which is a beige underworld endlessly furnished in sofas that swell even more as you look at them, the Edwardses, or the Whiteses—Shiltie and Millie, Millie and Shiltie—and is such euphony good or bad in their situation?—are having the morning meal. They've called it that ever since an interviewer, there at that hour with a photographer for Shiltie only, inquired: "And do you two always join each other for the morning meal?" and Millie, sharp-tongued even then, replied: "Only if after the evening bed."

Above them the ceiling, which isn't very high, is covered with gold-colored aluminum, said to give a softer reflection than mirrors. They never look up. The cups of espresso with which they start their day are on separate cocktail tables; there is no big table anywhere. Columned floor-to-ceiling all through the house there are sound tracks, which can boom a score to make a crowd of two hundred feel they're swimming in it easy—or whisper it just enough to cool your neck. Other communications must be in the main column just to the right of their facing sofas, all dial-fronted down its stack, ending in a small, red-lit one-line inscription that certainly isn't the time, isn't the stock market; what is it?

"The decorator's number, maybe," Shiltie said, first look. They'd had it all done from California, carte blanche. "For when we feel we want a change. I don't feel it yet, do you?"

It wasn't a telephone number, and no, Millie didn't.

"Just don't say the word 'beige' out loud, though," she said, "things might shatter. This furniture is still looking for itself."

Later, after a couple of Morris Louis pictures were brought in, and made into walls so that they wouldn't look too much like pictures, the sofas grounded.

Between their two is a patch of bare butternut-colored wood floor. Two four-to-five-inch metal sound pipes, alcoved at the top like smokestacks, rise knee high in the middle of the patch. The kitchen is designed entirely for caterers, which is as it should be. They bring any large tables as needed, and remove them.

"Nobody Home," Shiltie said in every room, that first time.

"I love it," Millie said.

Shiltie was only quoting his mother, who shortly said it for herself. "This is the kind of place always says to me Nobody Home. Who lives in such a place?"

Millie said lightly, "It's all up on the *fourth* floor. Home."

Mrs. Edwards, a straightforward woman, is much hurt because Millie has never invited her up there.

Millie's mother, who knows better, never mentions it.

From wherever Shiltie's on location—the Seychelles, Malta, all the other odd coigns producers go in for, they always come back here. They come back quickest of all from the Coast, where people have a tendency to press Shiltie to stay on alone.

"New coign!" Shiltie will call out to Millie, some day shortly after. Shiltie will put on hold the direct line to his agent's, which is inside that big dial-fronted column too.

"New coign," he'll say again—the silly word came from an awful script once—"Guess where?"

But Millie's agent, who called yesterday, has already told her. It's always very tactfully arranged. Perhaps that's what that bottom-line electric warning is really for?

"If you'll consider going," Shiltie always says, "I've a mind to."

Millie laughs, smiles, kisses, coming down neatly on his chest. Ending up there. "Flip a coign," Millie says.

She's tough, she's smart, the slight rasp that made her teenage voice is still there, and vivid in her face as well; she's never needed a psychiatrist. All through the *Boojum* years, while she cut other discs as well and made appearances, her father made her commute to Bennington or Sarah Lawrence meanwhile, and she is still harboring her resources.

Once, caught on a Venice canal in all that bubble-glass reflection on a warm evening, Shiltie, whose latest is by then already a box-office biggie though it also won in the art way at Cannes, says: "You all right kid, you really?" The sister-in-law part she'd been engaged to do has turned out to be a one-time bit, in a beauty shop. She trails her hand over the gondola's side, toward that much-used, knowing water. "Enough soul-muck down there for the whole Renaissance," she mutters. "Yeah, oh yeah, don't worry. I'm destroying my image. Good for me." She means it. Though back in the apartment, she will never say.

This particular day though, she's not on her way to a fencing lesson, or to N.Y.U. for art history, or even to the voice coach. Since she's too young for a face-lift unless there's a part in it, and won't go in for peels, she looks her age. Between pictures is when Shiltie flops, these days way down sometimes. Far down enough to need his highs. Though since he's had his eyes done he never looks it. Today too, they are: At Home. There's a third cup of espresso

on a third cocktail table. It's noontime. The new president
of a major studio is sharing their morning meal.

She's about their own age, which when you come up that
fast that far on Wall Street by thirty-five, you don't hide,
but she grew up in the studios as well, daughter of a director once on everybody's tongue. An unbeatable combination, this week's papers say. "Sure—" she's saying. "After I
took my mind East."

"To beat your image, huh? As your pa's daughter."

Coke takes Shiltie in his own way; he's an original there
too. He doesn't hit the serene like the rest of us. Coke hits
him contrary. But right for him. Or so far. What it does is
to make him more rubbery. Not only at the knees. On top.
In the nose, to say precisely. Where it hits all of us—but
not the same. Rubber—he's made of it. As all the world
knows. Knew.

She watches that nose activate. "Oh no, Mr. Shillitoe. For
my mind."

Now, nobody calls him that. Not since other little boys
beat up the runt for having it.

He knows what the studio calls the president behind her
back. Shortly he's going to call her it. But first he says, "I
appreciate their sending you." He's a mannerly guy. "But I
already gave Sandor my answer. Sandor knows I won't
work that throw-it-away, documentary-type sound track
he does, you never quite hear all the words. I'm an actor.
I'm in talking pictures."

That's all very well. But they all three know that voices
are important to Sandor, even if words aren't. And he is
known to hate Millie's voice. There's no part for her. Shiltie's just covering for her. Or the coke is, for somebody.
"So thanks," he says, narrowing the eyes but the nose following, "Poppa Girl."

Though in his mind of course he's still bargaining. The
way you do when you still think you have enough clout
even for presidents.

Now this is what nobody knows. Did the president of that studio come to ask him again to do Sandor's picture? Or what she did ask for? Or did she just then think of it? She is smart.

Millie meanwhile says, nervously—you can hear—"Have a croissant, Mrs. Ingalls—Prue. I mean—I'll ring for one."

They never have croissants, you get nothing but coffee there. So, do you think Millie already knew? What was coming?

Anyway, the president says no on both accounts. "Oo noo—" she says, "I don't do Sandor's errands. I came on my own. What we have in mind, what I have—." She takes a breath you can hear all over the tape. Of course she had one on her. That echelon they all do, they're like in the public domain. Plus she played it back for some of us. Anyway, Prue Ingalls has class. She says, "Why no, why I came for both of you. You're both so wonderful."

And that's how *The Story of Boojums* is born.

Afterward, Shiltie says, still high, "I wonder, Wonderful. She come for you, Millie, because of me? Or for me because of you?"

It's not the Polo Lounge yet. It's not the Four Seasons again either. It's the Tea Room, where it's Christmas all year. In New York only. That little banquette was Harold Clurman's table. That over there, Mr. B's, Balanchine. Whatever time it is, it's the night that the opera, the ballet, the play, the picture—opens.

Three men have come from L.A. for it. Not the same three. And in this place, don't call them numbers. Call them: An Oboe. A Tuba. And an unidentified Brass.

"She was simply—!" the Oboe squeals. "How they ever got her back down to fourteen. Sixteen."

"That medic down in Argentina. She was never lifted before, so he had a clear field. Then Makeup could age her along with the script. The last part, when she's older, they did first, natch. The voice she did herself, almost all the way; only once they used the record." A Brass is always informative.

"Why'd they ever let him play himself?" the Oboe mourned. "God, it was sad. But what could they do? It's his life too."

"I hear they couldn't have got her," Brass said. "Not without him. But what's on the cutting-room floor, wow. They're ditching Prue Ingalls for it. It wasn't only he was spaced out for every shooting. He's all—"

"Rub-bah—" the Tuba said.

Easter morning, you wouldn't want to be in either of those New York restaurants. There's a lattice-y green about this place that holds up the season properly. The avocado comes in like a piece of Crown Ducal, primed with shrimp. Ever notice how the food tinkles here, like tender majolica? There's a fish-gill ripple table to table each time the aquarium is entered; either you know who, and don't give a, or you don't and you do. Sure, the place can brink to the top with envy, and has corner squawks of vulgarity which fall heavy as nuggets, but all the beauties swim through it like carp. Even old people's ankles feel light and cool. No one can have a cold here. Everyone is newly risen today. This place does not support agony. This is the Polo Lounge. The polo ponies, if there ever were any, are back in Kipling where they belong.

Why have individual voices ever anyway? Why not just tracking?

She comes in, Millie, with the new musical they want her for gathered in drifts around her like the most becoming of boas—though she hasn't yet signed for it. Or been signed? There's a rumor she's more interested in the artistic. Or he is—the new man she's temporarily leaving them for. Going back East is always leaving.

"Bye-bye, Moe. Hello, Angel. Dear Moneybags. Darling

Prue." Her voice still has the rasp, like lime in sherbet. Those aren't bat squeaks behind her; a component must be out of synch. Or the tape is too worn. "No, I'm considering a script about an older woman. Lovey, that doesn't have to be art."

Someone asks, "And will there be a nice little something for Shiltie, baby? Hear he's on exercises, snapping back strong."

From another corner a technical murmur: "Under the face powder, along the jawbone, see there?"

From yet another: "Well, dimples. After forty they make a face look like apple pie."

It's a Moog medley now, half ugly. And the theme very beige—if you go in for these audio-visual crossovers. And why not?

In the apartment, Shiltie is reading Rimbaud, a mean colorist of a poet, if only with the vowels. There used to be so many colors, so many more of them, in voices too. Shiltie hasn't yet got around to reading him aloud again, like when he used to sneak practice in some empty echo box in his father's joint. He's only letting those vowels sink back into his character. Shiltie has been harboring his resources. Which, thanks to early training, Off-off and Off Off-off, are considerable.

The sound track is meanwhile playing from every stack in the place, all three floors. You might think a party was in progress here, for two hundred pairs of feet. What he's been doing is playing all his and Millie's party tapes, while he does his two exercises. Tapes of all their parties—they have a full collection of them, it being a matter of honor never to erase.

He began today as usual, by playing his and Millie's favorites. Something happens on each of them. On Millie's, a Spanish *zarzuela* singer brought over to record, a huge man used to great popular adulation, suddenly stopped treading the pale, heavy water-music going on here, cried—"This is a truly classless society!" and was found in the men's room weeping, head on arms, in sobs as regular and glutinous as a bullfrog's.

On Shiltie's choice, a waiter mistakenly hired from an agency catering mostly to Hasidic weddings breaks into a wild kazotski dance which brings him by heel clicks, Cossack jumps and suspiciously Russian yelps, to the top of the stairs, all the while wheeling on his raised palm a tray of smoked salmon sandwiches, which he then eats, all of this to the crowd's cheers.

But more generally, things so flow and register that listening is half looking again, at the young beauties in fish-scale chiffons always on that wall sofa, holding their elbows well up to show their pectorals, the spotlights barbering all the advancing men to peach color, while their speech melds to one sated blur like the tearing of gift packages.

The two exercises are the simplest and hardest of those tricky bits of business Shiltie learned from his first acting coach, his initial year out of Jersey in a class held in a hole-in-the-corner at the Hotel Seville. The coach was a seedy-famous actor so old that he had never been on anything except Broadway.

One exercise went: "You are coming up the palace stairs. You are a starving man. Hold it—I'm not through yet." The class was always so eager. "You are not in rags. You are wearing a tux."

The second exercise was a physical feat once common on the circuits: focusing every eye on you, both onstage and out there, by holding your breath. The old boy could turn red as a turkey-cock and hold for what seemed minutes. It was always a show-stopper, like real tears. Nowadays you rarely saw it in the theater. Body-to-body audiences of the old intense kind were needed for it. It was no good for film.

Neither tape has brought Shiltie's talent out. As the mirror has shown him, he does not pinken, he does not starve. He is not surprised. But his agent has just called him. It's for a musical, not a big part, but a solid one. He has a small singing voice, just possible. He thinks he'll mostly talk it, like Rex Harrison did in *My Fair Lady.* Talk himself back into life. What the call really means is that Millie's due in from the Coast. He's been practicing for that too. There she is—hear the door? And that snap is where he closes the Rimbaud.

He lays his head on her breasts. Those'll never be major, but there's quite enough room for such as him. His nose looks very refined in this coast's dim light, hollowed some but not too damaged for the kind of actor he's got to be from now on—one with only character. The nose goes with the knees, no longer rubbery but limber enough for art.

"Ah, here you are," she says. "In your coign." She always likes these verbal signposts. Over and over. It strikes him she's like a girl stuck in what used to be called the vamp of a popular song. Very faintly in the background, her own theme song can always be heard. It strikes him— hear it?—that in time she may have a little trouble following him.

She doesn't think so. In the stage-light always here, she goes to bed with her new man. She doesn't wince at the sight. He was always dynamite with older women. Nor does he fail her. He does the reminiscence bit better than anybody.

Next day, they come down as usual. On the little tables the espresso cups are waiting, set there by that maid one never sees. Like everybody here she is real enough at intervals, but has acquired certain habits. And like in any decent play, she knows all about her employers. A pity she can't be brought in, in her winged black Sunday hat and good cloth coat, to correct matters in certain restaurants.

The Edwardses—or the Whites—are standing on the bot-

tom step of the narrow, pie-cut stairs which lead to the
duplicate floor above, and from there to the one above that,
where the stairs end. Carpet runs like cream under everything except that one patch of yellow slick between the two
biggest sofas. Millicent and Shillitoe sit down, one on either side of it. Those two metal stacks, which rise from the
floor like periscopes, are in between.

Amazing, how this place has never soiled. Parties don't
do that, not where corps of cleaners can be called in afterward, or a decorator given carte blanche. Anyhow, the little, piggish, smeary acts of living are absent here. A sound
track certainly makes no dust. They have it turned off at
the moment, or think they have. That line of random sym-
bols at the base of the big column, like one vital red capillary from an oculist's chart, has never been explained.

"I knew where you were all the time," Millie says. She
doesn't have to say. She shouldn't say, not for Shiltie's
style of things. Nor for safe keeping. But that's Millie.
"You've been up on the fourth floor."

He sees she hasn't touched her coffee, and is staring at
the patch of bare floor, just as he used to do when he was
down. Worse yet, she is carrying a purse in her own house.
Yes, there it comes, the same little bit of business she always maintained he acquired under the stresses of the West
Coast, or the statuses. People do it just as much here when
the money palls, or the stress does, but Millie has her
images. She takes a dainty pinch, then another. He sees it
isn't the first time. What interests him—he'll always be interested in her—is that she doesn't close her eyes. Or even
lower them. He worries about her nose; she's never had
much of a one.

"Don't worry," she says. "I'll be going up there for a
while. But what goes up will come down, huh. Isn't that
the way with us?"

She shouldn't say it though. They may be overheard.
She's sitting very straight now. "Shillitoe?"

He straightens to it. Only she is allowed.

"You destroy an image, you have to put something in its place. Ask any shrink."

"Did you?"

She smiles reassuringly. Though not quite at him. "Out there? Out there even the shrinks have astrologers."

They laugh, almost together.

He waits tensely then, to see how it's taking her. If it takes her the same as it did him. The way everything they've been through always has. He will join her as he can.

"So I had to come home," she says.

"Home?" He sounds just a little like his mother.

"To see how you were doing it." She doesn't have to say what, but she does. "Coming down." She glances over at the Rimbaud, whose theory she doesn't see for beans, but nods. "Keep it open," she says.

He takes her hand. They don't have to wait too long.

"Beige, beige, beige," Millie cries suddenly.

The sofas, which were never much more than balloons, sink down with a bloop and float calmly offstage, or up the stairs. The sound track, which may have been musing along after all, certainly stops. Several other changes occur, which only they see. Both of them.

"It's all new coigns here," Millie calls to him brightly. "Come look." She's very literal about the products of her imagination, just as she was at thirteen-really-fourteen. No wonder those crowds of kids tagged along after her. Like him. It all began with her. Begins. He's the actor. And like the finest, acts hardest for himself.

Rubbery, he follows her.

It doesn't matter that they're sitting exactly as they were.

"I don't mind if they do overhear," Millie says. "Even this part of it. What I can't stand—is to listen to *them.*"

He nods, holding on tightly. "This is the quietest place. We were wise to take it. Even back then."

She's dreamy now. Though never serene. "And up here, it doesn't in the least matter, does it. Who has the coke."

He shakes his head, with great verisimilitude. That is the other word he got stuck with, from that script.

After a pause he says, "My agent phoned today. There's a part for me in a musical, it seems. Small, but kind of solid."

She nods. "Mine'll be phoning soon. I'm on, if you're game." Or should it be the other way round, this time? She's confused. "Anyway, they'll have to take both of us."

Have they ever been so frank about it before?

"Why—you're tall," he says, as if looking up a staircase. "I always thought you were just a little thing."

She grins, as if looking down. "So are you. Tall. So are you." Her voice has a husk to it. "Pretty soon, I suppose, after this pic anyway, I'll be—well, I won't go back to fencing." She rubs a thigh, shaking her head. But I'm sure going back to N.Y.U." Lifting her head, she chuckles. "I left art at a very funny place."

After a while she sighs, and opens her purse.

He puts his hand over it. "I can't, you know. Follow you quite that far. Not just now."

She nods. She does know. She closes the purse. "I'll be coming down too, you know—in time. Just in time. We always do."

He can let her hand go now. "I want my coffee."

"Bet it's cold." But it isn't. Since she left, there've been improvements. That maid knows her job. Each cup, still on its separate table, has its hot tray.

"Well, here we are." He smiles. "The morning meal."

She darts a look behind her—nobody there, nobody listening, and smiles back. "That's breakfast!"

They lean forward, to and from their secret life.

The story is too well-known not to repeat.

The Passenger

I HAVE JUST SETTLED in, in my roomette on the Chicago-to-New York Amtrak train. Back at the television station, over coffee and crullers in the hour-long warmup with the camera crew—one more short, intent membership in a guild I will never join: tea with nuns, sandwiches with workmen on the Acropolis—they were surprised to hear a girl like me wasn't making a plane. Their phraseology, not mine. They wouldn't hear tell of how many wintertimes I have been grounded at O'Hare. After the program, the minute they put me in a cab, the snow started, from a sky like sludge; if the cabbie hadn't rolled off at once, I could have called out "See!" and vindicated myself. I could have shouted "And for God's sake, why are your snowflakes square?" They were. Something more than ground swell must be going on in the nowhere territory outside our cities. Prairie rusting through on this one, looked like. And more coming. Yet when we got to the terminal, the train was there.

I have a reason for taking trains. Overpowering. Not easy to make emerge. Though not impossible; there are words for everything. Meanwhile, I have other vindications al-

ways at hand, and very useful too, since everybody uses
them. Not four days ago for instance, we had waited seven
hours in Rome airport for the New York plane, unable even
to use our lunch tickets, since the restaurant was just then
closing for siesta. *"Responsibilita? Niente!"* the pint-size lady
floor cleaner threw at us as we were turned away—"We are
the syndicate!" I enjoyed that. I enjoy all transportation.

The airport was full of Tunisians, many of them paying
court to one very old dignitary hunched with his feet up in
the scant hollow of the chair opposite us, who at intervals
retracted into his hooded cloak of chalky-fine gabardine,
eyes closed, hands folded, head down, one clawfoot left
hanging, the yellow horn on its big toe scratching the air
like a thumb. Next us, a young black madonna of the desert
breast-fed her baby in beautiful style—how many nursing
mothers have you seen in a sequined veil?

As more and more Arabs, from other delegations perhaps, crammed round us—dark faces stamped with Egypt,
white turbans unstained with an oil every Westerner sitting
there could see—the strutting pairs of Italian guards, hol-
sters at hip, grew even more hysterically rigid. On December 18, a month before, we ourselves, by a last-minute de-
cision to stop off at Vienna, had missed being in that
Rome-bound Pan Am jet, which, already safe on its run-
way, the terrorists had bombed-burned. Oh, I enjoy it all.
But you will accept the vindication? Granted, the rising
indignity of air travel, to say nothing of the dangers, is
unbearable.

For shorter trips, I have more intimate excuses. All real.
The sudden pressure drops in our domestic planes often
deafen me for two days. Penn Station and Grand Central
are only twenty-three and fifteen blocks from my house
respectively, as against the ride from Kennedy. I plead loss
of time to some people, money to others.

Reflecting afterward on which to which tells me a lot.
Down at the bottom of my vindications are the sleeping

cars I remember from childhood—enchanting, dark-paneled cells of half metal, half plush, with tiny brass sinks like chalices, tiny pee-box below. And the morning breakfast car, still rockabye but sunny, seemingly made of white linen entirely, from tablecloths to porters' jackets, out of which came the cooling black voices, sternly solicitous. "Sober as a judge" my father used to say of his favorites. While eternal beside us, and dripping like a font, the silver coffee urn.

All my reasons are real. But are not the real ones. Don't think I am here, for instance, just because when I am on a train, the dead come back.

I yearn for trains because of what happened to me on one, fifteen years ago. Since then, trains have grown rarer. And my need stronger. Now they return in some number, and I am grateful. This is my second one, after a shockingly long interim. As for this roomette, engaged as a matter of physical convenience, it is excessive for the basic angst, you might say. The train of fifteen years ago was a suburban one, of perhaps four coach-cars unadorned with extras, which ran from town to town, around a bay. Do I desire merely a replay of that wildly extraterritorial moment? Or do I also hope against hope to lay down, while still alive, the burden it left me with? All I can tell you is that on Amtrak, whose acronym might just possibly include answers, I might just possibly find I have a ticket honorable to the syndicate.

So I've taken a train. Knowing beforehand that it will be some prison shape of gray modern, already seedily breaking down in the socialist way that our modern comforts do. The broken rubber fan stares down at me with an air of "Aren't I good as you?" But the air-conditioning works. There are these alternatives. There's always some point at which modern design deserts human nature altogether. Here it is that once you have put the bed down, you can no longer use the toilet. The old Pullmans had been more re-

sourceful—but by now, of course, so am I. A drain under
the water spigot, a good supply of paper cups—and me still
limber; we have a sixteen-hour night before us, and what
else to be done? So, still dressed and in my chair, leaving
the aisle curtain slightly open for air, I settle into my book,
with that railway dusk of old, marvelously transient and
gleaming at my window. And that dollhouse sense of everything provided within reason. Any terrors will be my
own.

"George—now you take good care of my wife, see?
Screwed up the reservation, they did, but not your fault,
George. So take good care of my wife."

Country-club voice. And yes, my ears, working while I
read, have recorded the tail end of some conductor to pas-
senger altercation just over, up ahead.

I look up in time to see a man pass the curtain. Big, well
set and well clothed, tailored to the voice. Has had a drink
or two, and is pushing his wife before him—her head was
down, and all I saw of her was the back side of it, blondish
but not blond. And the dress, a white-collared print, not
dowdy, but genteel smart—the kind certain suburban
stores sell. Main Line, or near it, I think, catching an accent
from a place where I had once lived. And settle again to my
book. But it's amazing what the off-eye will pick up, when
unpressured. From first to last—and I only saw her once
again the next morning, she kept her head down.

"George. Meer a minute, George. Now you take good
care my wife, see, George."

Half under, not seeing, I feel the unmistakable exchange
of money. Or dream it. From father hand to porter hand.
That practiced-traveler's exchange between collaborating
mutes. Men who keep saying "My wife" though—it marks
them. In her presence or out of it. She must know she is. I
am sure she is. My father, a great traveler, never took his
wife along, rarely took us—when he did, it was a dream.
Still is, like the dusk at the window, now dark. I go back to

my book, where the unmarried English girl, a virgin, is just being impregnated, in a flawlessly asexual paragraph.

"Okay now, George, you take care my wife—honey he take care you—you don't mind my calling you George?"

Kind of question requires no answer, but I hear the mumble. A second later the porter passes me, staring straight on. One of those Indian-faced ones who used to be a feature of the Philadelphia-Washington run—and when I was pregnant the first time used to serve me turtle soup on the way to Wilmington. But do I impute the expression it has now?

I hate my liberal consciousness. As leftover as the white man's burden. And about as socialist as that fan. Yet it's true that even fifty years ago, my li'l ole Southern pappy never called a Pullman porter "George." After a while I put down the book, good and true as it is, and promising to be a flawless exposé of female nature, not through sex, but maternity. A new idea when you come to think, and I look forward to it cozily for later. But first I have a fancy to have a drink in the club car.

The car is all smoke and guzzle, and already swinging. No seats. Some girls at the biggest table, nursing beers. Men lining the sides, still talking only to each other, some going to stay that way, some alert. Down at the end, the big man is still having it on with a conductor about something, handing over some bills, making a scene, and proud of it. Already the focus—he has the air of a man who has always lived up to his physical appearance. He is the man your eyes pick out—what has that done to him? A heavy drinker, but holding it. "That's all right then, Doctor" the conductor says. Doctor—as if he knows him and believes he is one. Not "Doc."

I've known coarse doctors. In the Middle West particularly, where a farm boy can still rise like quicksilver to be king of some small mountain financially and socially, even with a gloss of culture from his researches at the state hospital—and still keep less than a veterinarian's temperament. In upper New York State, the medical lout is different, running around for antiques, which he buys to hide fees in from the revenue men, so is a sucker for anything outlandishly priced, as the dealer will tell you, pointing with a grin to a pile just set aside, which includes maybe a porcelain chow, a Sheraton knife case, a tester bed, and a long bar picture of three Victorian nudes. "Doctor came in, cleared me out." Those like that I've known have all been casualties of success. Not casualties at all really, except to some poor slob of a patient who maybe has only intellect. Who if he shares a town with such doctors has to come to them in the end. I myself am growing older, and I wonder—all of us who survive on—as we grow older, aren't we casualties of that success? The young must think so.

Drinking a club soda while I wait for my Bloody Mary, I stand at the bar, a tall woman, commanding by now (it was awkwardness once), with the remains of a dancer's waist (amateur only), and actressy hair, which as a matter of fact comes from God. Hagar-in-the-desert hair, which under the dresser's hand will not subdue, but only elaborate. I am assumed to have worn well; that's because no one but oneself so accurately remembers the size of eyes or the clean swoop of chin. And to have kept a youthful empathy. What they mean is that I remember my humiliations. I have kept a child's faithful memory of those.

"That's all right, Doctor." The conductor strolls out, leaving the big man center of a crowded banquette, his hands spread on a table strewn with silver packets of those smoked almonds Amtrak awards drinkers who order lavishly. The watching beer girls have none. He is now wearing rimless glasses that keen his eyes over the slur of voice; the head, bull forward, knows we are all watching a scene we ourselves would not make.

I know that tantrum power well, or once did—of the demonstrator willing to make a scene over what others—

parents, husbands, children, friends and waiters—would let pass by. Rages for which I never needed drink—no credit, no excuse—and to which no elixir I know of can return me. What I remember best is how, underneath the wild epileptic pride, the ecstatic shame, in which I am the seized, lording it over those whom excess has never shriven, I yearn secretly toward the silent nonhagglers of life, worshiping them.

A shadowy man gets up suddenly from Doctor-doc's left. Not an easy seat, probably. I am offered it. I set my Bloody Mary on the table and sit down. Isn't this what I have come for?

"That's right, honey, sit down." His arms are spread, the table is his, cordial to the swimming universe. I had a drunken lover once; I know that easiness, which they must drink to get. Never mind that I can't and wouldn't. It's the ease that can say "Let us love one another" right out loud in its slurred way, or in the body english of its joint glass and backslap. And I envy it.

"Is there room, maybe?" A woman's voice over my shoulder.

"Sure," he says, "sit down, honey."

Even before I see her, I slide out so that she can sit between him and me. Once she sits, I see she is the kind one can do this to.

"Hello, girls." He leans forward. She and I chat at once, heads turned away from him, like women anywhere who join up to ignore a man. That easiness we both have. She doesn't have much else, perhaps. A long, fiftyish face made more ocher by very black, oiled curls of the corkscrew kind once worn by little girls, Saturday night farm wives, and country whores. Horn rims, though, and the sweetly engraved smile of dentures. She is naïve, wholesome (probably), comes from Spokane, state of Washington, has never been East. When the white-jacketed dinner porter comes through, tinkling his bell, she asks timidly do we have to leave? Never been on a train before, she says. But handles her glass well. Sunday afternoon in the kitchen with the neighbors, I should think, or after dinner in the local—a family bar. A few miles out of Spokane.

Why do I think I know so much about people and the probable? When I was thirtyish and still hadn't figured out how to be what dreaming said I was, I thought of training to be a psychiatrist. There's a prescription for that. And I so wanted to be something other than a mother and a child. At college they had said I ought to. Then one day, a canny woman doctor to whose poet sister I was showing poems, said "Really want to be a psychiatrist? I'll stake you." She was "calling" me, as they say in poker. Because whether or not the poems were bad I couldn't shift the dream, and she knew it. I didn't want to be anything there was a prescription for. Then I found out there wasn't any for what I wanted to do—and started being it. Now I am here. When you're a success at being what you should merely do, then you begin to be a failure, right? Like growing old.

"What's your name, girls?"

As if we had only one between us. She and I grin, acknowledging that in a way this is true of any two women in a club car.

"We get to Washington at ten, don't we?" She whispers it.

"We get into New York at ten," I say doubtfully. "And D.C. is still some hours from there."

"Oh, dear Lord. And my sister-in-law's meeting me at ten."

Yes, she is wholesome. "The Washington sleeper must split off in the middle of the night. That must be it. Don't worry."

But she clasps her hands. "Oh. Must I get up and change with it? How will I know?"

"No, you won't have to do anything." But am I sure of it?

In Paris once, I had to run the whole length of the station, to transfer to the boat train. While the porter scolded. I am never really sure of what happens in boat trains. Until I was forty, I never traveled without a father or a husband. Or a family. At twenty-four, when the new baby and I followed her father to his new job—a six-hour migration, not a trip—the roomette was as crowded as a stateroom. My parents, and that woman doctor too. She called me "the rabbi's daughter." I wrote a story about it later on. My father was not a rabbi. The story was about a girl who had been given everything, and a conscience too.

So that nowadays, when, though I may be of an age to live on a while, it is also proper to think of death and of the old, I begin to understand why, in spite of all vitality loved, one might let go the thread quite willingly. So that the dialogue might at last rest. So that one day, this dialogue may rest.

Looking at me now, though, you would never suspect anything but what is also true, that at forty, I flew around the globe alone. And around and around since. But does it take?

I look for the conductor. "I'll ask."

"Harrisburg," the head of our table says. Ignored though he is, he knows he is that. "Middle of the night, Washington sleeper unhitches while we're asleep. If we are."

He leans across her to me. He's had a good face, which sixty has perhaps softened and jowled. But it can't leer. It's not villainy he's got. Merely a face which can convey that he's chosen me—as well as hint at the assured practice he has had at choosing.

I lean back. The sexual explanation of me—aside from the lineaments of desire at long last satisfied—is very simple. In youth, thinking myself ugly, I was gauche—and not often chosen. But I have had an attractive middle age. Truck drivers have whistled at me late, but not early.

Sometimes still do. Yes, it can help keep you young, you see. An uncertain vanity.

Have I described the club car? Can one? Oh yes—that gray, depressive blue or mustard brown rubbed chair seats, atmosphere-stained walls; they bring out your view of human nature. Either everybody's taste is as bad as this, or nobody's is. The porters are the only stylish ones here— black skins and white, maestro linen. The rest of us are soiled travelers, sweating for home. Drinking ourselves naked. When you drink in such public confine, you have to be coarse enough to survive, meanwhile knowing yourself more sensitive than most.

But I have to be quick now. Doc is going to speak. He leans forward. Indeed his linen is the best in the car. Among the guests. He speaks. "You girls seen *Deep Throat?*"

I see she knows of that movie, whether or not she saw it. Who doesn't know of that porn movie, a "blue" one, as they say—more pumpkin and California color, as I recall it —where men are serviced by mouth? By a girl supposedly looking for her own satisfaction. Linda Lovelace by name, I believe. I had a typist with that same surname, once. A cool, blond, fortyish woman, wistfully stilted, out of *Jane Eyre.*

"Do you always address women you meet like that?" I have an Anglophile accent which comes over me when I must put on the dog. I have lived in two countries where manners are elegance, rote and nerve—but I can't speak Thai.

There's a funny class shock at the back of his eyes. He's misjudged.

"I heard you back there in the sleeping car. Calling the porter 'George.' Thought I dreamed you. Didn't know there were people like that anymore."

Lame, lame-pontifical. Only sex has saved me from the ministry. I read Jeremiah as a child. "I heard the conductor call you Doctor. Are you one?"

Is he redder? Or only drunker? "I'm a psychiatrist."

Behind us, the whole club car is our audience now.

We two are with Freud. Who must see the class shock in my eyes.

"Oh yes, oh yes." And now he is like a salesman, reeling off contacts, names. Or like an applicant for good grace. Columbia Medical School, he worked with so-and-so, and so-and-so. Back then. No, he doesn't know any of the names there that I know, as I too reel these off with an aggression that shames me. But finally *I* know some of *his* references. So it's true, then. He watches me grudge that.

"What's your name, Doctor?"

"Warren."

"Last name?" I say it like a schoolmarm. No club-car first names for me.

His eyes measure me. "White." Then he shrugs, like a schoolchild released. "Have another drink, girls?"

She accepts. I go to the bar and pay for my own. Without grace. Come back to him. He's got me in his game. Or I have him.

"About that George," he says. "I was in the Air Force."

"What do you do now?"

He's looking at his shoe, a big, gleaming black brogue. "I testify at murder trials."

Down, down he goes, down the Columbia staircase. I went there. And to many other universities. Teach, teach. There's an academic pity we have, we save, for people who stumble and lose their category. Or their right to it. I don't know what Freud would think of that pity. I know what I think of my share of it.

"The Hall trial. I did that."

I can't tell, quite, whether he is proud of it.

"Oh, I remember that," the woman at our elbow says. "Hall something. That's a long time ago. That tells my age, doesn't it?"

"Hall—Caine," I say. "Oh no, that's a novelist." I must drink no more.

"I can tell your age," he says to her. "Anybody's. Doctors can."

"Astrology helps you do that," she says. "I'm very interested in it. Are you interested in astrology?"

"Astronomy, yes," he says, "but not that other stuff. It's not scientific." He offers me a joint scorn.

I turn it down.

"Are you?" she says to me.

"In astrology?" She hopes. I see that. "I'm interested in people who are."

"You do something," she says, "don't you?" Humbly. "I can tell."

Of course, I meant her to.

"She dreams about people. Who call sleeping-car porters George." Is his grin really intelligence? Or drink? I know it's both.

"She's going home to New York." The woman is eating all the smoked nuts the porters toss at us. I've been opening them for both of us. "She did business or something in Chicago, I bet. Didn't you."

"Maybe she did," he says. Funny, how his face is the part of him that can't leer. "Did you?"

A television show, I could say. But it always gives the wrong impression. That's not my category. "I'm a writer." I bring it out badly, proudly. After all these years, it still seems to me like a boast.

"Are you?" she breathes. "What's your name?"

I tell her.

"Well, now," he says, using it as familiarly as if I had given it to him. "Well, now. Do any screwing in Chi?"

I sit back. But not because of insult. It's because I see—the way I see. Have gone on seeing, so many times. For me and them. For all the club car behind us. *"Hall-Mills,"* I say. "He and she murdered her husband—that case. Yes, that was a long time ago." The past is a light, I think, looking at him.

"I can tell *your* age." Swiftly he picks up the back skin of my right hand, drops it again.

Tell me an hour ago this man would get as far as touch me, what would I do?

"Fifty," he says, grinning scientifically. "Fifty-two."

What thralls me? Vanity? "Five years short."

"What do you know. Marvelous. I'm sixty-two myself." He knows he doesn't look it, either.

"And you are a psychiatrist?" I know he is. Marvelous.

"Yes, I testified, that trial. Lot of them. Since."

"That's what you do?"

"That's what I do." He dares me. To think of it. I do.

As I sit there, a short man weasels his way between us. The woman has faded. Gone where ladies do.

This man tells me his story before I can say pop-go. He lives on the Eastern Shore of Maryland, has all his life. I have lived there once too, "That makes it easier," he says. I say no more. He says that just before he goes off to war—the Korean one—he and his wife tell each other their marriage is over. Just before he gets on the plane. "Just like that, we know it is over." He has lived all his life in or near the town where he was born. Weekends he can go fishing, sailing; he wouldn't live anywhere else.

"Turtle soup," I say. "You get it all over the Chesapeake." I used to have it in the dining car, coming down to Wilmington, to the new house, new husband, in the weeks before my first child was born. When I was twenty, and had a job as a social worker, but could still get them all off my conscience, any time.

He has a girlfriend now. "That makes it easier." Safer, don't I think? No, he and she are not marrying—the girlfriend works a way away, and he still has the wife, still has the wife.

We are rocking very fast now. "Turtle," he says. "We

used to say that in the war. 'Are you a *turtle?*' we'd say. Anybody know the answer to that?"

Behind me, at a table for two, a young, blond man has been sitting with his girl. He has the kind of face and stance, tough, short-nosed and horsey, like the cowboys you can see coming out of the Garden—Madison Square as used to be—when the rodeos are there. Horse cherubs, who know everything. He and his girl have been to college though—probably; they have been reading the New York *Times.* "I know the answer," he says, cracking white teeth.

"Okay, then," says Maryland. "Give me the right answer. Are you a turtle?"

The boy eyes him, smiling. *"You bet your sweet ass I am."*

They laugh together. Neither explains. The boy's girl says nothing; neither do I. Some fleck of a war we'll never hear about has passed over us.

"Buy you a drink?" says the man from Maryland.

"Thanks, no; I have to get back to my car." And to my book. Where the girl is almost certainly going to hang on to that baby. Without the man.

"What are you going to do there?" The doctor sways with the car, and a little more so. "Read a book?"

"Guessed it the first time."

He smiles. His teeth are white, small and even, and when you see them, it fills his face in for certain. He's smart. "Write any dirty books I can read?"

I get asked that. At the most ordinary party, there's sometimes a club car. Turning away, I talk to the boy and the girl. They live on his parent's ranch in Colorado. Cattle ranch. My husband is from near the Dakotas, I tell them; his cousin runs a cattle ranch too. The boy says, "I came back to the ranch—after 'Nam. Couldn't settle yet on what else to do." But he has something else in mind, you can see that, though he doesn't say. "What's your last book about?"

I can never say. But for him I try. Passing them the nuts now. They are drinking beer.

"About the ones who *didn't* go to 'Nam?" he says. "Yes, I could have been one of them. Then, all of a sudden—I went." He rolls his tongue like an Irishman. But not quite. "Yes everybody tells me, my accent. The whole town I come from's Norwegian. Maybe that's why." He has a story he thinks maybe he ought to write. He tells me some of it. It's about his luck, his war, and how he weathered it. He has more than innocence.

I'm not sure he can't write the story or won't—but *I* have forgotten it.

A touch at my elbow. "No, I'll never leave Maryland . . . Have dinner with me, huh?"

I gather my purse. The girl glances up at me after all. "Thanks," I say. "I have to get back."

"Buy you a drink then?"

"Boy, bring me one, boy." The doctor shows those teeth at me. "See? I didn't say George."

We are rocking so fast now our faces bob in unison. They are tossing their stories in my lap like flowers. People do, means nothing. Not the same nothing to them though as to me, that's all. I haven't opted for this consciousness. I stand up. Now I have no lap.

"You a turtle, Doc?"

The doctor looks down at the man from Maryland. They are sitting side by side. I hear the listeners behind us. "I was in the *Air Force*." He grabs for me. "Let me see your hand again girl. No? There's life in the old girl yet, though, isn't there?"

I see him tumbling down staircases, up stag lines, charm-over-charm. A Deke I knew squeaked through medical school, singing "Sweet Georgia Brown." Then went into surgery, learning in his war—World War II—to lop rather well. This is a frat boy too, surely. Back when the gray hair was fair, and the red cheek was pink—from good air. Not

Main Line though after all, probably. When was his fall? And when did I settle for this consciousness?

"See you after dinner, honey," he says. He doesn't stand up; why should he? My drunk never did either. "After dinner, hmm? Since we're in the same car. Bet you shake a sexy book."

I remember what I came for. Though the focus has changed—as a focus will. "Yes, I saw *Deep Throat,* Doctor. With my husband. You see it with your wife?"

I hate that grande dame voice of mine. That's not consciousness.

Across the aisle, a little man flutters his eyes at me. Nodding, he keeps fluttering them. Haven't seen him before. Is he really fluttering them at me? Or has he a tic?

"No." The doctor flusters for the first time. "But only because she was in Pompano. I was somewhere else, that's all." Who's he making his excuses to?

"Good night." I nod to the boy and girl. And to Maryland.

"Watch it, miss. Stand back." The porter shoos me. "We got a break in the ladies room. Mop it up in a minute. Stand back."

"Anyone can be somewhere else," he says. "I'm a consultant."

"You still do trials?"

He mistakes my interest. And yes, he's flustered. At last. "I'm chief consultant. To the chief of police. Of Pike County, Pennsylvania."

It's those two chiefs get to me, when I think of it.

Two porters are mopping. I am immured between the banquette and the doctor's outstretched shoe.

"Your husband from the Dakotas? I heard you say."

Standing tall as one of those Lutheran silos they have out there, I nod. Sweating for home.

"My wife comes from there. Farragut."

It's what he said next that stays with me. I must have

been looking hard at his shoe. Thinking of the trials of ego we set for one another. His ego, that mouths sex. And my anger for the world—no deeper than a throat.

"Like these shoes, huh?" he says. Warren White is his name. "Like them, eh?" He holds a foot out to me.

I recall a time in London, standing marveling at a window of ugly hats in Selfridges, when a man sidles up to me. *Like them eh? You could have one of those.* In my middle age.

"They're the best," he says. His smile isn't smart now. His failure's in it, somewhere. "They're Nettletons."

As I pass the little, fluttering-eyed man, he says, "That's right—*give* it to him."

In the ladies room, the woman from Spokane is there with a friend she's picked up. They are giggling at the flooded floor. "We didn't do it, one bit. It just ran out." The woman from Spokane tells her new friend about me, looking up admiringly. "You sure gave it to him."

In the roomette, closing the aisle door, I decide not to go to dinner. I have food here; I never travel unprovided. Knowing how, among strangers, I fail for want of meditation. This thread, that I must keep. The girl in the book is keeping her baby at all costs. The baby she didn't want. She is not telling the man. I remember an old abortion, an old marriage. The dark streams at the window, concurrently. After a while I push the button for the fan. Those are the matters I forget. The broken fan looks down at me like a commissar. Still in my clothes, I open the curtain for air, and read on. Yes, we are keeping the baby, the two of us. My first conceived would have aborted midterm anyway, the doctor said "We shall have to retrovert your uterus." He had to think about it overnight though; he was Catholic. So I had it done in a hospital after all. The second-first baby—*that* one I carried like gold. Eating turtle for her which I thought was for me, on the train to Wilmington. Which we shall pass somewhere in the night.

"I knew you were in this car, I smelled your perfume."

I look up. It's Maryland. He's harmless, and with a
friend.

"Dinner maybe?"

"Thanks, no."

After a while, I ring for the porter, who puts down the
bed. As the toilet disappears, I stand immobile. Between me
and the aisle-curtain with snap buttons like a child's sleeping garment, there is a steel door which I slide closed, but
don't latch, not trusting the lock, which may be a commissar. I stow my goods like a sailor—shoes in their cupboard,
slacks in their chute, coat hanging at the foot, ready to be
an extra quilt. I settle. Riding this way does remind me of
pregnancy; while you accomplish an act no longer in your
control, the landscape passes, delivering you to the foreseen
event. I never think this way in a plane. A plane is fully
conscious. And does not rock like childhood, but only rise
and dip.

The girl's baby is born and she keeps it, not telling anyone in her crowd. Not telling the man. She and it are having
a totally private experience. An afterbirth. As I read, I eat
salami and cheese and hazelnut wafers, out of my paper
bag. And almonds. The food I provide myself on these lone
travel nights is always adolescent. Little separate treats,
having nothing to do with meals. Bringing small guilts I can
support. The girl's child has a serious flaw; we are sisters
there. When she meets the father again, she doesn't tell him
he is the man. We differ there. Do all mothers in wedlock
secretly yearn for the totally private experience? As takes
place in half the mother animals of the world?

All night long, I read and rock, and sleep and wake. My
paper cups work well.

And in the early dawn we arrive at the birthplace, Wilmington. There's an outline, a shore. Marcus Hook Refin-
ery. Oh, I see you, your huge mists and tanks. What shall I
say to you, birthplace of a child who is now dead? (Not the
child in the book, who will remain forever young.) Dead

after a painful living, alone and between us. Finally alone and dead—a decade older than I was when I bore her. I must say something. This is the birthplace. And the train has stopped.

What shall I say to you, young women, young women flying toward this place? Holding your butter-soft toes high in the morning. That sex is only what we are inside of? That a woman is defined by giving birth, or by not giving it. And a man by not being private as she with his child?

I can't tell you for sure. Being still in meditation. And I left my uterus back there on the road, some time ago. For sure, all life retroverts into a hospital pan. Meanwhile, wear perfume for it. Have small, separate guilts. And sweat toward some one other creature—as toward home.

In the morning, the porter, putting up the bed for me, says "Your door slide open during the night. I close it for you. You were in some danger, girl."

"You don't mean it."

"Dilly, I do."

I point down the aisle, to the right. "That one?"

He nods woodenly, not joining my smile. Or not admitting what it's for. George has taken care of the wife.

I go to breakfast tardy by intent, but the time change has fooled me; looks like we are all here again, the whole club car. There's something encouraging about a dining car in the morning; forty years don't change that prism light on the water glass, this sense of newly washed journey. In the morning, we are all failures, hopefully dressed. Over there's that little crone of a child whose underfoot mewling made even the kindest grannies sit distaff-faced yesterday; now he's high-chaired and cup-cheeked with an orange in his fist and a fresh wicker sprout of hair—a little king we can all try to love. The granny faces are folded chicken-soft in the morning. What is the worst? Not to love a child.

Snow flurries along the rail, but we're running close to
schedule, the porter says; we shall make up for lost time.
All the time we have lost is running by us at the windows.
My father no longer visits there. He is back in his thirty-
year grave. Unvisited. The woman from Spokane has been
detached in the night.

The porter seats me on the aisle, next to the young
rancher who is riding in the window seat forward, opposite
his girl-wife. That is how she seems; they seem ever
younger as one rides. This morning she speaks, and we talk
of the music she studies, chewing it in mild tones with our
rolls; breakfast is encouraging. At home I have an old
Broadwood piano with a special sound, and have been
playing music I would like to talk of too, but careful careful, on these encounters one must never mention what one
has, for fear of boastment. And doubly so with the young. I
do it anyway, leaning on Lully as I go, and on Pachelbel,
whom I have been playing, but it's just as I thought—the
music dies. And I am left with only the Broadwood.

At home—the boy says, they live twenty miles from
anything; that's why they're coming to New York for a bit.
They're neither lorn nor penniless but I long to give them
some small treat. For what they are. There is a sweetness in
all the young that gets killed somewhere. Past what age did
I begin to feel responsible?

"Can I do anything for you. In New York?"

Thank you no. They have friends. His lips firm. Her eyes
grow green. Have I lessened in them? Or only frightened
them?

No, it's only that we have all almost arrived. On the
point of it, creeping slower through these strange, eaten-
away gray bulwarks, cables twisted by the windy past,
bunged-in scrap yards, diseased grass and reflected back-
water sky, which mean arrival by rail. And I cannot bear it.
To let them go, not knowing. Not having exchanged the
little spark.

"Can I—?" I say to the boy. *Last night we talked, remember?* "May I—know your name?"

I have variants of this, but always ask permission. On the train from Vienna to Arezzo, just two months ago, I said— formal to the formal (even though by then the five of us in the compartment were almost a family, and the woman I addressed had first begun our conversations) "May I have the privilege—" and was even awarded a card. Grudgingly, exactly as the boy now gives his name. Though last night, he told me all the intimacies of war and, scarcely waiting for my questions, all his meditations on destiny.

Because I didn't have his name, wouldn't ever, if I had observed the proper obsequies of the traveler's farewell.

I can't bear to, haven't been able to for years. Oh, I know the ethics of the short encounter. But I press on anyway. I always overstep. I saved that card.

I save them all, their shapes and faces, and spinning voices . . . Tall, high characters, with a kind of sparse info about themselves that lodges in their flesh like buckshot. Gross, cavernous faces, with mouths like half lemons, flavoring the tale. Young girls going nowhere, and asking. Men going everywhere, and advising. People who speak but do not tell—and hope their silences give them away . . . It's not gossip you hear on the short encounter, but the real rock-bottom groan of the daily, waiting to be redeemed. And my trouble, increasing with age, is that I cannot forget any of them. Flick me a life, and I remember it.

But the truth is, I can't bear this any longer. My consciousness is not my own anymore. My lap is full.

Want me to tell you about Miss Schild? The one who gave me the card—and one of the happy ones. (I don't save agony only. Merely—all probability.) She works in a beauty spa, and has a spa personality—nurseish, dietetic and silvery with massaged fact. The train from Vienna passes the hill where the spa is and goes right by her own house, to which she will drive back from the train stop. To prepare for the party she is giving for Sylvester, their New Year's—the thought of which ripples all through her, from neatly suited belly to tolerant mouth, tousled hair and russet hat. She opened the conversation when I took off my scarf, revealing the old scar of the same operation she had just had. Past a certain age, we have something for everybody. Though I don't know when I passed it. We exchanged thyroid dosages, her intimations of mortality, and my assurances on-the-record—mine. That's why she gave me her name later. But I should not have asked for it.

Forty people for supper, what will you give them? the Frau on my left said, shaking her head, but not so hard that the two tiny pearled combs, the only vanity on her round, pursed self, moved a minim in the bunned hair. She and the *papa,* whose Winterhosen were clipped neatly to his shoes so that he couldn't remove the shoe in the heat, as she had her lamb's-wool-lined ones, were going to Rome to spend Christmas with their only child, who had just got her doctorate—an archivist Frau Doktor who spoke sixteen languages—and only to cardinals. *Sixteen, ja!* And now the Frau's combs, lips, unshod feet and whole wren shape jerked as if in orgasm, her voice artificial as a pigeon's, denying glee but spreading it like a paste.

They were relieved when they saw we'd brought our own lunch; one could never trust Americans. I was embarrassed at having splurged on Austrian champagne and a tart from Demel's, then remembered that it was my birthday, and we drank to it. After further demurs, we quartered the cake, I citing the archivist. *"Demel's,"* the Frau said holily. When we passed the Austrian Chancellor's hometown, Papa, an even-faced man with a discreetly roving eye for Miss Schild and maybe even for me, referred to it in German as Yidville, then coughed—did we know the Chancellor, Kreisky, was a Jew? Papa had no politics, he said—

When they ask me what are my politics—he beat his breast daintily—*I say I am Catholic.*

In their cider, I drank to that. And the Frau and Papa open their bags to show four large blue needlepoint chair seats. *Nobody has a flat like the young Frau Doktor's, the Cardinal said to me he said to me* the mother said. And again that shaking, head to toe. She squeaked when she heard where we stayed when in Rome; it was the same priests' hotel where they stayed, had stayed, would stay—in eternal life. Amen. *Oh, the dear Santa Chiara* she chortled. Meaning: *Papa,* after all, they are possible. And when we left at Arezzo he helped us very politely with our bags. More politely than any liberal American.

Ah, so it's the little vignettes she does, you say; that's what she does—you think I do that? You don't yet understand. That their spirits haunt me more now than my familial own . . . When we got to the Santa Chiara ourselves, a month later, I had to be stern with myself in order not to ask the manager to be allowed to look them up in the Christmastime register . . . If I didn't do that—and I didn't—they would be lost forever, not to be connected with again except by endless research even I would never do in the whorls of Vienna and the Vatican. If I did have their name, as I have Miss Schild's, would I look them up someday? I doubt it. Though if ever finding myself in the neighborhood, it is likely that I would veer quite near—I would go ask the way on purpose—and then renege. As I have done before.

It's not having the name that afflicts me. It's a loss. Afterward, it's that much harder to gather them in.

I think that Miss Schild, after her Sylvester party, will have one person stay on, maybe for the night. And that this will happen Sylvester after Sylvester, although the person may not always be the same. I fancy she will come again to America, as she did once, though she will not look us up.

And I know that her operation will be a success, and that year after year she will give and take satisfaction, in the beautifying Alps.

But I am very much afraid that the Frau's daughter—the Frau Doktor archivist—will not marry. Someone ought to warn her about the cardinals and her chairs—a poor combination for maternity. No one is likely to. In any of her languages. I had a cousin named Schild once—Erna Schild. And a Tante Sophie, who wore hair combs exactly like the Frau's. Though I don't hang on to either of them, in the same way—I know what's happened to them.

How is one to hang on to all of them, that's it? And still get one's proper rest.

Nevertheless, I have been avoiding the table across the aisle. The doctor is there in the seat near the window, in his eraser-gray suit. His facial pink has not faded with the night. I can't see his shoes. But breakfast has not encouraged him. Riding backward, he is speaking forward, to his wife. Whose elbow is parallel with mine, but whose shoulders and neck swoop so low, low and toward him above the crumpled napkins, that I can see only the neat, tapering comma of her blondish hair. That must be the longest neck in the world.

No, that is what entreaty can do to a neck. For, within the train's rough rhythm, which we get so used to, his voice hovers thin as that telegraph wire sidling along with us. *I do love you,* he is saying. I do love you, he said.

Oh, Freud. That's the cancer in the tongue isn't it. Or the music that never dies.

"Hello, hello," he says, catching my glance across the rhythm, with no break in his own. Never a break there, I think. Caught in it. But catching others too. What does a drunken lover do at night? Goes whoring. Then whores with you.

"She writes books," he says to his wife across their table.

"Her husband comes from Dakota too." He doesn't introduce us. But she is required to look at me, sideways. She's younger than he, fortyish.

"Had a nice time last night, didn't we?" He's looking at me. He turns to his wife. "She's teaching me not to call the porter George." She keeps her eye on him. Yes. That is agony. How well I remember it. One abases oneself before the abased. Who is smart. How well I remember it. I turn away.

The young rancher and his girl have seen it all. They shoot me a look. In true youth, experience is seamless. But they are no longer that young. Twenty miles from anywhere, they must have had events.

The waiter, turning on his compass point, pours coffee, sparing none of us; they have their rhythm too. Sparing only my father, who is now sitting south-table to my north, only not rocking like the rest of us. I no longer know the location of his burial plot. Helped pay for it, left the certificate with my brother who went to war and have never looked back. If you're going to trust in the things of the spirit, have to start somewhere. I have done this for all my dead, and would not do differently. That way they can pop up anytime. Willing or not, they have got out of the flesh-trap; the least we can do is cooperate. The guilt about the burial plot is little enough to bear.

In Father's case, he can go on working indefinitely. Which is what he would want. *Alienists, my foot* he says, looking up from his newspaper, which if it isn't spread all over with the Hall-Mills case, I can't think of what other. The time zone would be about right. *Interpreters of the mentally disturbed, it says here. Ward heelers for the medical, why don't they say?* He wanted all his life to be a lawyer, but tripped over his own tongue so early and quick that the money came before the law did, and he got stuck for the rest of his life with the rhetoric. *Paid witnesses* he says now, and puts down

the paper. *Ain't nobody lower to the ground, is there?* He had a
sister who was mentally disturbed.

And Captain Dr. Warren White, late of Columbia University, the Air Force, Pike County, Pennsylvania, propri-
etary licensee of Pullman porters, consultant at murder trials and alienist of people, *Deep Throat* audient and customer
of the Nettleton Shoe Company, leans forward to me with
a grin at his wife. "Your books got any dirty parts we can
read?"

Maybe it was the "we" that got to her. His wife. Forcing
her to acknowledge me. Flexing her just enough—not quite
full face. Agony has its postures, as we know from the
saints. One cannot *not* notice them. The left side of the
doctor's wife's mouth lifts—distorted, obedient, sillied with
pain. So that I recognize her. Marital pain sillies some
women. Certain married goosegirls. Maybe they tend to be
a little silly-nice to begin with, but that's no excuse, is it?
Or maybe certain physical types tend toward the same agonies.

I know that the doctor's wife is not really my Mrs. Lovelace. Who for years has typed for novelists. Returning to us
the finished manuscripts—full of whatever eclamptic modern horrors or pornographies—with an unsmiling smile. My
Mrs. Lovelace has two daughters, for one thing—two
slangy message takers whose telephone voices don't respect
what she does. This woman here doesn't have the print of
real children on her. But maternity, if it doesn't get you in
the belly and loins, can get you in the head. *I* do *love you.* I'll
bet that under that country-club print dress across the aisle,
and under Mrs. Lovelace's genteel city coat, which is all I
have ever seen her in, the pink, flinching gawk of the two
bodies is the same. Sensually mouth-lashed women, who
don't need to see movies on oral sex. And have the same
long, agile neck.

I know that the probable history of Mrs. Lovelace's coat
wouldn't fit in here. The cloth part was probably bought at

Loeser's or Alexander's, a designer markdown, and that fine fur collar added by a tailor who got it for her wholesale, in the Brooklyn way. The economic part of these two women is localized, that's all, in proportion as New York is to North Dakota. But if the doctor's wife here were to fade, slowly fade—as married goosegirls tend to do—and if Mrs. Lovelace, even in that coat, were to take her place here, I think the doctor would not much notice the difference.

I do not want these connections, any of them. I don't approve of them. Dead people sitting at present tables. Analogies between people, who may distort the same only because one sees them under the ooze of time. Birthplaces returning on schedule. Old abortions revived by books. All this cropping up—I am opposed to the whole idea. I haven't pity enough for all of it. These things follow one after a while, that's it. They recognize one's astrology. They seem to get the blood scent of somebody like me. Who, after a while, will give in and follow them.

When did I give in, accept my lot you might say? As you might guess it was on that train. Fifteen years ago. It doesn't seem possible I have carried the burden that long. Of course it didn't seem a burden, then. More like a mystical light—or let's say atmosphere—of the kind that at death is promised the faithful. Never having been one of those, I'm almost ashamed to speak of it. But not quite.

It's nothing to be ashamed of—that long, foghorn moment when you agree to believe in your own death. This having nothing to do with the hypochondrias that bloom like briar bushes around the ankles of all of us—whose flesh isn't pricked with that? Only a charm against death, that is. I don't mean that. Fifteen years ago, when for a month I was having to go twice a week from Palo Alto to the Stanford isotope lab in San Francisco to check thyroid dosage—forty miles and return just to swallow what looked like water in a doll-sized paper cup, then pass under a machine—I was really only under a half-sentence of death. Only for two weeks of it, really. And nothing to do with the isotopes. "Fifty-fifty chance at the most," the examining doctor said when he discovered the other thing. But I believed him, one hundred percent.

It's impossible to kid with, that sensation. That *is* the sensation. Nobody's kidding you. You're not kidding yourself. You're not pretending anymore. Needn't ever, about anything. Especially on a local train. Maybe especially there.

The days of Palo Alto come one after the other out of the honey box, as fixed in their amber as glazed fruit. Out there, I used to tease that I couldn't tell the people *from* the fruit. The color of youth can be very trying, year after year on a countenance. Blandness petrifies. "But we are semi-tropical," they retorted, calling my attention to the night change—that ice cube of cool at drinktime, only as serious as the sweater-need on the bare forearm, once a clockwork night. I found their certainty frightening. The puritan Easterner depends on a little climate torture for the good of his soul. To guide it decently toward universal dark.

Certainty is the real dark. And (if it doesn't kill you at once) the real aging—ever see those dry, twin pairs, baby blue Jacket and powder pink Jumper, on the Miami train? "There's the Washington Monument," Jacket said to Jumper, on that Amtrak. "See, it goes up and down." And we laughed at the mentality, but shuddered at the certainty. My one creature and me. Who am his. This being the one certainty we do trust. Since it has so little power against the final dark. Which is surety indeed.

Once, I thought I wanted that. The one house in the one street, forever and alackaday. When all the time it was change that was the devil-wine in my veins; half the young mothers in the world are legionnaires in nursing bras. Oh, ambivalence isn't at all the rack they say it is, but the heart medicine for going on. For dancing on the piano in the moving van. For walking on the bridge that could have been the other one. I saw a sad bridge in Vienna recently. There's always a blind quality about viaducts. At the head of this one was where the Russians settled in. No, our friend Hannah said, there was never an alternate bridge here. And now, raze and rebuild as one may, that foreign sadness still comes out on it. Like a lot of Alt Wien, they say. There was never a choice.

Not like on the fifty-fifty-chance train.

The day I walked slowly down the hill from the Stanford Lab, and then ran with the wind at my back all the way to the station to show I could, the train was still a local. I was merely riding forward, going back. On the local train to the days of Palo Alto, and all my days before. Carefully thinking of nothing larger than the distance between forefinger and thumb. Stockings to go East with, if I'm going back to have the op. Hospital bed jacket to buy, if I'm to have it done here. "Shouldn't I go home?" I said to the two doctors. "Just in case." But secretly, I would like to stay here and spare the children, both in boarding school. Yet can one really be sick in this climate? Surely this sunshine is inoperable? "Maybe you better go home," the melancholy doctor says—the one who discovered it. Surgeons are merrier. "Nahh—here's fifty says you can stay."

The things we do to make do, how I depend on them. To put a public glaze on a meal, set straight the past in the button box, swab down the wall under a dead girl's drawings, so that I may stare at them blindly, within the fold of the task. The art needlework of the daily, that serviceable cover for what's boiling below—women of my generation were taught it early. That night, I clasped my arms over my suspect body and read a cookbook. Now and then, patches of sorrow for those I loved flowed over me. And for myself of course. But there was no other burden of consciousness.

Any mysticism I have comes to me in the early morning

with the orange juice and the fresh-baked pavements. The owl hours breed in me comfort or anxiety, satire or sexual excitement—but no piety. Nowadays, I know my habits and am resigned to them. But that morning, I merely rose betimes, my head reeling with recipes, put a jacket over my arm for the sure-to-be winds of San Francisco Bay, which even pleased me, and took the train again, as specified. Just because one was standing by for an emergency hospital bed, could one put a halt to the mild, astrological message that a set of lab tests for lifetime thyroid dosage might bring? Scientifically not.

So here we are, in two trains simultaneously—one now arriving in New York, and one then starting out for San Francisco. Stand by, Dr. and Mrs. White, man with the fluttering eyelids, young rancher and wifeling, man from Maryland. Porter George. And little tuft-haired royalty. You'll all follow me soon enough. You'll leave your mark on me. As for me, I know I've left no mark on any of you. Not in trains. Not even when I transgress the strangers' agreement insistently enough to cadge your names, your business cards. The one mark I can hope to leave on you or anybody is here. Where I shall already be to you like the dead, who that first day on the fifty-fifty train, swarmed to me out of their cold book of receipts.

The more reason I can't lie to you. All during my life, words have been honesty to me. Defenses of the un-churched spirit. Panoramic flags furled round the study chair. Buds in the window box, waxing against the grain of hope. And yes, if necessary, the truth-cancer at the tongue's root. Above all, I believe that if you say radiance radiance radiance often enough, you will come to see it as the blind do, in your own style. Or, that it has to be said for you, in certain sharp, historic voices. In whose shadow I crouch.

Yet that moment of transfiguration which will overtake

me on the train to San Francisco will be entirely wordless. Perhaps that's why I can never summon it back. Or because I got it cut rate.

I am just sitting there. With the expectation of Bay winds to come kind on my sweatered arms. The towns passing on my left as we go northward are so subtly rich that one can scarcely see them. Or recall them. Menlo Park, was it? Atherton? Scenery never gets to me while I'm in it. Later maybe, in the mind's eye. In museums, I watch people. Crowds in flow are my rescue; they will not be intellectualized. The usual crowd would have been on the train that day, the usual people, never quite explicable. No more reason for empathy that day than on any. Or no less.

I can describe them, in the abstract. Across the aisle, maybe two huge youth-boobies, purpling with health, and high on themselves. Women of a very certain age, with gray crimped hair, and the presbyter faces that go with it. Children with cowlicks and without—a large difference. A man with a narrow face and medallion lips—an icon from the Abruzzi. Four fat women, hung with uniting jewelry. On two of them it celebrates the flesh, on the third it is as competitive as her fur stole—and the fourth, only a girl, quivers her chains for confidence. In any crowd one beauty is to be found, and one monster—until you see the eyes of each. Turn for relief then perhaps to an old persimmon of an Asiatic, with meditative hands. The mix is getting richer everywhere. Might even have been a person with a tic; there often is. Tics are for what's been lost and cannot be hid. Or for what one has, and cannot find. There are crowd samenesses, always. And the unconquerable differences. Which I love.

Such would be par for that crowd, that day. With me myself not quite as charmable by the gems tossed the eavesdropper, my eye turned inward by its own circumstance. Would you say you are a sympathetic person? So am I, very. Full of compassion. Though on occasion worried by the quality of it. Villainy these days is already so corporate, I'd like my compassion to stay personal if it can. And unprofessional. "I'm working toward more compassion in my work," a writer once said to me. I could never do that. I can't feel that the act of recording absolves.

That day I was sunk in my own cells. Feeling one's own feeling tones; I have such a dirty talent for it. But the moment to come will go below that. To the root-inevitable. Of dirty circumstance, that I would now officially join. Hadn't had much yet, you see. Child hadn't yet died.

Or do these baptismal moments at the ego-base of existence have nothing to do even with that?

We were near Frisco now. Almost there. At a siding, we stopped. Not for a station. For one or the other needs of trains. Steam. Signals. Silence, maybe. In these moments when the train stops, high over a chasm at an overpass, low in a brook-ribboned blur of grass or by a brown cow pool— it sometimes seems to me that the train itself reflects.

This time there was a train opposite us, going the other way, but stopped also. People in it gazed out, or dribbled out onto the platform, or sat as we sat. Nobody communicated. Yet after a while it seemed as if we might be in international conference. Across a track. Or in a pause such as must take place at treaties signed by names like Talleyrand and Metternich, where, as they say, the peace of Europe is insured for fifty years. All scurry it would have been—then a huge pause. Lasting at least as long as a greeting of trains across a divide—the passengers being ignored.

Some of those on the opposite train were recruits. Recruits always make a train look crowded. Sprouting out of the windows, faces that don't yet match the uniform, though army rig is still the best mass tailoring in America. Each face a long dimple of concentration, like that of a boy beginning a table game. Below one of the windows across the track, an elderly dude, in one of those western cord ties with fancy metal points, is offering up an apple. Three boys, one apple—it's a problem. To their right, a broad-hipped old body in a knitted cap hoists herself up the high step of the coach with beldam vigor, and hangs by the handlebar, shouting something. Not to them, not to us.

I had a Daumier print once, of a crowd streaming past a railway carriage; an old dame in a mobcap hangs in the foreground, her harridan mouth stretched wide. Can't hear what the old girl across from us is shouting . . . In the Daumier you can hear. There's been time . . . But the main fact about us, two trains of us or one, give or take a touch of Chicago, a Sierra Club tie or even a veil from Tunis—for I concede the plane too, really—is that short of a slight similarity of destination, fragile and nonlasting, we are all here at random. Absolutely at random. There is never a choice.

And so, both trains here concerned with are arriving. Back there, we have left the siding, and that treaty by which maybe only engines were switched, and are slouching into San F. Here, we are in the tunnel, grinding toward Penn Station. There exist trains where there is no immediate bustle to leave; these are never New York ones. In spite of the conductor's chugging " 'Eep ya seats; 'eep ya seats!" the aisles here have been swollen since Newark; one man rose to get his hat, and we were done for. I myself have left the club car without a backward glance and am outside my berth, foot on bags, coat on shoulders, chatting with George. He lives in Philly, but says that New York's where the life is that's worth living for. He seems to think I'm an expert on the fast life. By now, maybe it's true.

Back there in Frisco we have left the sun for the winds, and are maybe sensing that. Or are there trainfuls with more delicacy than most? Who maybe do not want to break the interim world they have made. Out of the random given us. Do they feel that too? There's a tic we all hide—what is it? Or is it that near the city as we are, we've stopped again, tantivy, tantivy, just in sight of everything.

Great sight. We have time to feel our destinations. I have a chance to feel mine.

Suddenly—I believe in my own death. Nothing to do with the Sunday lip service, that potluck testing—of luck. This is the bottom of the wormy barrel, comes only once. My eyes are underwater wide. All the iron girls I was or hoped to be are drowning past me—iron dancer, iron lover, iron mother. And all the floss ones too, in the silly-silky rustle of the humors we used to have together. Angel-jolts of music I heard early spin their barrel-organ in my ear; down, down we go with all the words since—a cloud of gnats over the head, a curd of fish food under the nails, a snapped string of pearl bubbles, chuckling to the sea floor.

And there I sprawl, with my wet little bladder of ego in my hand. I am the goosegirl. Approach.

I open my eyes, which have never closed. Like a child, I always cheat. All I've loved is still with me. They've stayed with me—the whole coach car. Clinging to its window ledge, I resist them, snarling at Jahweh, with whose word I have never made bond. If this is how the saints feel, I'll have none of it. I don't feel in parables—sorry. Clean meaning is my prayer.

Sitting upright in their pocketbook crimps, wild boots, bear beauties and reasonable hats, the coach car waits with me. Iron children, in all stages of the cracked, floss body, their eyes join mine. We are arriving. They know. The experience is seamless. Acres of the self-concern that I can never free myself from drop from me. That I was bound into at birth. Like them. They are the scenery I cannot put by, the museum in which I belong. Of how brave it is to be at all. And how we go on with it. Oh, iron children, who walk between their own murders—this I know. Yet I could plunge my mouth on theirs, vampire to their bravery. They believe in my death. I believe in theirs.

Down the length of the train, the simple facts extend and

pass by me like fans that open and close, held by hands I cannot see. These are the dead. That is what they do.

I believe in all our deaths.

The sight of everything is a great sight.

Fifty-fifty is something else.

"Sorry to've put you through such an experience," the first doctor says, postbiopsy. "I'm a little downbeat these days. Maybe I put it on you. But recently I've lost so many patients I like." Smiling at me wistfully, he twines his psychology with my nondeath and offers me the bitter-almond bouquet of it.

What a peculiar compliment, I think, looking out the window at the dazed air. Maybe a California one. Do they all die in full amber here, longing for a little dark?

"I hope you don't resent. That I liked you that much."

I do and I don't. But I know what he's dreaming of. Death is so much more symmetrical than life.

"You couldn't help it, I guess. Wanting every one of your patients to be a movie star."

When you're like me—humble to the big things but self-righteous about the small ones—it gives you a bad tongue.

The train back to Palo Alto was of course full of light.

And I am left with the rhetoric. Fifteen years later, on the New York train.

I want to be visual in the next life. Words are too much love for me, and too much vanity. I become a basilisk, adoring its own eggs for the pearly membrane which gives it back its own stare. The dialogue of compassion merely rests that. Oh yes, George, humanists rest remarkably well, for a while. Until we learn that nothing rests us from the dialogue. Nothing, George. Except the dark.

This porter's much more of a liberal than I am. He's known he isn't perfect, from the first. So can speak to me as an equal without half trying. Even my good tip hasn't poisoned his humanity against me. Though it may not have convinced me of mine.

"Got to watch it in the big town, girlie. But who care, it such damn fun. Who want Philadelphia? Got to watch it everwhere, don't we? We the kind."

Is he smiling like a father? Not quite. I lower my eyes. Only remember; people are not probable.

"Watch it now, girl," he whispers. "Here come trouble. Here it come. Woo-ee."

My father used to say that. In between the goddamns dropping like tobacco juice—that low, pure whistle at the profanity of life—Woo-ee.

The crowd from the rear cars is coming forward. From the club car too. George stands tall, reminding them. A porter has to remind us. Of last night's beds. The oncoming feet make a massive shuffle. I shan't watch their faces. Can't expect another baptism like that San Francisco one. Fifteen years later, and I'm only dying gradually, far as I know. Nowadays I don't watch faces as much, nor hands either. When I was thirteen I thought that the entire spirituality of the race was evidenced in its sensitive hands, not excluding mine, and wrote one of those bad poems to them. Now I prefer to notice shoes. They are what God did not put into the world. When well and fully worn, they are not symmetrical.

A pair of them stops in front of me. Nettletons. New. I shan't look up. Maybe they can pass me by this time without something dirty coming from them. And a pair of goosegirl shoes can't be far behind.

The emptied berth isn't mine any more, but I step back in. Its window is black and still. No more to be heard from it.

"Morning, George."

No answer. Got to watch it. We the kind.

"Here you are then, George. Here you are."

I hear the rustle of money.

"Put it on a horse, boy. A big smart dark—horse."

My father was never shy on trains. Once, going through the Rockies, he spent an afternoon in a compartment with the diva Galli-Curci. She sang for him. But to the end of his life, he was shy when giving people money. Furtive about it —for them. To the end of his life he was a small-town Southern boy who believed more in swap. To the end of his life.

Father, when do you dead achieve symmetry? I fear it is only in the past—ours. Which can mean nothing to you. For it doesn't happen because of our hearing best the pain that's nearest us—not at all. It's just that the family in all of us lasts a long time afterward. Your death was rather kinder to you than we ever were—two short, surprised grace notes of cough, and a clutching at an eighty-year-old chest—but otherwise a death ragged enough. My mother's death was a pain-by-the-yard I can still see unwinding, all the way to the lumps and knots in me that confused California—but in itself a coda to a beginning that never had a chance.

As for me, whether or not I find a cab at Penn Station, I'll be home soon enough to dust beneath a dead girl's drawings—a dailiness that does not comfort me. Oh, flying girls, dead and alive you are all my daughters now, and I say to you that in our deaths we are none of us symmetrical. It is the past that mists, and churchifies.

The shoes are still standing there. I half expected it. No, I won't look up. They're alone. I'm not surprised. Some of us never see what we step on. That's you, Nettletons, but I'm past hating you for it. Some of us can't stop seeing what's underfoot—that's me, but I take no credit for it. I didn't opt for this consciousness. And I can't keep it up. Please move on.

The other day, walking on Ninth Avenue, I almost trod on three patches, each a paving stone apart, that at first I took for pizza. Then, chicken fat. Then I saw that they must be human flesh, brown-white and blood-riddled.

Vomit and spit are more ordinary for that turf. The police
cars were just then whining away. Must have been an accident. Maybe one day soon, while tracking my way over the
forest of bodies always just below our feet, I won't rear
back in time. Bending over just too late, I'll see the smashed
palette of an eye. And it may not be an accident. There may
even come a day when I may not be able to move my feet at
all; oh, I understand the catatonics well. Walls of their own
pity, closing in on them. Watch my shoes though, and
you'll see nothing. They're as new as yours.

You'll see mouths, I think, Doctor, if it ever gets to you.
The mouth of a girl in an erotic film, stretched so wide to
accommodate love that any smart boozer can take her from
behind. Meanwhile, shove on, will you. I won't look up at
you. I might see your face.

I see my own hands, the young shape of them corrupted
but still perceptible; right forefinger bent from early suck-
ing, sixth-grade bump on the middle finger that has
scarcely used a pencil since then, slim left thumb that always seemed to belong to a more graceful twin sister, and
the small fifth fingers, so bad at the piano and still so innocent. Why do I pity my own fingers? My own shoes? Is it
pity that's corrupting me, or the desire for it? These days I
don't want to do anything with a sentence except pour our
blood in it. Peoples' agonies are like dunes I stumble in,
always falling with my fangs in my own wrist. I did not opt
for this symmetry. A live one. Heavier and heavier, never
enough.

Why do you go on standing there, head hanging down
like mine? Lips sealed. Oh yes, I see them. I always cheat.
But I won't testify. What could I tell you? Hew to the one
creature as toward home? And hope each morning, that the
creature is not yourself?

Move on then, shoes, will you, suit of eraser gray? You're
standing on us. We're standing on you. And I already know

what you want to say to me. Did say, really. I'll even say it back to you. Woo-ee. Woo-ee.

Please move on. Please. I don't have pity enough.

I'll never have pity enough. Never.

Not for you.

Not for me.

Woo-ee.

The Tenth Child

ABOUT SIX YEARS AGO, an ad appeared in the *Times* for the sale of a triplex on Park Avenue which had Closet Space for 1,000 Dresses and Room for Party for 100 Children—in that order. No mention was made of how many adults could be housed or entertained, nor of what was happening—Estate Sale? Owner Transferred?—to the family giving the place up. But I couldn't forget them. What was this crisis in their lives? Was it a modern one, as most crises these days seem to be? Or had it been a very old-fashioned apartment indeed, in which the dresses had worn out one by one, and the gamboling children were too many ghosts to deal with, what with the cost these days of even ghost-help?

I never called the real estate agent. To see these By Appointment Only specials, one has to have references to show one is serious, which means rich enough. I wasn't—and after two Sundays the ad was withdrawn. Gone, that place—snapped up. The special ones always are. These are never places people need. They seduce by vision and metaphor: such as choosing a dress to go with a lover, a lover to go with a dress, from a wardrobe empowered for any eve-

ning, any reverie—or calling in the hired magicians and caterers, and the children, from coast to coast. And they ap-
peal to those who have always lived by the multiple
decimal, or are newly able to. Some nouveau-riche couple
who want 1,000 children, perhaps.

I never worry about the purchasers. They release me to
the next proposal. An ad can be like a bad painting blowing
a real wind. Or like that single cloud, rounded like a sheep,
in a dream copied from Magritte. Or bring to mind the very
pattern of use the kitchen dishes assumed nightly, in the
house one could no longer bear. The people I keep in mind
are the relinquishers—and none more so than the family—a
special one too, I think—who gave up that place. Over the
years their story has become clear to me—and perhaps even
their fate.

It would be the children who started it. Deirdre, the four-
teen-year-old, from the first concerned me most—named
for no one in particular, not even Irish, unable to pronounce
her name intelligibly until she was four, the braces on her
teeth still no help with her r's, and eldest of a brood who, as
they came along out of the ether and that little private
hospital in the East Sixties, had their family-linked names
inscribed with a diamond-point on the northernmost pane
of the tower of the triplex. For of course, though there
might be other comparable apartments in the building,
theirs would be on top.

Although she and her siblings were quite used to decimal
living, actually there were only nine of them all told. Sometimes they feared their parents had given up, there in the
master suite, which in after years would fly into the children's heads whenever they heard the sweet, nostalgic
rumble of slightly ill-fitting closet doors. For although their
mother's closets, which would run all along the fifty-foot
length of the bedroom, were equipped with those silently
swinging metal-armed installations such as garment cleaners have, all moving like the solar system at the touch of a

finger, and behind quiet doors hewn by that original builder whose sacred name was on a brass plate in the lobby, Mr. Higginson's walk-throughs—C. D. Higginson, if you know Boston—would have had to be installed extra, and ill-advisedly had been, by the carpenter son of his senior partner at the bank.

Now, a walk-through is a closet with a door at either end, and these had been constructed on the damp opposite bedroom wall abutting that side of a terrace whose usable footage—owing to extra piping added to supply a swimming pool known in the family as the Missolonghi because a beloved cat named Byron had drowned there—had declined to ninety-eight, making only four closets possible instead of five. These flaws in a family metric system will recur. If you want to know how a cat can drown, that comes later, but I can tell you about the sound of those closets.

The young carpenter, a graduate of Phillips Exeter, the shop courses particularly, had had the idea of making this line of walk-throughs so that the children's father might commute from master suite to terrace in order to view his hobby, a small but exact replica of the earthworks at the Battle of Chancellorsville, during a war where an ancestor of both of them had been aide to Joseph Hooker, the commandant. Since C.D. was indeed always walking through one or the other of these four exits, each of which commanded a separate scenic or strategic view, that explains the constancy of the children's memory. Since the young carpenter, though handsome enough, had not been a very good one, that explains the rumble. An even more grating sound, of their father yelling to get back in when the outer doors from the terrace got stuck—cries not always immediately heeded—is not reported.

None of this appears in the ad.

The children's names, after Deirdre, would be:

Hedwige—their mother being a semiretired (but not

quite, hence the dresses), part-German, part-French (hence the combo of Hedwig and Edwige) and still quite pretty movie star.

Abigail—C.D. would be a descendant of the Adamses as well.

The twin Annes (for a great-aunt with a double-frontage property in Belmont, Massachusetts). One of whom has another name so similar no one can recall it, and they always answer in congress anyway.

Ermentrude—in response to a reasonable protest from maternal grandparents in Westphalia.

Mireille—after a counterblast from ditto in the Bordeaux country.

Patience—a sentiment for which it seemed safest to return to New England.

Griselda—self-evident.

And at long last, the year before the ad: C.D., the floweret, the Junior—though never so called.

At the time of the ad, Deirdre could have been a day student in her third year at Brearley, where she might have instigated herself as a mere Dolly, or at Andover, where she could easier have slipped off her braces now and then, at either place probably being sent to nurse to be checked for anorexia, until they would discover she eats around the clock, costing only a little less to feed than a quarterhorse.

Actually, she is taught at home, as they all are, because of the symmetrical views on education that unite their parents even more than love and the bedroom. So Deirdre, now and then yieldingly called Dee, keeps her marred water-baby smile on until after dinner. She is writing an Elizabethan-style drama, inspired, she says, by the juvenile productions of the Brontë sisters (though it is not known that they ever wrote a monologue about a young male child who vanishes in a tarn)—and is without excuse my favorite.

The other girls are rather bores; their names would have

too much influenced them. Hedwige is sulkily stage-struck, vaunting a waist and pelvic measurements even smaller than the maternal ones which have so remarkably produced them all. Abigail writes letters in the eighteenth-century style of that ancestress who was a President's consort; unfortunately, since she is only twelve, she writes them to boys. Ermentrude will no doubt be a literary scholar in the Teutonic tradition, but right now is confined to crushes on authors beginning with E, whose hems she wishes to kiss, and if possible snip off an inch of. Mireille has only enough esprit to collect dish towels with maps of the wine country on them. Patience is the real trial. Even in other people's living rooms she finds monuments and sits on them; of course the Higginsons' circle would have these in good supply. Griselda has taken the opposite course from what her name would indicate; she is a five-year-old feminist. The Annes? One is always forgetting them. They would do nothing overt.

C.D. Junior? He is a boy.

All in all a very literal family we deal with here—as any whose destiny is converging on that ad would have to be. All the girls would have bubble curls the color of fresh wood shavings, exactly like their mother, and a couple of them are already wearing her old pop-up bras, still perfectly good, since only worn by her for a day. Only Deirdre wears herself straight as you might say, from lank hair to size ten loafers, but that's all right; you know who she is. She is the ugly duck.

Six birthdays along, or say ten to keep the numbers clean, which would bring her to age twenty-four—on a Park Avenue corner, a former British rock star, formerly of Budapest but soon to be formerly of Ottawa where he is now a film director, will sink into the arms of his dress-designer companion, crying: "I just saw Eternity." The companion will mutter, "That was last night," but will cast a look anyway at what has just emerged from a marquee—

and will let his friend slide. And Eternity Dee, once Deirdre Higginson, will next day begin both her career and her wardrobe of 5,000 dresses.

At the moment however, she would take after her father. He, even if something of a history bore, would be the type of looker with money who could keep a girl like their mother pink and happy through ten planned pregnancies, all except the last one being ten months, or some multiple thereof—apart. So in all probability he would be the kind of generalized American Adonis—with maybe one bevy of great-aunts painted by Sargent, who could hope to project his own image and bone structure at least once, even on Mrs. Higginson, their mother—who is never called either.

Mother is Katya. Daughter of a German ski instructor and a French lady barber, she would be the sort of Mittel Europa light-opera singer (movie star courtesy of one film made in Croatia on Mr. Higginson's money), who would be a ringer for Sonja Henie, if she could skate. Still, with that figure of hers, all ins and outs, topped by the nose that would be tip-tilt and the eyes of trout-*blau,* she could look very *hübsch,* even in the wrappers she would wear around the house to spare her celebrated wardrobe—which is being saved for the costume wing at the Metropolitan, though they would not yet have accepted for sure. She is indeed very pink, perhaps a trifle more so from health than from happiness, though one hates to say. Yet to get such a robustly equipped family on the road, there would have to be something. In fact, with Katya one may have to desert the future imperfect tense entirely. Katya is.

The wardrobe hangs muffled in satin, perfumed with rose, on those giant-armed mechanisms, one for each walk-in. There are ensembles enough for three years to come, which as simple arithmetic will show, calls for a surplus above 1,000 of 95. This may be one of the Many Extras the ad did mention. Actually, the 95 are Katya's theatrical costumes. Why these had stopped at that awkward semidecimal, with only five to go, remains obscure—perhaps in the future imperfect of Katya herself.

Each daily ensemble is just that, complete from head to toe to jewels and then some, so as to forestall all forethought, for each day of the three years. Some attempt would have been made to grade them seasonally. That done, Katya wears what she finds decreed for that day, and all that day—and night. Short of bed, that is. What she wears there is kept separate, and is not on the inventory. And not for the Metropolitan.

Such strict adherence to what the calendar decrees can cause oddities of garb—an antique riding-habit with three foxheads and a trailing skirt, say, for Mr. Higginson's ecumenical breakfast for the bank's cleaning women, but her faithfulness has fostered what is admittedly one of the world's great styles. When her Marie Antoinette picnic outfit, complete with panniers, basket and cake, and all of a clear plastic made by a subsidiary in which C.D.'s bank held the controlling shares, had to appear at the opera, all the patrons in the boxes, most of whom knew her, applauded intensely, but the rest of the audience had not, a matter of concern to those of Mr. Higginson's stockholders not geared to the popular ethic that less is more. Yet he has always stood by her, later explaining to his board of directors that his wife, like all young matrons of means, has to have either a charity, a cause, or an art, and that she has by temperament chosen the latter, parlaying woman's natural love of dress into what amounts to theatrical engagements.

There are days of course when a star must rest, or cannot face the calendar, perhaps when it has puce on it. Or when she yearns to wear what must lie fallow until next spring. Any woman who has to wear what she has in her closet to wear will understand that entrapment. So on those days Katya retires into one of the plain wrappers once worn at her old makeup table in the Kleine Schauspielhaus at

Scharaffenland—a comforting supply of which she keeps in with her bath towels—and simply stays in.

Recently Mr. Higginson, who would be one of those husbands who are as deep as they are amiable, has jokingly suggested she hire an understudy. Katya had refused, saying her wrapper days are good for the children, though she hadn't said why. Those days—when they are not likely to be picked up at the dentist by a mother in whatever—are the days they love her best. Mr. Higginson may have replied that he didn't consider this a direct answer, which it wasn't.

Somehow Mr. Higginson, who would be as slow to change as he is deep, would come out of this interchange with the conviction that to hire some blond Katya-replica to accompany him on his own calendar might be a service to the entire family. As the birthday party for those 100 children draws near, perhaps he is still thinking of it.

From the ad, one might infer that space alone had dictated that number, but by now you and I know our couple does not act on shallow excuse. Up to now, though each girl has had her own birthday celebration annually, the flat's capabilities have been modestly used. Each has had the privilege of inviting one child-guest for every one of her years, plus whatever extra would round off the list to the power of ten, Deirdre's fourteenth, rounded to twenty, having been the largest to date. There was always a magician. At Griselda's party, the most recent, there had for the first time also been a ventriloquist. Still, none of them had ever been allowed 100 of anything.

But with the advent of the tenth child—and heir, the decimals would naturally take over. Since his arrival, although several of his sisters have had anniversaries, these have risen only to cake and presents at early dinnertime, in care of their own nine nannies, the new one and her charge making a token appearance. Our couple are not insensitive. But their way of life has always been multiple. So, until the heir's first anniversary of his own, all parties would have been—delayed? Submerged? Abrogated?—in favor of this cardinal one. At which each child will have the privilege of inviting nine friends and their nannies, with little C.D.'s nanny to exercise her choice among selected nannies and their charges from the park.

Nannies of course don't count. In the count, that is. But with that largesse common to the very best ads, there would have been plenty of space in the foyer—indeed extra, for ten baby carriages.

Otherwise, the amenities would remain much as before, though Mr. Higginson's offers have been generous. Ten magicians perhaps, so as to sequester the fun by ages? Katya says no; too many illusions would not be good for anyone, would merely confuse. Then—another ventriloquist? "Another?" she would say, startled, and he would answer, "I mean—an extra?"—but she would veto that too. On the grounds that good ones are very hard to find.

"The children indeed told me—" Mr. Higginson said, "how much they admired the birdcalls." For, owing to business abroad, he had not been at Griselda's birthday.

Meanwhile, Katya herself, it seems, is going to provide the extra that a party such as the great one to come must have. She will appear in one of the 95 costumes—the bird costume with a breast of sequins, a scarlet tail and a cap with a twenty-inch aigrette, in which she once sang Papagena, in a not quite Mozartian version of *The Magic Flute* at Der Bühlerai Brauhaus in what is now East Berlin.

"Ah yes—" Mr. Higginson would say "—you must sing."

Perhaps they both would have their hopes?

Of course she would. Remember the ventriloquist.

Of course he would. Remember the understudy.

And what of Deirdre, Hedwige, Abigail, Ermentrude, Mireille, Patience, Griselda and the always misplaced Annes—all so numerically reared, and so rudely awakened to what a double-digit child can accomplish, particularly when his name does not have to be spelled out? Wouldn't they have had their hopes too?

Of course they would. Remember the cat.

While I apologize for having let us get almost to the party without describing the heir.

He would have been born, little C.D., nine months to the day after the last party, that one for Griselda's birthday which Mr. Higginson could not attend, he having been in Switzerland for a month prior, and in fact for a month after. Griselda had been mortified, though when he did return he brought her a watch that kept the calendar. Therefore, nine months after to the day, when the baby was born, she was able to point out the connection. Mr. Higginson, who wore an old-fashioned watch, would also have the habit, strange for a banker, of counting on his fingertips. Perhaps that would be why it had taken him so long to conclude his business in Lausanne. "Clever child," he would say, kissing her—for all the girls would that day have been ranged around Katya's bed in the modern way, to watch the home birth.

Katya would be lying back on her pillows, cleaned up but not really too exhausted—after all, ten! They would be waiting for the baby, whom the midwives had snatched away to be cleaned up too.

"Yes, clever," he would say, bending to kiss his wife, and to whisper in her ear. "But it can't be, can it, my love? I don't recall you and I having any *Bühlerai* around that time."

Katya sits up. She would not wait for the future, or the subjunctive either—remember? She is. Added to which she has the serenity of a mother whose children have always looked like her.

Just then the senior midwife brings the little boy in. Of course they all already know it is one.

Eight bubble-cuts the color of fresh wood shavings, and

one head with no-color hair straight as string, kneel to peer at him there in their mother's arms. Mr. Higginson, his own pale hair now slightly silvered with banker's gray, and his complexion perhaps a trifle heartier, would be the most eager of all.

C.D. Junior—for we must call him that at least once, is indeed a darling. They always are. So were the girls, but not like him. His nose, tiny as it is, is curved right up and under, like a darling little beak. And the nostrils—like darling little snails. What workmanship a baby is—and this one would be. Most of all his hair, which stands up, black and affrighted, all around his darling head.

The midwife, the senior one, takes it all in. She's a smart one. "With boys, you never know."

Katya, tightening her arms around her wee newest, hums to him *"Kommt ein Vogel geflogen,"* and stares full at her. "They all look like this in Westphalia."

"Who do?" Mr. Higginson says. He too would be choked. "Boys?"

Katya has a cadenza laugh for great occasions. It comes now, trilling up at him. "Only the special ones. This is a ten-month child."

O—the midwife's mouth would say silently—O.

But not the girls. They would be more daring.

"What did mother say to it in German?" Mireille says crossly.

Ermentrude answers quick. *" 'Comes a bird,' "* she said. " 'Geflying.' " Ermentrude has a kind of genius for translation. "It's from a poem. A song by Heine. Fräulein taught me it." For of course her nanny would be from there.

Hedwige says, "Can I hold him?" and does so, posing him against her waist, and maybe squeezing too tight.

Abigail says nothing. She is mentally writing a letter.

Patience comes right out with it, as the long-suffering eventually do. "What in tarnation"—she has an antique vocabulary—"is a ten-month child?"

The midwife vanishes. Her task is done. And she can't wait to have a chin-wag with her second-in-charge.

Mr. Higginson is alone with his family. Like many who have more ancestors than they know what to do with, he would know his Bible rather well. Or think he did. "It's a very wise one. Who knows his own father."

Griselda, who is still sore at him, and maybe at all males generally, says: "Wasn't it lucky though, Daddy—that we had my watch."

As for the Annes—children beginning with *A* tend to be withdrawn, something to do with their responsibility for the entire alphabet. All the more so when there are two of them.

Remember Deirdre? She writes monologues. Wouldn't she say anything?

She says: "He looks scared."

A glorious ripple from their mother. "How could he be? With nine loving sisters to watch over him."

A *frisson* passes through all nine. Perhaps a cadenza should never be repeated.

C. D. Senior would nod slowly. If he is thinking that now his initials are no longer only his own, in some cases a father may be forgiven this. "Oh—I'm sure they will."

All that a fond mother with one eye on her fledgling would be likely to see is that her husband's clasped hands shake meaningfully at the girls.

But one of the paternal advantages of having one's girls look alike is that one can seem to stare at all of them at once in a single commanding earthwork glance, and have that glance returned, as from one tenderly pledged understanding.

"Kiss us, Papa!" all the girls said.

Now we can go to that party, which takes place ten months from that day, this being the birthday, according to Katya, that a ten-month child would have. We won't be among the earliest. Better to arrive at a party's height, at that moment when it would be about to topple into the memorable.

One hundred children of all ages, from the screaming rosebuds to the solemn sailor-suited, to the smoky T-shirts with the maws of rock stars on them, have been getting to know each other very inventively, yet only one Louis XVI cabriole has so far been busted, and that one a fake. All the nannies, both Home and Park, are in reasonably good array, and though out of voice—"Angelique, *tu a un mouchoir pour cela!*" . . . "Nicky, pull down your skirt"—are still able to yearn audibly for when the parents or chauffeurs will come to rescue them. It is Saturday afternoon, and even the best people rarely have the chance to leave the children where so many nannies are; they may have to wait long. Parents have not been invited. "At a kids' party they are always so nosy," said Katya. "Always poking at your arrangements. Criticizing the drapes. And hiring away the help. So we will put champagne and macaroons in the foyer. Not too many. Not too much." And on the invitations she had written: "Children and Nannies Only." Though on the cards to little C.D.'s own guests she had added, "Nursery Naps Arranged."

All has been, by many hands. In a few minutes or so Katya, who has been upstairs in her great walk-in closets getting into her costume—and by nanny opinion taking far too long at it, will emerge to sing. The magician, Mr. Paltenghi, actually the children's white-moustached old piano teacher, who seldom gets them past the Esmeralda Waltz because he is so kind about teaching sleight-of-hand to them, is just sawing Nicky in half—or is it a rabbit? A sailor suit has grabbed Angelique's *mouchoir* and is about to be hit in the eye. Off in the den, the teenagers are playing video games, or watching them through the smoke, leaning back thigh-crossed, with their chesty rock-star allegiances prominent. The pairs of thigh don't always match.

No young Higginsons are among them, or in the ballroom where the dais is set. Where are they? By the time
Mr. Higginson arrives from his office—he would pretend to
be a slave to his accounts but would be socially shy—he
sees that they are going to miss their mother's aria. Rude of
them. Yet he does nothing. Taking a peek round, he sees
that the nannies, who have a natural contempt for parents,
have been into the champagne. He is not worried. They are
all of that expensive sort which may get hazy if the wine is
good enough, but where a child is concerned remains as
responsible as Nelson when he defeated the Danes at Co-
penhagen, claiming not to have seen the signal to cease
action, having put the telescope to his blind eye.

They are also too old or too ugly even to attract a chauffeur. Not one of them could go to be an understudy.

There was once a Higginson nanny, almost a governess,
who could have, but where she is now nobody knows, perhaps in some pretty little leftover castle in Malta, or some
other tax-free island, the kind too where a man joining her
would not be extraditable. Katya has hired all the present
Higginson nine, and they in turn have carefully selected
their park friends. But where is his own recent choice? "We
must really guard the heir very carefully," he had per-
suaded his wife, and for once would have had his own way.
Where is the peerless Nanny Ten? And where is the birthday boy?

He would not be worried. Katya may at first have suspected he wished to employ one of those too modern grad-
uates of the academy that had supplied the British royal
household with a guardian almost as blooming as the Prin-
cess Di herself,—but had been reassured when she saw his
candidate. Nanny Spry, according to references which only
he would have seen, must be eighty, but one would never
know. Tiny and doll-jointed, she is loved at once by all
children, and when awake is as agile as her name. She has
that dun hair, neither gray nor yet dyed, which used to

mark the aristocrats of her profession, and if the Pendartin children were not all now sixtyish and too poor to pay her pension, she would be with them still.

Only her last mistress and first American one, a not very gung-ho snip from New Canaan, Connecticut, had reported that at night, and at nap times insisted on frequently, she rubs the infant gums with paregoric, an ancient soother derived from opium, and allows the elder children a sip of her sloe gin. Today, as Mr. Higginson would happen to know, she and the heir, and the heir's young guests, after the one party activity she had prescribed for them—"An early crawl-about, sir, madam, and one-half ball of vanilla without thingummies in it"—are all dozing in the nursery, which would be plenty big enough for nine cribs hired extra.

He would know this because actually he had come home early and unnoticed, in order to commune with his earthworks. Doing so, he would have heard from his terrace certain goings-on in the master bedroom which would have made him sorrowful, but not surprised. Cracking the inner door of one of his walk-throughs, he would attempt to see the bed, fifty feet away, but try as he could, would only be able to confirm that second pair of struggling legs. At a moment when all was quiet and covered there, he would find himself able to pad shoeless along the near wall of the master suite to its sole exit (he would not have been a courtesy runner-up at the winter Olympic trials of the St. Benedictus Altar-Boys Alumni for nothing)—and so had made his descent.

On the way down, coughing an Ahem, he would have heard that unmistakable silence, as of giggles being swallowed like mashed potatoes, which means children are in hiding. His dear girls, whether or not they are his—and how can he ever tell in their case?—are still loyal. And passing the nursery of the only child he can at least be sure about, he would observe that the heir and his friends, and

Nanny Spry too, are all mum. She in particular would be slumbering like every such nurse in history, *Romeo and Juliet's* included. It would sadden him that all his life is so conventional.

And now he is sitting in front of the ballroom dais itself, on one of the fourscore and twenty folding pews. Though such pews are a great rarity, the ad has not mentioned them. They come from Katya's hometown, where all her relatives had them for quick getaways, though she has never said from what or who. A few stray parents, of the worrywart kind or else Saturday afternoon singles, are already sitting on them. They seem to have managed a few macaroons.

Paltenghi seats himself at the piano. He has finished sawing Nicky in half and has put her together again. Now all the nannies except one are trouping into the pews, each with her flawed group of nine. For none has a Higginson. At the piano old Paltenghi strikes an A. Or whatever would be needed. Mr. Higginson would not be considered musical here. But this is his moment of truth nevertheless. Nicky, open-jawed, pulls down her skirt.

From the wings, the downstage left one, that is, Papagena appears, shimmering to the tip of her aigrette. She crosses the floor seemingly on sparkle only, although Mr. Higginson recognizes her garnet wedding shoes, now rather overstuffed. She looks ageless—that is, too much like the girl she once was. She stands on the dais, bosom ready. It is a full one, the kind always receptive to a little *Bühlerei.* The aigrette is alop. Mr. Higginson would then close his eyes— as he has always done—for her voice.

Now Paltenghi is playing, the aria has begun. Yet Higginson hears no other sound. He opens his eyes. Why—she is merely miming it.

But then. Ah, then. Truth can also be sawed in two; a stage has two wings. From downstage right there comes a divine trilling—the aria. A small figure trots out, seemingly following after the melody like a dummy butterfly, diving into it and out again. By the time this swallowtailed figure has reached center stage, the melody appears to be coming from Katya's mouth.

Well, one did say to remember him. The ventriloquist.

He is wearing Katya's sole relic of her father, the *Chapeau-croque* left behind at a final getaway.

And how these two must have practiced. Tremolos and headlifts crisscross interchangeably. As they sing and mime, mime and sing, they are in absolute synchrony. Perhaps they have been that way before.

Now it is finished, to shouts of "Encore," and "Pwease more." The ventriloquist bows, and sweeps off the top hat. It is a collapsible one. As everyone knows, those are the sneakiest. Not a breath has been seen to quiver those snail nostrils shadowed by its shiny brim. No coo has seemed to come from that curved bird mouth. Though as the figure bows again, its dark hair springs up artfully. The hair is collapsible too.

Katya is quivering all over. Mr. Higginson sees that this has indeed been an artistic engagement. Not a duet quite as the composer intended. But it would be exactly what her husband had had in mind.

"Yes, encore—" he says, standing to clap politely—what a sportsman he is. *"Brava,* my dear." He would turn then to the other figure. "And—*bravo?"*

Though, as he adds, he cannot stay to hear. "Unfortunately I must catch the Concorde, then go on. Phone you, my dear, when I get to Switzerland. Apologies to all. But yes, encore. In fact—pwease."

Of course he would not really go to the airport. Switzerland is for some other less usual day. He would go back upstairs to commune with history, looking in at the nursery on the way.

"All sweetly sleeping," Nurse Spry, now awake, whispers, laying a forefinger across her lips. The forefingers of

such nurses are always extra long for this purpose. "All
except your darling boy. How the music has excited him.
Listen!" Then she falls asleep again.

Mr. Higginson goes down the line of cribs. In all except
one a deliciously ordinary child lies moistly dreaming. It
seems to him that only a mother could distinguish between
them. But even if the tenth crib did not have a canopy, no
one could mistake little C.D.

At less than a year, he does not yet speak intelligibly,
though he will coo back an echo of any language in which
he is addressed. But now, the small nostrils are working
like bellows, the wiry hair is electrically stiff. Even the
crystal lunettes on the crib's canopy are tickling one another. Is it from the two bottles on the mantel, struck by an
invisible tuning fork, that this echo is coming? From the
one marked GIN, which contains the paregoric, or the one
marked PAREGORIC, which contains the gin? For such is the
habit of such nurses. Or is it from the round mouth, yawed
again in sleep, of Nurse Spry herself, that Mr. Higginson
hears, wee and far, but veritable—an aria from *The Magic
Flute?*

He would put his face in his hands. Would tears slide
from between them? One is never sure of the paternal emotion, especially when musically accompanied. But what he
might mutter would be, "All he needs is a hat."

Mr. Higginson would then climb again to the master
suite. No sign that anybody had been dressing here, or re-
versing that process; Katya is winningly neat. Perhaps a
scatter of blush powder on the beauty table. But the long
wardrobe gapes open, showing fifty feet of garments hanging motionless on the great bronze arms, these now motionless, but geared to dip and spin and loft past one another to a knifeblade clearance, at the press of a mother-of-
pearl button switch in the mirrored wall. There are four of
these apparatuses—examples of the Nu Dri Kleen: Suppliers to the Trade's most advanced equipment, but done over

in custom Italian Renaissance, which has caused problems. Crumbs of gilt and gesso, seeping into the housing of those computer-chips which would otherwise elevate and efficiently whirr forward the one pair of black-on-black harem-pants that Katya might specify, now and then cause these burdened arms to start up nervously of themselves, or to whirl neurotically faster. The children have been trained from infancy never to go near.

And what good girls his girls are—if they are his girls. They never have.

But what is this? The last apparatus at the end, the one that dispenses those smartly humdrum travel garments which make women incognito, including those raincoats and ponchos which obligingly turn themselves inside out to do so—that one's arms are stark bare. He would know why at once. That section is the one Katya filially calls her Getaway Closet. Besides, across the vast rug, in his own line of walk-throughs, where his mere fifty suits and other gear are disposed on spartan pegs, he has one section like it, unnamed, but now in the same condition. Packed.

Except that on the floor of that closet of hers there is one perfect sequin. Shed in what haste? He bends to it. In its minuscule silvery face he can see his whole marriage. To the woman who has taught him the sole three foreign words he responds to with feeling. *Scharaffenland*—Fool's Paradise. *Bühlerei*—fooling around; illicit intercourse. And that ridiculous word for top hat, with its suggestion of pasty-faced, raisin-eyed, paid applauders in the boxes: *Chapeau-croque.*

So from now on he will tread cautiously. And so must we. For with the current cost of newspaper linage, and the competition from Owner Anxious and Forced Sale, even an ad set in block letters and separately boxed cannot afford to tell us all we should know. Yet we absolutely have to be in possession beforehand, of the logistics for a denouement that will take some dashing about.

How wide was the master suite precisely? A triplex can be stingy there, narrowing as this one may, toward the top. We do know that the master, standing at his earthworks, can see through and across the room to the mistress's closets, as in any household. Providing, that is, that both the inner and outer doors to his own closets are ajar. But whereas from that position, or even inside one of these walk-throughs, he would not see beyond the bedroom to the swimming pool on the other side of the wrap-around terrace, Katya, standing inside the bedroom, could. Thirdly, what we may never know is whether those apparatuses could in some manner be guaranteed to misperform—or was it a matter of temperament? Children of course often have an affinity for such matters. And where, precisely, was the pearl-button switch?

What we may guess at, for pity's sake, is that in a room already so confused with mirrors, people might not merely lose their sense of direction momentarily. A mother distraught might even confuse impulse with ability. And a man be transfixed, by sheer opportunity. Particularly when both have already packed.

What we can and do know is that this particular Saturday was a beauty, with little breeze, and that the blue-tiled Missolonghi was serene.

Yet a swimming pool is never so personalized as a closet. So, one last question. Do honest commercial machines, perverted to vanity, get nasty-tempered? Or is there a much gentler yet broader key to them? To fine-grained steel at first tempered so true, then projected into that bloody era, the Renaissance—and then made witness to so much.

Anyway, remember them.

Now then. Up the iron stairs to the swimming-pool side troop nine girls, their heads shining in the afternoon sun. Their steps make a harmonious clang; they are not in hiding now. In their center, a pair of twins appears to be carrying an infant angel—as the next penthouse north, always heavy on the field glasses and the mythmaking, will one day report. Actually they are carrying a ten-month-old, to whom they have attached water wings of a lovely orange color. For a birthday present, they are going to teach their baby brother to swim.

To their credit there is some discussion on the matter. For now that he has sung, he is peacefully sleeping.

Abigail says conscientiously, "Shouldn't we wake him first?"

The tallest girl says moodily, "The Annes didn't wake my cat."

Surely cats don't have to be. Not when water wings have been tied on them. Not that these always help.

Nobody says this. The two Annes hang their heads in a neutral position. They could go either way, and often have, there being one of them to spare.

Griselda looks sternly at her watch. "Time's up."

She's right. Laughter is sifting up the inside stairs to the master suite, then a scuffling, then a few leftover trills, the tired but happy ones of duty done. And pleasure beginning?

"There's always time," Patience sighs. "But be quick."

The Annes are the ones to place him on the water. They have the spirit of inquiry. And the experience.

Hustled onto the iron outside stairs again, nine girls look over their shoulders. He is still afloat, the winged baby, lying on his back.

"Not to wowy," the tallest girl says. She hasn't worn her braces in weeks. "My guess is, he can fwy."

Once again the iron steps clang.

Meanwhile, on the other side of the terrace, Mr. Higginson would be studying his Chancellorsville. Like all history, from time to time it appears to be in need of a little renovation, but he is waiting on harsher concerns. He hasn't to wait long.

In the bedroom beyond the terrace, what nymphs and satyrs are dancing, now that they have sung? Or is that pair once again occupied—and at the eleventh hour, in what may one day forever blast the decimal order of this house?

The weathered-gray outer doors to his closets, the ones that too often stick, are today propped open, each one of the four with a stone taken from the breastworks behind him, from in fact the exact point where his own ancestor fell. But Mr. Higginson is not going to walk through them, or on through the glass-transomed inner doors, which have always opened easily. He would not want to catch that couple in flagrant indelicacy—a straightforward action on his part which might have saved all. Instead, he would peer through each transom in turn, for its restricted but powerful view.

The first transom is a clear amber. He would stand there in and among his camphored winter suits; it is June. Katya, yawning, is already nude. Her companion, trouserless, is still in swallowtail, a plump sack of serge on skinny legs. Not the sort one would think a Sonja Henie look-alike, married to an adequate if generalized American, would fancy. Katya's body is what any one of sense would expect the body of one of the best-dressed women in the world to be. It looks better unclothed. In the nude, to look too much like the girl you were is not that bad. What unsettles him is the pair's peculiar air of domestic intimacy. She is wearing the top-hat. The ventriloquist is wearing the aigrette.

Mr. Higginson next moves to a transom of cloudy blue. He stands there in the starchy ambrosia of all the summer suits he may not be going to get through in their usual modest sequence, at least not from home.

At the bedside table of countless amiably shared breakfast trays sent up by cook, that couple are now hunched over a cardboard tray from the caterer. On the floor beside the ventriloquist's chair is a squat valise with too much personality. Beside Katya is her Hartman. The swallowtail dips rhythmically. Her elbows waggle as she chews.

This blue honeymoon light is not the kind in which a man's wife should be seen eating with such smear. Nor is it the color in which a man watching should feel only the gnawing reminder that he himself has eaten nothing since a sandwich at noon. Yet that is all he feels. By the time a man gets to a transom, he would wonder, is nothing spectacular enough to satisfy?

The third transom is soft rose to vulgar red, depending on the angle of the sun. His hats surround him, and those long tongues silkily whispering of other days, his ties. What is that pair doing now?

In the horrid, lurid red of sunset, they would be lumbering hippily down the fifty-foot length of Katya's walk-ins, playing naked hide-and-seek among the clothes. Now they are two russet bears, plumply off-color, now two whitishly conniving blobs that match too well. Imagine them at the beauty table, exchanging wigs—though Katya never wears them. They could be understudies. Of one another.

Mr. Higginson would turn away. He would think that now he knows what transoms do. No spectacle seen through them can satisfy. No emotion can survive their glass, no prejudice. A transom serves one purpose only. It ruthlessly tailors love.

He would be wrong. In a minute, a shriek would rouse him. It does. For Katya, now forty feet along in the wardrobe, deep in ballgowns with her buttocks tilted and a kiss to them on the way, can now see the swimming pool. "That's *our* baby out there. On the water. What have those girls done?"

He will raise his head in time to see the pink swoop, like a comet's tail, that would be forever Katya—who cannot swim—running toward the pool. He hears the splash. Over and above it he hears that *our*—a red knell.

To his everlasting honor, he will pound on all the tran-
somed doors. Perhaps not so much to his credit, already
subverted by circumstance and a young carpenter, he will
anticipate what could happen, what does happen to damp
wood when it is tried too often. They will all stick.

So it is that although he will never actually see the fate of
his Katya and his heir—left alone, the babe might have
floated on, if not flown, but a mother must save her child,
so the two went to the bottom together—he will witness
the end of her lover.

Are all ventriloquists prim? Or overly concerned about
their stock-in-trade, those forever pursed lips? This one
would seem to have been one or the other. For, refusing the
kiss as proffered, the second figure had run on ahead to
catch Katya from the front. So doing, it had reached the last
section of Katya's walk-ins, the one that is now all arms of
bare steel. Empty ones. The closet whose provender has
been packed.

Through the clear white glass of his own fourth closet,
cleaned out too down to its pegs, Mr. Higginson sees those
arms shift, reach, engage—and clinch. As they rise and fall,
swing and flail, upending a pair of ankles, closing like a
meat-press on plump white, and turning Mr. Higginson's
clear pane a bright burgundy in the process, they would
seem far hungrier than him.

Then the cycle shuts down; the doors of the wardrobe
mercifully close.

Or has somebody once again pressed a pearl-button
switch?

For a couple of hours, until the superintendent, phoned
to by the man with the binoculars, comes to the rescue,
Higginson rages. Using the sharp ferule of his best English
umbrella, he strikes to kill at those transoms; they must be
plastic. He pounds on doors until his knuckles are raw. Was
his own good enough body and the plain life he provided
not blurred enough for her? Who are the shrouded fathers

of his other nine? What if, even now, she is not an Ondine in a Lethe of chlorine, but in a rush of remorse and adrenalin had learned a last-minute breaststroke? Would she then pack C.D. Junior with her? Why, why is it so dangerous to achieve all one's decimals?

Much later, when the time comes to place that ad, he will be able to say to the real estate agent: "No need to mention the transoms." Though she obeys, he knows that he might as vainly have instructed her not to mention that the place is a triplex, with space for all that it has had space for. He is merely now able to recognize how his architecture has influenced his life.

For after those two hours, where we leave him for the nonce, he will never again be a would-be. He has attained to that cleft between the past and the future where we all strive to be. Higginson is.

Remember Deirdre? Sorry to have to ask again; she may no longer be your favorite, if she ever was. She is like her mentor, Emily, who out of the wettest moorlands and maladies in Yorkshire always bounced back to be the movie star among Brontës. One may grow to like Charlotte better, but there was no Charlotte among the Higginsons.

On the day we caught that premature glimpse of Deirdre on Park Avenue, she was on her way to see her father. He would live alone now—sorry, does live—in a spacious but essentially one-room studio in a bachelors' co-op—not having married again and being slightly wary of numbers, though careful to observe anniversaries. Deirdre, like all the young, thinks that this practice makes one old. But it is the tenth one of the tragedy, and though she no longer believes him to be her father, she is devoted to him. They have the following exchange:

"I saw this ad, you see. In the *Pennysaver.*" In Southern California, she explains, this is where all the million-and-over house ads are. She shows him the clip, which reads:

"Park Avenue Pied-à-terre. For those who can afford one-of-a-kind unique. Roofgarden can be restored to original landmark earthworks. Master bedroom has wet bar. Restorable closets, setup suitable for seraglio. Antique machinery for same still in basement. Main rooms will accommodate movie premiere. Many Extras." She broods. "They added their own. Ours had become part of the apartment."

"Extras tend to do that." He wonders privately whether this ad would be accepted by the *Times.* Seraglio!

"I saw that," she says intensely. Her esses are subtle, her *r*'s lightly present, the occlusion of her teeth a sight on which to dwell. "I had to see for myself."

"And how are your sisters? Did you go see them?"

"Oh, they're fine—exactly as you'd imagine. In their same styles."

After searching without luck for their putative fathers, he had kept them all on, as too young to desert and maybe too familiar to let go, only farming them out to schools, camps, and other youth-developmentals, as these parking-places were now called, of which he had had to have lists as long as his legs once were. For the homesick girls were always leaving these euphoric hostels, on the grounds that they didn't fit you for ordinary life. His legs, now up on his gout-stool, have meanwhile shortened considerably.

"Now they are all well-flown," he says. All of them having indeed managed to become as ordinary as only a very few people are. The only one he misses, with the nostalgia natural to us, is little C.D.—always to have more possibility than the rest.

For Deirdre is claiming to be a better researcher than he. "In fact, as such things go, I am the pimpernel." She shows him her documents, ream after ream emerging from one of those clever loaf-size knapsacks he avoids, in which one can carry the world and Atlas too. "That's it, Dadda; there were eight of them. The fathers of the Annes were twins."

He glances down the list of fathers only slowly enough

to see that they are all foreigners, which she knows would best accord with his preference. All the credentials are fine. Can he believe in them?

"Well—you sure have inherited my feeling for history," he says, almost proud. He now limits himself to reading it, a sad replacement for what cannot be restored. "And so— you are my only real daughter." As he suspects she always wanted to be.

So, Deirdre will not tell him. That she is the daughter of that one of Katya's lovers who, as with many a first lover a married woman takes, was the one who looked most like him. Indeed in this case being related to him. From her earliest childhood she has with reason suspected all this— and all carpenters.

"How did your mother ever manage?" he marvels. "To make all the others look so much like her?"

"I think it was why she had so many mirrors," she says sourly. She would not be her mother's child if she could manage it. But has not been able to prove otherwise.

"I don't keep mirrors here. That's why I don't shave."

He looks it. In her travels, even to Westphalia and Bordeaux to search out the unknown side of the family photographs, she has not found one in any way resembling that beaky little baby. The Higginson side is of course already in all the books. But now, seeing her father, shrunken as brown as his leather stool, and with the beard she has seen him clip with a twirl toward the nostrils, while listening to the recordings that keep him hour-long company, his mouth meanwhile rounding to an O—she shivers. Noses thicken with age, a physiognomist has told her. But do they also hook? Would it be—could it be—that C.D. Junior was Mr. Higginson's only natural child?

"Good!" she manages to say. "Don't. They're bad for you."

"Not for you?" he says, smiling.

"Ah well," she says with a weak salute, "we all know who I resemble."

"Good enough. So I can always look at you."

They both laugh.

But is no one going to mention C.D. Junior?

No one. That would be bad research.

"Who's selling the flat?" he says idly. "Same two men who bought it?"

"Mm. They're moving to the West Coast. Agent showed me the place, but I met those two out on the street later. Anonymously." Then she tells him about their plans for her being Eternity Dee, negotiations for which had been finalized by stages that same evening, in a disco in TriBeCa, a soul-food place in Harlem, and a pancake joint in Riverdale. She still has her appetite.

"Fine terms," he says, when he has looked over the contract. Then he bristles. "See here. This clause marked 'Agreed Upon Family Background.' Your mother was no gypsy. I saw the whole family tree. You come from wholly conventional families, on both sides."

"That's the trouble. They can't publicize a girl brought up so traditional."

"Well, you certainly were. I won't apologize for it."

Nor will I ever explain, she thinks. They stare comfortably into the fireplace, which is a gas one he can reach to turn on and off from his chair—nowadays his sole exercise. And he is only forty-eight.

"You know—I'd like to see the old place," he says. "Maybe I'll go have a look."

"Father!" They exchange wave-lengths. Theirs have always been in touch. "You're not—thinking of rebuying it?"

"No-o." But it is half a question. "Or not for me."

"For who, then?" She sits up, outraged.

"Oh, I won't marry again. Unless I find the right woman. Which isn't likely now. My tastes have become rather perverse. Or maybe always were." He gets up suddenly—he can still move fast when he wants to, and when he does not think of doors. He puts a record on. The voice, or voices, come oddly, a whole forest revel of them. "I dream of one, sometimes. Found this in a secondhand shop." Not true; he's had it for years. The record finishes. "But it's by a man. With a name—ah, half like that German poet, half cereal." He checks the record as if to recall it, but she is not deceived.

"Rainer Mussli," he says then. "A Swiss. Sometime worked as a female impersonator too. And damn good at it."

"Oh, I suppose they can be," she says. Especially when they already are female. "Sometimes they even go to be governesses."

His foot gives a twitch. Gout can be a very present disease.

"Oh, Dadda. Perhaps I should find you one. A female ventriloquist."

"Oh, if I bought the place," he says lightly, "I would buy it for you. But could you be a movie star from here?"

"No problem. Haven't signed that contract yet. We could put it in."

"Only one thing still wonders me," he says, looking into the gas aureoles. Is he aware he sometimes talks like Katya? "That pearl-button switch. They don't by chance still have it?"

"I told you. It's all a wet bar now."

A vision comes to him from the phrase. Two little waterwings, like a split cherry tomato, perched on the rim of a glass, or a swimming pool. "It still wonders me. Who could have pressed it?" If anybody did.

"One of the Annes," she says quick. "You know how you could be staring at one and think there were two of them. Going down those stairs, one of them could've simply snuck back."

She will never be an actress, he thinks. No matter, there's her face.

"If I could be sure."

"Oh, you can," she says passionately. "They were the only unconventional ones of all of us. Remember what they did to my cat."

Now he is pressing the button for the gas fire. It goes out. It goes on again. "It could be a deal. I buy the house. You marry. Somebody like me, if you must—or from Yorkshire. And restart the family. For I shall never. I shall travel intermittently. To keep *au courant.*" And here is where he ventures into fantasy. For among the girls, she is still his favorite. "And you would manage to make all the children look like you."

And if by chance a family beak comes out in them—the one that skips generations and is never painted by Sargent, by that time he himself will be gone. For of course he would have—does have, a little pocket mirror, silver-handled and palm-size, suitable for trimming one's beard by the light of a bivouac. In it he can see any time he wants to the long-sought face found in secret papers finally ceded him by a remorseful young carpenter. That curly mug—in morning light somewhat puddingy but by bivouac time even somewhat bankerish, of their common ancestor, the aide to Joseph Hooker, at Chancellorsville. Who would have been—had been—a ten-month child.

Who but Higginson has been the best researcher of them all?

"One's children are one's real genes," he says, choked. "Who can trust either of them? And for you children, parents are the same, aren't they. So be content for the nonce —which is the best place to be. And one day—we'll have a party. For your premiere, say. For 500 of all ages, and well mixed. No, to be safe—499." He has come to mistrust decimals.

"Oh, Father," she says. "Dadda. Oh—Papa."

But when she can say it casually, she says, "Thanks—no. I have to live in the present."

The gas fire burns well, lurid through its amber glass.

"Yes, do that," he says. "Perhaps it's easier in California." He gets up and goes to his desk, where the contract is. "But couldn't you keep a New York place, our old one say, as the ad says? As a pied-à-terre?"

He won't tell her that this bachelor setup is only that. Let her keep her idea of him. But she is staring at him, sly. "Why—C.D. You'd like me to keep up the past for you, wouldn't you?" She's never called him that before. "That's a parent's job!"

"Oh—I now live in the present entirely," he says. Keeping a spare in Switzerland, as I always have. "Though small items come in from time to time." He picks up a letter lying near the contract. "The Metropolitan is finally going to accept your mother's wardrobe for their costume institute." He folds the letter back into its envelope. No need to reveal the rest of their remarks. That after a second cleaning done by their own experts, some of the collection, the laces particularly, had attained that marvelous ecru luster which only hemoglobin gives—and would he care to tell them whose? He has replied that he is researching it. "They say though, that one of the theatrical costumes is missing. There are only ninety-four."

"Why, don't you remember? The Egyptian one, with the belly-dance stomacher. We buried her in it. It never became her."

"None of them did," he said. "That was her charm."

Before Deirdre leaves, he lets her sign the contract, after making a correction on one clause only. "Five thousand ensembles to be provided, eh? Let's make it four thousand nine hundred and ninety-nine." As she signs, he looks at her fondly. Her clothes become her, although they never fit. He stops short. In the tearful nature of things, who he really wants to warn—is Katya.

"Well—C.D.?"

He senses she'll call him that from now on. Not sore anymore, just patronizing. That's healthy. That's young.

Never put them on cycle—your closets. Is that what he wants to say? And skip the machinery; maybe use just pegs. As for doors—there is no solution. No solution being in the nature of doors. Yet none of this is really what he wants to say to her. Dear Deirdre—he wants to say—dear putative child. For of course he suspects her parentage, remembering the remorseful air of his very adequate replica. Yet being as he is, he will always have hope. Never believe that much in button switches, is what he wants to say. Or believe in them only as much as you believe in your children. Which is never enough.

"Empty closets yearn," is all he says. "I'm convinced of it."

She pats his shoulder. "Tell that to the ads."

They kiss.

Is she hard or is she soft? What hurts her most, of all her upbringing? He'll take a flyer at that.

"Try to forget him," he says. "The cat."

She smiles her water-baby smile.

What a start that gives him. Should he hope she never sees that brotherly resemblance? Or that she see it always?

Perhaps they are all his children. Nine of them, born like most people, under care of the conventions. The true ten-month child requires more confusion—as to term, time and tenses. Yet that is the very nature of the decimal life.

After she goes he puts on the record again. Yes, he was always musical. With a taste formed late—more for the understudy than for the star.

What he misses most in the present life are his fake battlements. Those in Malta, which the gardener always mistook as being from a British war, or pretended to, for a joke. People don't joke enough. That gardener understood his temperament. And those larger earthworks in the house in

Lausanne, on a workaday afternoon, in the quiet nearness of his bank accounts. And, never forgetting, the final ones on Park, which will always be home. All his ads have done too well for him. As with so many extras, they should.

What can he tell the Metropolitan? That a certain tint of the magic cognac always gives the past a luster without name? That the past is in part always minced ventriloquist? Shouldn't they know?

Now the record is over. Lost once again, that far caroling.

Carefully he lifts one foot—*pied,* from the floor—*terre,* then the other. Keeping oneself in the present takes keeping up. It is what gives him the gout. His bags are always packed. Always empty. When he arrives, he always peels the labels from them. When he leaves, these have grown again, a chattering of names and destinations that a wise father—and maybe even a foolish mother—knows will never end.

He picks up his bag. Empty again. The present has drained from it. The trouble with this place is that there has been no ad for it. To concentrate life, there is nothing like an ad. Soon again, he will have to reappear in one.

Remember then, Mr. Higginson.

Survival Techniques

T RUTH IS NO MERE feature story. It's what happens to a man, his wife, and a street. My vice is to sit here and think about it. Though if it is my wife who is saying those things in the newspapers, don't discount them. Only stop in your tracks now and then, as some of you do, to watch me think. As long as some of you do, all is not lost.

See that apartment-house door halfway down the block on this side, going east? She and I have lived there for thirty-five years. Up this hill in the other direction, just back of the subway entrance on the next avenue west, used to be the stationery store my father kept before me, coming to Manhattan out of that same entrance every morning at six. I always meant to turn it into a bookstore. Selling newspapers, I admit one learns from them. After I was interrupted by a war, we had to take it over as it was. Still, that was when we got the flat here, on a tip from an old customer. Two and a half rooms, the bedroom on a court, the kitchen with a wall common to the back elevator, but the front room with a view of this famous cross street. Look up four storeys. That window there.

During our first years, such a mellow time, my wife often

remarked to favorite customers who lingered that we
"maintained an apartment" just down the block, a phrase
she'd picked from the magazines which were now our main
stock-in-trade, along with lighter fluid, Scotch tape, and
similar notions, as well as in those days also a friendly
stamp machine and neighborly telephone booth. Later on
she mentioned it less, afraid we might somehow lose the
low statutory rent which was allowing us to buy the weekend cottage in the hills around Carmel, New York, even
though we never had a car to get to it and must take the
Harlem Line train. Still later, when a young man, choosing
fancy paper napkins, hand towels, candles and place-cards
from among the party goods and greeting cards which had
taken us over, exclaimed: "Why you live in my house, too!"
she hushed him, for there were transients in the store, and
though we still kept its door unlocked, each evening now
we took the after-banking-hours receipts home with us. As
we went down this long block—"artery of music and art,"
as the city calls it, what with the last one of its three old
concert halls still going—and reached our own door, which
has a doorman, we still happily dropped the street-fear behind us. Who could get at us now, on our fourth floor? The
house, old but well tended, has such fine security, with
alarms from basement to roof. In all our time there had not
been one robbery. So, at The Eclair pastry shop farther up-
town, where my wife, who is Viennese, still meets her lady
cronies, she could still boast of living on our block. Being
Viennese, she respects not only pastry but art and music
too.

Yet to the very last, with our minds so much on what had
come to be called "violence," we never suspected our
block's true claim to fame-to-come. I don't know what the
modern high-risers like the one down the hill there on
Sixth do about their boilers. They give no outer signs of
their warmth. But we older houses and office buildings run
on what is called New York Steam, which comes from be-

low. Slums too have their gypsy heat-crannies, from old cellars to restaurant exhausts. But in all midtown, as I now know, there is no other street so brilliantly prime for certain conveniences, for certain people.

Two blocks north is the park, for summer mainly, but in all seasons always free latrines. We are also in the center of four entrances to the huge midtown subway complex, including the one right at hand in front of our old shop—for whenever you have enough for fare, even though a toilet or a bench is all you are after—or in extreme weather, a roof. For company, passersby are stocked until very late here, and many of them the best types and the cheeriest, with theater stubs in their pockets and reservations for the Russian restaurant. Yet there's also a nearly all-night dairy, with coffee and food take-outs. And to all this add the four winter jewels of our street, those four warm spots where a body can maintain itself, even in rain. Even in snow I have seen it done.

Two of those four are pavement only, two of them grills through which the heated air to the legs or the buttocks comes up direct. In the beginning of course I did not know this, nor that the prize one is curbside. You may sit there with all your equipment at your side and enjoy a cigarette as much as in front of most home fires. If you are likely to sprawl with a wine bottle—though this street doesn't much run to that, the wallside one is best. The curbside one is only available when the woman who has dibs on it is off to one natural function or other in the places I have indicated. The walls either side of the dairy's window are also warm to stand against, maybe because of the roast-chicken spit turning inside. And finally, near what was once the old Aeolian Hall, there is a handsome brass stanchion, polished at all times, narrow for a bottom, not warmth itself but near it—where, if able, one may sit with dignity. Almost as at a sidewalk cafe, except that it may be winter, and there is no glass enclosure. And it is free.

And you will have with you everything you now own.

Often quite extensive, even well packed. The woman—see her there on the grill, a familiar sight to the hundreds who pass daily, has I suspect the best-planned equipment of all, though no one has seen it entire. The first one to come here, she has kept to herself, but we know from the famous snowy day that it contains a ratty brown fur stole—never much, my wife said, probably muskrat. The man standing against the wall—I have never seen him sit—has a supermarket cart neatly loaded in both baskets, in the upper one a cloth overnight bag so tightly stuffed that when he takes out his drumsticks, as he does at intervals, and performs a roulade, meanwhile twirling the sticks in the air and deftly catching them, often to crowd admiration, the bag itself reports like a drum. As you see, his bald head has a V'd black wig painted on it, as are his broad, squared brows. Hard to say whether the cheeks are red from exposure as well as rouge. But it's quite possible that he may once have been a performer in more than his own head. The drumsticks are professional.

Not much beyond features tangled in beard can be seen of our wino, the only one I have seen use the sprawling spot. Normally he stands. Observing closer one can see that not only is he a fine figure of a man, or was once, but his long formal topcoat is really very adequate, like the mountaineer-style boots, even if the boots are not a pair.

As for the man sitting on the brass standpipe, observe for yourself.

So how can my wife—look sharp up at our window there and you may see a figure move—how can she say these people are bums? That's a word from our shop. She says that what has happened to me is because we sold it. After that, she says, I lost my shopkeeper's mentality, and she may be right. There were outside and inside people then, just as now, but I was tied to the shop. After that I had more time to see. How a shop itself can make one introvert.

Once we retired, I did the marketing; that was only fair. Besides, the supermarket was west of us, and she didn't like to pass our former shop window, now a barber's and bare except for a potted plant where we had had all our paper nutriments. What I hated was the supermarket. As a proprietor I had been so safe, all sell sell sell, and I knew what every item cost wholesale. There in the market it was a wilderness of buy buy buy. But of course I did that. One must survive.

Those mornings, she cleaned the house, now that we no longer needed a maid. A house too could make one as introvert as a shop, she said, so afterward she would go off to The Eclair. A man like me doesn't have afternoon friends. I used to have my weekend poker nights, but once we had the cottage that stopped. I didn't know whether any of that crowd were now retired too, or if I had, companionable for what? Men like me don't lunch, and drink was for after work. What it came down to was that my wife and I had lived two by two. Now more and more we were one and one. So I did what a city person does. I walked. After a while, when one walks the same route, as men like me do, it's a little like work. After a time at it, a street is a little like one's shop.

Yes, I think it was the woman who came here first. I may not have noticed her much at the outset because she too was still walking. Or it was light weather, when our famed spa spots are not so necessary. I do recall passing her, a dumpy woman in navy coat and hat not yet dirty, toting some bags but not yet for sure classifiable by them. Then one spring night she was on the brass hydrant—as I then thought of it—with her bags beside her and smoking a cigarette. She smokes jauntily. She still might have been taken to be pausing there from work, a cleaning-woman or dowdy nurse.

Come summer, I forgot her. It was to be our first full season in the cottage, and the last one before we rented it out. In time it too would have to be sold, as my wife would not yet accept—for we hadn't sold the business that well. For the same reason that had caused us to sell it. The wrong outside people kept coming in, even in this brilliant neighborhood. Wanting our money, not our stock.

Then, one dusk in early autumn, I saw the woman from last spring. It was about six o'clock and I was coming home from market, arms loaded, for I am not a man to push a cart. As always on that walk, I felt weary and lone, not from my burden but from its repetition, which would go on and on, and when I got home the two of us would not be cheerily in from the day's earnings and events; rather, my wife, who now spoke of sewing for certain ladies at The Eclair, would be checking every item's cost.

Just then I went by one of the gratings, and saw who was on it. She has an unmistakable silhouette. Short, yes, but round at the bottom, like one of my wife's dumplings, which swell once more at the second boiling. There's something touching now in the way hat and coat match, and the hat itself is no casual woolen cap but cloth, with a neat crown and brim. She even has a certain style. One thinks of Maine, or Ireland. A pipkin face. Afterward, one recalls the eyes are blue. But of course she had passed over the indefinable line. I was sorry. Except in death, or at the very least a coronary, one does not sit on the city's floor.

A few steps on, I turned back to look at her. I couldn't help it; the load in my own arms turned me like a counterweight. At that distance I could see how the hat helped hoard her glance. She could look at us or not look. The arms too curved in a certain unmistakable way. She was carrying the burden of herself.

As the weeks went on, those of us who had to pass her daily learned both to accept and avoid her. In the apartment house we older tenants, who often chatted a bit, did not speak of her. She was too near. Winter would remove her, we may have thought, as in my childhood it removed the beggars from the streets. Though she did not beg. My wife and I never spoke of her either, even in our now rare walks together.

One day I decided to patronize the barbershop which had replaced us. I have a good head of hair. The barber was slow and glum. While the cuttings drifted down I had time to think of the history of stationery stores. In my father's time there had been a whole wall here of earnest aids to ambition, from spring binders to lined account books with hard red-ripe covers, to the glossy flipover pads children were then required to buy. On the lighter side, we had had the candy counter and certain simple toys—tops, balls, jacks, skipping ropes. Cold air, door always half open, a smell of news and of public school. The worst event a small hand pinching a chocolate bar, and the name of the parent often known. Had I and my wife gone wrong with all those party whatnots and gift items? We had only gone transient with the times; I knew that well enough.

We had had our glories. If the barber had looked Italian I might even have told him of how the opera singer Martinelli looked in retirement, a great flourish of a man with a head like an emperor's, twice the size of mine.

"I come to buy the evening—" he always said, there then being a raft of newspapers for it, to which he would add a box of our best brand of boxed chocolates, for the mistress perhaps, and the Havanas we weren't sure he himself smoked. "Do they affect the voice?" my wife once dared. Though eightyish, he smiled at her, flirted his cane near the ankle on whose pretty shape she wore and still wears a gold chain, and gave a retrospective hum. We had others, too, from the concert world, who maintained us in our own eyes even if they never bought from us—once Van Cliburn himself walking into the Hotel Buckingham, his long piano hand carrying a brown-paper sandwich bag. My wife couldn't believe her eyes, but I can; we all have to live. Our store's last claim to basics had been the candles; during one blackout, by staying open until twelve midnight we had supplied the neighborhood.

It would be about there, in front of the first barber chair, that the man with the knife had one day pushed past two customers going out; that's the moment of risk, as all shopkeepers know. Buzzers and locks do only what they can. There was nothing this man with the drugged stare could want to buy from us, what with no newspapers stocked any more, no cigarettes. My wife kept telling the story afterward: "And this man, my husband, this man quietly reading in the back like he does, this man with a heart condition"—which after the war was why I kept a shop of course—"this quiet man—overpowers him." Well, I had resolved to, after the third of them. But seeing from people's headshakes that such accounts only bored or disturbed, I would say, "Well, I knew he couldn't want a card that said 'Luv A Bunny, Luv You.'" But I had known it was the end. Over there, where the fake shaving mugs now hung, had been the one shelf where we kept the autographed programs of the concerts we ourselves had been to, plus a few ballet and opera books to sell. I took the knife from him just there.

The barber had finished. I admired myself and tipped him for the privilege. Pocketing it, he stared out the window, over the potted plant. "Look at that guy. All week he haunts this corner. And you know something? The police can't even chase him. He don't beg."

I saw him first through that clean, well-known windowpane, now prismed with afternoon sun. Perhaps that's why I still can't bear him though I appreciate him—the man with the drumsticks.

"Do you know—the woman down our block?" This was the first time I had mentioned her to anyone. "Toward Sixth?"

"No, I go home Eighth Avenue." He put his scissors away. I'm not a man for clippers. "But there's a guy on crutches. Stands outside the bank, going toward Broadway. Him too. Never asks for a thing."

Yes, it was disturbing. That they didn't beg.

"Disability," a customer said through a hot towel. It's a good barbershop. "They get pensions somewhere."

"Street people," the man with the manicurist said. He held up his diamond to her. "What you wonder is, where they go for you-know-what."

That's what an investigation would turn up. Pensions somewhere. Places for you-know-what. Only the technique. All the things people don't quite know and I didn't yet. Do you or do you not get welfare without a residence? Where do they pick up the checks they do get? Where does one find a muskrat stole? Or mismatched crutches, one wooden, one aluminum? What moves you, to move? Or to be permanent, on a particular city block?

—All that I didn't yet know I wanted to know—

It was winter by then, but the woman stayed on. Passersby stopped to marvel, hesitating, appalled. I walked on steadily, for I knew the routine by now, hers and mine. Days she had a cigarette I felt better. Under the hat, the nose was jaunty. The hat continued to remind me of Maine, though I had never been there. People were hardier up there, weren't they? I saw that even in the bitterest weather her hands were red, never purpled. She never wore gloves, but by now I felt this was by choice. She had her resources. Whenever she was not there I was sure she would be back. One day I saw her stand up. That dumpling swell of hers was surely clothes. Once a man gave her a coin and I thought she smiled, but more for the deed. She never talked, so far as I saw. The drummer did, talking busily and proudly to people as he drummed for them. He came and went; so did the wino. Though I never saw him with a bottle I continued to name him that. I was a trifle nearer their days than most, but I got used to it.

So the winter passed, and the spring. We sold the cottage and it was autumn again. Summer lifts all hearts, but toward winter, couples like us begin to watch how the money flows. My market bundle, though each week composed of the same, grew heavier, my wallet lighter, yet we were still reasonably all right. Three years though, until the Social Security would take over from the savings in what the bank calls their "golden" passbooks, plus a bond or two— for the cottage had sold better than the shop. Our possessions meanwhile grew dearer to my wife: her Bohemian-glass decanter set in its majestic box, and my folks' table silver, one fine spoon of it even from Russia. Sometimes she evaluated them. We allowed ourselves no more anxiety than most people like us had. Still, I was glad there were no more poker nights, even at the stakes we had played. My wife polished the decanter's box ever harder. "Of course, they never give you what things are worth." I was doing our accounts, a habit I could not break. "This desk," I said. I loved my desk. I only said it to comfort her. "These days a roll-top desk is like gold."

One day we were returning from our monthly movie. The film club in the basement of Carnegie Hall is cheap and cozy. After a modest membership fee for two, a double feature cost only a dollar each, and pastry may be bought. Once in a while we hit a day when one of the features would be a French one without subtitles, but even that was gayer than the television. Extravagance is necessary. Going home in the false starlight—for our street, though usually too gas-fogged for the real stars, is remarkably well-lit—I watched the two of us in the windows of the stores we were passing. Women more often do that, but I was beginning to. It was darkly raining, which improved our images under the glare from the Hall's great brow. I saw how my wife's lustrous raincoat and my serviceable dun one were still part of the throng. We had bought well.

Ahead of us, we saw the detour just in time; the crowd

was managing it so neatly. Except for an occasional Sunday when odd-lot concerts or out-of-town graduations take over the Hall, our crowds are businesslike.

"Let's cross over," my wife said suddenly. We were already on our own side of the street. I glanced at the dairy, framed by its own signs like a proscenium arch. Often the drummer and the wino flank it, both standing. Neither was there. But even the one time I saw the wino sprawled he had hugged the wall. Whoever was lying on the ground there now would be a stranger. There had once been one of those. I forced my wife on. "It won't be one of ours," I said.

But it was. The woman sitting on the pavement had merely opened an umbrella. Some of us attempting to pass did not have the luck to have one with us. Gazing back at us, she might have been in a deck seat, or on a *plage*, thinking exactly that. Always before, her stare had been self-centered or remote. Or hidden. Now she was out in public, but sitting on her own pillow. There are some articles which should only be on hire. Also the hand holding the umbrella was blacker; one could scarcely see last year's reddish skin. So that was how skin became without washing. But the umbrella was perfectly good.

I think she saw me making these divisions. I had never stopped in my tracks like this before. Her glance was quizzical. My God, my God, I thought. She's sane.

"Come away." My wife had to tug my arm. "Don't look."

Elevators emphasize how we live cooped. I disliked ours more and more, never now speaking in it. My wife blamed this on the sale of the cottage. But that day she too went mum. When we got upstairs, which usually freed me with its familiarity, she gave me no time to thaw, turning on me. "What did you mean—one of ours?"

My coat was dripping. She snatched it from me and went to hang it in the bathroom, not waiting for an answer.

When she came back what I said was strange even to me.
"I don't begrudge you The Eclair."

She will sometimes take a few drops from the decanter.
She did that now, trembling. "At The Eclair they always
want to treat me now. Now that I sew for them." But she
was crying for me.

"Tell you what—" I said. "Why don't you do the marketing for a while? We'll use the delivery service, even
though it costs." I saw no solution unless I got off the
streets. "I'll do the housework."

She's Viennese, remember? "No! I'll do both."

"As if I were ill?" I said cannily.

The stopper of the decanter, carelessly placed, rolled off
and broke.

But so it was settled, for a while. When I did go out she
was careful to go with me, though that is not the same as
together. Always we walked east toward Fifth Avenue and
the fancier streets, but already that no longer applied, as I
could see. Where there are warm spots, those who are cold
will fill them.

Each day, after the rest of the house shone, I finished up
with the bedroom window. Our rooms are small, but so
strung along the building's side that while the living room's
one window overlooks the street as I have said, and the
intervening kitchen has none, the bedroom at the rear has a
view through the areaway, of three façades on the far side
of the next cross street north. Farthest left is the firehouse.
In the middle is an old carriage house with a peaked roof,
long used as a practice skating rink. Last comes an ancient,
small, four-story apartment house with fire escapes running
up its old yellow-brick front, and a stone crest at the top
with a worn name in large letters, SIRE or SIPE—probably the
builder. The third letter is obscured by the thin railing of its
top fire escape. Unless I asked to see it from the next window right of ours, which belongs to the unknown tenant
around our building's back corner, I would never know

which. Now that I was doing the housework, the placement of objects had begun to interest me, also the aura they bring with them. The placement of people is behind it all.

I knew I hadn't yet begun to make the right divisions in that respect. Each day, as I stood there with my box of rags, lemon oil and wax, Brasso and ammonia, I thought of it. There was a day when I imagined calling the city, if I could find the right department, to demand attention for our street's derelicts, that being the city word for them. On another, I saw myself campaigning among the tenants, either to help those people, or to remove them. We could take a vote. Though I knew how it would go. The real word for it is "cleanup." I would vote against it—and submit. At last the day came when I thought of the church in the middle of our block. Why of course, mightn't that be why those three haunted us? On the worst nights, wouldn't that be where they disappeared? With Christian coffee in the morning, to send them off.

"Call the church—" I said to my wife, who was home that day, sewing. "Maybe we can volunteer." Though I had said it out of the blue, she understood at once. But she answered that it was my idea, and went on sewing.

A phone solves nothing, but you can clutch it. The first voice said no, they had no feeding program. Where was the nearest? I was shifted to a second voice, which said, "Water Street." That's rather far, I said. "I had hoped to serve locally." I gave my name, and where we maintained our address; it's the only way. Unless—it occurred to me while waiting—one has none? There was a silence. "I am not a communicant of your church," I was suddenly prompted to say. Nor of any. But that is a word in their language. They would put me on to the pastor now. In truth, I was trembling with excitement, as if I was once again to be confirmed.

"Pastor—" he said, giving his name. He had been told of my inquiry. No, they could not provide.

"I thought if there were neighborhood volunteers—the church maybe could act with us?" With me.

"Food and shelter? No. We have no administration for it."

His voice was reserved. I felt for him. "I understand some of your problem, Pastor." I did.

His voice lightened. The Bowery Mission was the place, or Water Street.

"Well, you see—" I said "—I live on your block." There was a silence. "Do you know—our three characters?" I said into it.

He did. There was nothing to be done.

Oh, but there is, I thought. This is how one comes to it. "Do you know anything about—the woman?"

He did. "Some. I—understand she lost a child. But she's very abusive."

I said I had never heard her speak.

"You're lucky," he said. "The line of filth she hands out. No, we've written her off."

I could understand that. I had kept a shop. I thanked him. "I just had hoped to do something—locally." He gave me the number of the City Council of Greater New York. They would refer me. I was shaking by now. Confirmation is hard. "Those three—how do you pass them?"

There was silence. "That's your problem," he said. "We'll deal with ours."

When I left the phone my wife raised her eyebrows. A woman who hand-sews is a beautiful object. I had had such an object once. That was how she now looked to me, each day receding. We both knew. When a man like me volunteers, he himself may be drowning. I shook my head at her. "Nothing doing. They're in the middle of the block."

So, I returned to the bedroom window. It's the thinness of the pane that gets you. I should add that when I first decided to stay indoors my wife transferred the thick bedroom drapes, which had for so long greened our private moments, to the front window, so that we could no longer see down in the street. At night in the bedroom we must now use the old roller-shade. She leaves the daytime choice —up or down—to me. The Viennese, where they are not frivolous, are very literal. The view exposed, with its neat stone riddle, is the same as in the early days of our marriage, as is the shade. Sundays after love, she used to lie in the pink nakedness a man does not forget, watching the firemen below bring out the engine and polish it. A celebration which present traffic no longer allows them. We are midtown now. Back then we were only the West Fifties.

Later that day, I heard the front door close. The sewing must be ready for delivery. On those days she still permitted herself The Eclair. From now on I would let the window grime. Some things must be written off, so that others may be attended to. My stay up here was only a hibernation, in which the vision of the street was always with me. I can't tell you what a bear dreams in his hole but I know what a man may, and that there is no one season for it.

I went to the front room for our little red street guide, though I knew I would never get to Water Street, or to the Bowery either. Those streets are for an era long gone, or for pastors. But coming out of the hole is slow. The flesh has to decide whether it is a sitter's or a walker's. My wife all these months mistook my staying in for fear. I had let her think so, the way a devoted husband who has found another woman to love stays in safe night after night. In the hall she had hung my hat and coat for me to see, each day brushing them. I went back to the bedroom to check the weather.

It was high noon. One of those bright, blank days when from indoors it might be any season. I would have to wait for a passerby in order to see what was being worn. Sundays and holidays are slow; today must be one or the other. But presently a man came along, in jacket and cap. Just between the firehouse and the skating rink he stopped in his tracks, then went on. The next, a lady in a fur, did the same, and after her a young couple. Then, another man, then a boy. I watched for a long time. A few did not stop. No pause was long. Because of a car at the curb I couldn't see what they were passing but of course I knew. I saw now that the deep-recessed door of the skating rink was newly secured, the way empty buildings are. Windblown papers lay against it, and it had that secret, tempting look. I thought of leaving the window but knew I would return to it. When the car finally moved off, I was still watching that interrupted rhythm—of people who could still pass a body by.

There was a grating to the left of that recess, but he was not on it. I am farsighted; it's my wife who needs her opera glasses, even to look down from four storeys.

I can see him yet, that stranger. He lies face up, in that tangle of hair and life-scratched clothing which at last obscures identity. I had never seen one of them in the center of the pavement before. So they inch their way up from the bottom of the island, and in from the curbs. But it's the rhythm of those who pass, as seen from above, that is so breast-haunting. A kind of subtraction, the way we used to do it. Dot and carry. Dot dot dot. And carry over. And carry on.

At last I moved. I could already tell I wasn't going to be a walker. I took my hat but not my coat. It must be a fine day.

Outside, the day hit me like a kaleidoscope. This will happen more and more by the way, and on any kind of day, but with persistence one learns to separate the street from the people, and in time that becomes permanent. Having my three mentors, I was already halfway. I saw that our block had many more than previously noted, of what I had called "hydrants." They are not that of course; they are standpipes. The highly polished one belongs to an insurance company now and is marked Auto SPKR. I sat down on it. I dared not look at the other three, but the presence of all those pipes meant I wasn't usurping. In my fedora, shaven and clean, I was as yet not suspect, but I already felt a stealing peace. Tomorrow I would bring a pillow. By the wristwatch I still wore I sat for an hour, and was rewarded by a few askance glances from office workers who had passed me twice. I made it home before my wife.

I managed to sit there all autumn, yet to evade her discovery, meanwhile groping my way toward a balance I now know so well. One must acquire a wealth of lacks, yet keep an iron grasp on a few indispensables. I would try out book bags, vinyl-lined knapsacks and several styles of shoulder bag in hunting for the ultimate one, before I realized that, hoisted as I would always be, between the immediate comfort and the hour-long needs, one requires two bags—and that a money belt, even if empty, has its use. I found nothing wrong in drawing on my present riches to equip me. I was not aiming to be pitiable, only never again to have to be a passerby.

I still was clean. While at home, it was pointless to be otherwise. I wished to spare my wife any such rehearsal, and would have had no hope of concealing it, as I so far thought I had my sorties and my purchases. Now that our rent had gone up again, as even a statutory rent does, she was going to homes to sew, and often kept late. Sooner or later one or other of the tenants who must have glimpsed me at my post would speak. Though what I intended might eventually work toward her own financial welfare, I doubted she would see it as my way of being provident. But I couldn't conceal hope. One day she said, "You seem so—so—." She flumped her hands. She used to know me as she knew our inventory. "Anyway—could you take back the marketing too?" I hated to; it binds you to the other life. But of course I did.

All this time the three others on the street had been watching me, with a strange tact. Several times the one I

thought of as the wino all but nodded his John the Baptist
head at me. The drummer restrained his flourishes. The
woman, lighting her eternal cigarette, gave me a bold stare.
They were waiting to see whether I would qualify.

And of course I had my own doubts. I could never brave
the city at large. Could I leave my wife? With my heart
condition to consider, and a woman's superior life expec-
tancy, we had bought her our sole annuity, as the better
investment of the two. As only one person she could live
without the sewing. But I would be bringing her a terrible
social status. For, brave as she once may have thought me, I
had one great cowardice which would directly affect her. I
could not bear to leave our neighborhood. I had to make
my stand here. What it came down to was that we would
still be in partnership. We would have to see what each of
us could bear.

Meanwhile, a real beggar had come to our street. Even
when my wife and I were courting, he was already in the
theater district, in his leather cap and plaid shirt, whining
his angry *Aaah, ma-aaa, naaah.* He was written up once as
being the true sound of the beggars of Naples, and the
owner of a Bronx apartment house. A professional has no
trouble switching his beat. His arrival was disturbing. Ob-
viously, he did not live out of doors, was no derelict. But
that regular if various rhythm of our onlookers had been
interrupted, the eyes that lower or avert, the head that
shakes or the rare foot that stops—all to my mind an ac-
knowledgment of a common ground. Whereas this man
corrupts. One can give to him.

Then came the first snow, the famous one of—was it the
year before last? A first snow is normally just a freshener,
nice on the face, even to a storekeeper. No shovels yet and
a kind of childhood ring to the conversation. This snowfall
came very late in the year. When I opened the bedroom
window, as I now did each day, a morning damp with
promise entered my nostrils. The sky was a heavy gray,

intimate as a room. As I leaned back in, one of our earliest wedding purchases poked me from behind, a wooden hat-rack with pigeon-breasted, chignoned brass women for hooks. We used to laugh at a certain resemblance. Only last week she had said, "How they shine these days." Though they do not do so as brightly as my standpipe; the brass is different. When I had told her that the piano-stool cushion had burst and been disposed of, she hadn't complained. We had after all never bought the piano. This morning I had awakened sexually able, the blood gruff in my ears, a pride at sixty, but I hadn't awakened her. As I shut the window the snow started down.

"Shall I go or stay?" she said from the bedclothes. Aghast, I gave her a poor smile. One of her ladies was having a birthday luncheon. But that was my question, and the weather had already answered it.

All day the snow fell, like a secret granulation in the body. She left at noon. I was in the bathroom and stayed there until the front door shut. Afterward I ate the soup she left. I wanted not to be romantic about the small things. I might not be callous enough for those which were coming. At about two o'clock I had wound around me all the clothes I could, had laced the strong shoes and checked my two packs. Across the way the fire escapes were already crisscrossed black and white, like a forwarded letter.

I have a small disability pension. The Army gave me rheumatic fever and a runny heart after. That would be my budget. Without a place to keep up, it might be done. I made the bed. I left my watch on the dresser. What else was there to say, unless I said everything? Under the watch I left a note. "Sell the desk."

You may remember the radiance of that day. A real snow makes old New York emerge, an iron railing here, a stoop there. Its muffling cloud heals the sound of trucks. I walked slowly uphill. In the elevator a delivery boy, seeing my wool helmet and scarf, had said "Ski?" Our block, going

west, is on a grade. Toward the middle, all its outside people were there. As yet I have no better name for us. To
some we're the city's sores, from the general disease below.
To others we are its first line of filth. I say we are not a
crowd. Take us as you do yourselves, one by one.

I find the drummer in his favorite spot, on the uphill side
of the dairy window, with his cart. On that side there is no
overhang of signs. Snow on his black-painted pate and
rouged cheeks gives him a fine health. On the window's
other side the tall, bearded man stands in his niche. Though
he may drink, he is not a wino. He has the disease of sleep.
Today he sleeps standing up, like a horse. The woman is
the only one of us who smokes. One must have some vice
to get through the hours. As usual she is on one of the
gratings, today a wallside one, near the church. There are
several more such on the block than first appear. One learns
their cycles and degrees of warmth. On weekends, that one
near the church is the warmest. Today she has a blanket,
folded to a peak like a tent's. She can make a grating seem a
household. Like me, she sits.

When my wife comes up the block, traffic has long been
hushed. One can hear every footfall. There is no beggar
today, though it does not seem very cold. More like a cold
which one hallucinates. In time any cold weather gets to be
so. It is now so late that we four have had the street almost
to ourselves. We do not talk; we have never talked among
us. The two other men, one in his niche, are motionless.
The rounded woman is a shrub. Snow lazes down past the
closed, illuminated dairy, falling in front of the windowed
take-outs; roast chickens no longer turning, spare ribs, ears
of corn. In the morning I will learn that two of the dairy-
men are our coffee Mission, bringing it outside. They never
ask for payment, never refuse it.

My wife, plodding slow, is the only beggar here. *Ahhh-h.
Shah-h-h. Why?*

Tenants had phoned her. I found I could share her misery

but not her shame. An audience of three, silent as three city-battered trees, sustained me. Two trees, rather. And a shrub. When she left I steeled myself. One knows when one's wife of years does not really leave.

When the ambulance drew up, she was in it. I looked behind me. Those three had been quick. I was alone.

"Gone, are they?" she said. "How I had to explain. The hospital thought you were one of them."

So they already know us. Roosevelt is our neighborhood hospital. A fine one, and very near. The crew and the driver gave each other looks.

"This man has a heart condition," my wife said.

I fibrillate. I wasn't doing that, then. My pulse was firm and all my vital signs. They shook their heads at her.

Her sewing never crumples. Her face does. "Take him to the mental ward, then."

"It's going to get colder, fella," one of them said to me.

"I have on battery-warmed socks."

The driver laughed.

"Look into those bags of his," she said. "For months he has been storing them. Soap. Underwear. Look where he sits. My piano pillow. We live up there, I tell you. There." She pointed. "In three rooms."

They looked into my eyes instead. Perhaps they thought I was sane. When she began screaming, my poor love, they left.

She took my hand. "No gloves. Ah my God." I had simply followed suit. I didn't yet know why. Bundled everywhere else as we are, we do not wear them. Our hands are our thermometers and our only nudity. They give us both our inward and our outward state. By now the woman's are black and scaled. My wife's palm is soft with rooms, her fingertips nibbled by the needle.

People have begun to pass; it must be about 4 A.M. People with room problems often stray by at that hour, sent out by themselves. I squeeze her hand, signaling her to note a man

who has just circled around and past us with his dog. Bare-
headed, loose-jointed, he is stopping at each store window,
maybe to stare at the dream he has left behind. The woman
has returned to her spot, but he will never see her. He is
one of those who are safe, who will never see any of us.
Behind him, his small dog is as busy as the leash allows. It
circles the woman, sniffing, but does not lift a leg. They
never do. My wife is choking, on my name. "No, I can't,"
she says. "I know what you want. I know. But I can't. I
could never."

Was that my dream all along? That the two of us? What a
man like me dreams!

She looked into my eyes before going. I don't know what
she saw. But I knew when she left.

For a time she and I were still in partnership. She brought
me a fur coat, saying: "Only from a thrift shop." And that
was winter. She brought me cookies, brittle with love,
though one's taste for sugar goes. And that was spring. In
summer, when the newspapers grow thin and philosophi-
cal, she began clipping items on what shelter the city
planned for us open-air residents. In the domestic pages the
word for us is now "homeless." They will use armories. In
the foreign pages the word is "displaced." They use tents. I
saw that she and you would do anything to get me under a
roof. "Tents—" I say "—will there be any on this block?"

When I asked her to stop reading me the items she was
angry, saying I would not help myself. But when people
like us become topics there's no percentage in it—not for
us.

"Could we not move?" she said at last. "Out of the city. I
wouldn't care now, how far." That—from a Viennese!

How could I tell her, that I had long since tried? How—at
that farthest Long Island Railroad station to which I had
made a trial run, when some boys hanging over a viaduct to
stone a train targeted me instead, I was invigorated enough

to give them all my abuse—but returned here anyway. How in Jersey, where I had gone as far as Cape May, I sat all day lone and peaceful by the sea, wondering if I could dispose of my bags in it—and at dusk took them up again. How, returned to the city, I had stayed away from here, until at last, in ever smaller concentric circles, I had homed in. How—once over the line, the gnawing doubt is that you may be doing all this for yourself alone.

She still stood there, the soup plate dangling in her hand. I refuse anything else, but I cannot resist her soup.

I still volunteer, she always says. My eyes were lowered too. Foot-vain as she is, she will not wear overshoes, though the snows of this year are once again mud. That stubborn gold anklet is still there. I know she is looking at my hands. Thinking is my vice, and thought needs dirt to help make it slide.

"So you won't?" she said. "Move?" Then she put her hand on mine.

I shuddered for her. No one had touched me since she last did. I look at her rival, the woman in the hat. At all three of them. I am their city. They are the warm spot beneath me. "Can a sidewalk move?"

"Then tomorrow I will take down the front-room curtain," she said. "That is the best I can do."

We both know what she can bear. I keep my eyes lowered. If she looks into them, I will overpower her. But that day she had the misery, I had the shame.

See up there? The curtain is gone. Now and then you may catch a flash at sundown. She has hunted out my old binoculars. They are sharper than the opera glasses. I can see what she sees without their help.

We are like a wooing, this curbside, wallside guard of four. Once we were three. Five would not be too many. You yourself have faithful feet. Each day stopping longer. As if we were the authority to complain to. Dot dot, your rhythm goes. I recognize it. Dot, dot. And carry your bur-

den on. For we do not beg. If we would beg, you could get
past us.

I could tell you how.

The best way is to know nothing about us.

That is why I keep my eyes lowered. Never look into
them.

Better still, seek pastoral advice.

Yesterday—or was it yesterday?—my wife came once
more. She was empty-handed.

"Don't look," I said. Or thought I said.

I advise you to do the same.

Saratoga, Hot

Tot and his wife, Nola, are sitting at the kitchen table, just before dawn. The excitement of being in their own house always gets them up early here. They are waiting until it's time to go for early breakfast at the track to watch the horses work out. The August meet is already half over and they do not intend to miss a morning. They will do the same at Aqueduct, Belmont, and Lexington; as Nola says, it makes a calendar, both for the day and the year.

Tot worries sometimes whether since Nola's accident she has ever really wanted to live out any kind of calendar, though she would die rather than say. Or rather, since he was driving that day, she will live, for him.

Up here Tot is always encouraged. They are drinking champagne from the two six-sided blue flutes Nola used to tote everywhere, until they were able to afford this house, minute as it is, in which they will live one month. This is the only place in the world where he has a drink before breakfast, or where she cares to have even the one drink a day. The fizz lasts her, she says, right through coffee, and for the two and a half hours she is now able to spend draw-

ing the regulars at the track's old wooden-buttressed clubhouse.

Drawing, she can sit in an ordinary chair and appear to
be handicapping her bets for the real races later, but those
in the know are aware that it is the only hour they will see
her at the track. As she draws, the horses fly around the
oval, but she never looks up. Even the track itself gets short
shrift, though in the paintings she does at home it sometimes appears in the background, like a geranium-dotted
recurrent dream. Here she has eyes only for the tables of
the owners and trainers who have a stake in these tryouts,
and their seasonal followers, thinned out with maybe a few
of the owners' houseguests, still rubbing away sleep. The
tourist tables she never notices—and she has her own inner
stopwatch, rising smartly at the last half hour's edge. There
will be a murmur after them, often before they fully leave
—which takes some doing.

Yes, Tot has good reason to like it here. Three Augusts
ago, after five years in a wheelchair, Nola got rid of the
chair for a walker, which a year later, on August 31, she
gave to the Salvation Army in exchange for a cane. At the
time he had no idea what they had gone to the Army store
for, thinking she was hunting something for the house,
though with all the cast-offs from his several cousins who
keep August cottages here, there was scarcely any need.

The cane she chose, dark brown with a leatherbound
crook, was surprisingly one of six for sale. "End of August,
we get a lot of them," the Salvation Army worker said.
"Racing is an old man's sport." When they got home, using
the walker which would be picked up later in the week
when she thought she could dispense with it, she showed
him how the cane's crook snapped open above a sturdy
steel joint to form a seat. "Why, it's a shooting-stick,
haven't you ever seen one?" he said. "Rootie used to order
them by the dozen." Then both of them had clammed up.
She because she still has her troubles over his horsey fam-

ily, whose rich members give this poor one the jobs he is almost too right for. He because with a damaged spine and one leg encased in electronically activated braces, she is not likely ever to use the cane to sit on. She has little hope of discarding it.

"Canny girl," was all Tot said. He hadn't recognized the stick as such because all of Rootie's—who was known as Top Cousin in the family—had been of a yellow malacca bought in England by the lot and dispatched from the house at Epsom to the houses in Westbury and Lexington, the flat in River House, and the former long-time family seat here in Saratoga. If, instead of the cane, Nola had been holding a florist's long wicker basket of flowers marked PLATFORM—like the one she had carried up there just before he and she and that eager claque of the presidential candidate's young camp-followers had departed for the highway, she would still look like that girl. Even leaning on the walker, she had. Maybe that's why Rootie, whose son Budge had died in the crash, is so stiff with her, though somehow not with Tot. Budge should have been driving, but had wanted to be in the back seat with the girl of his choice. So Tot and Nola, met only that week, had been up front, in Budge's Porsche. How childish it all sounds now.

Especially to have been starting out from Bedford-Stuyvesant, that battered slum-end of Brooklyn where all the young friends of family friends of the candidate had been campaigning, Tot in from a Philadelphia cousin's horse farm in Wyncote, where he had been working out his incompletes at the university with a tutor his farm salary paid for, Nola not part of the in-crowd, there with a more serious bunch of do-gooders from Swarthmore—but all of them learning how to talk to black lawyers who had Phi Beta Kappa keys, the girls with their twee-twee boarding-school or Sacred Heart accents saying, shiny-eyed, "Bed-Stuy!" All of them cold sober with Christian charity—and then to end up on a tacky Long Island Expressway, like a

crowd of rich collegiate drunks. It made no difference to the
papers that they had been smashed into from behind.
"Wealthy," the papers had said.

"Nice—" Tot says now, nodding at the still life propped
on the mantel in front of a picture which hangs there regularly. For weeks she has been painting how a striped plastic
dimestore tablecloth looks through blue Steuben glass.
"Nice you painted both glasses."

"Harder."

To compose, she means. He knows enough of the lingo
now to sell her work, if she would let him. Good for her,
for both of them. But she won't; she knows who would
buy. Now and then one of the racing crowd took up painting—Main Line houses in cotton snow, or other recogniz-
able property, or portraits of friends easily spotted, though
with the hands usually concealed. After which these efforts
were bought in at some benefit by the gratified or obligated
sitters and house-owners, never for less than a thousand
bucks. Nobody ever painted a horse.

"Besides, one of the glasses may break," she says. She
always gives him two answers, maybe because in the kind
of life they lead there always are two. Or like to a child you
don't want to lie to. Her mind is better than his, which only
makes him sorrowful for her. Stop it, Tot, she said, outraged, the one time he mentioned it. My mind's no great
shakes, only different. In his crowd, now hers, he watches
her hide possession of it the way his Philadelphia grandmother would never mention underwear. What if one day
"the horse people," as Nola calls them, prove to be more
than she can bear?

He stifles an impulse to break one of the glasses and get it
over with, though he likes using them. She shouldn't have
to bear with having so little, and such stuff as they've
grown used to having; no wonder these bits of her own
home become tokens, always in the end cracked or lost.
Look at this place, their first and only real home. As only

half a Tottenham, the other half an actor who had happened to pass through Sewickley long enough to marry his
heller of a mother, he had grown up with just such stuff, in
between one or another of his mother's marriages which
had now and then done better for them.

The secondhand largesse of the rich is so often insensitive. Over in the corner is an easel so huge you could only
put a Veronese on it, Nola says, or else a founder's portrait
before it went off to hang in the bank—which was what
the easel had once accommodated. And how many bed
trays, from all the houses where one is no longer served
breakfast in bed or is ill at home, do his connections here
think one month in Saratoga can require? Or that Nola does
—who cannot eat easily lying down. The mahogany what-
not Rootie had sent when she sold the house here has, as
she'd said, "a sweet dimple of a mirror for your lovely girl"
—and a secret drawer to keep one's diamonds in. When
Rootie is here in whatever house she and Wheatley may
rent, she keeps hers in the safe-deposit at the local bank, to
which the August ladies are let in by special arrangement
after late parties. All Rootie's good tables and chairs had of
course had to be included in the auction in New York, and
the housekeeper had somehow sent all the bedding to the
Salvation Army, before Rootie could say boo. Anything left
in the huge cottage had been servants' stuff, his cousin said.

"Ours is a servant's house," Tot had replied. "Or a stable
hand's, from the days when the stables spent the winter
here. One of those shacks on one of those funny little lanes
behind the houses on Union Avenue." But Rootie has always thereafter referred to it as a carriage house.

If they all wanted to save his pride, they have done so.
Never send money; arrange jobs. Continue of course to
send roses for any family mishap or event—a blanket of
them when Nola got up here after the work on her second
hip. "I believe in roses *now,*" his cousin Tansie, Rootie's half
sister, always said. "Why wait for the grave?" And charge

them, letting the shop dun you. One season overdue being decent practice, Tansie running at least two. "Oh, the little people in Saratoga"—meaning the merchants—"they love us. They'd better."

But the family men—Wheatley, head of all its inherited operations, and the others through their special interests: Gifford at the Racing Museum, Courtwell at the Adirondack Commission, Bailey in Lexington—have all conscientiously done their best by him. Narrow and inbred just like him, if a tad prouder of it, they understand the dignities of patronage—and how for him it would have to be horses, not stocktips and a city berth.

"You know, there are still two more glasses from that set," he says now. "I was—kind of saving them."

"Where? Not here." When she sits up that straight it will always hurt her, the hospital said—can't be helped. She won't let on, but we think you ought to know.

"Uh-uh." No hiding place here except through a trapdoor to a storage space under the roof, from which he sometimes climbs out the dormer to the roof itself for a bit of air on the worst hot nights, locking his legs around the kitchen chimney. "No, at Grayport. In that closet where your mother keeps the cracked stuff. But *they're* not. In September we could pick them up."

"What a sap I am about it."

But it will be the first thing she'll do when they get to Grayport, the dilapidated fifteen-room house near Groton where her mother manages to live on, though penniless, three of her five children refusing to sustain her drunken ways with funds from their admittedly small inheritances. Nola, the youngest, named for the song Vincent Youmans had played at her grandmother's debut—and of course for her own mother, is one of the two who do help. She and Tot pretend to one another that they go to Grayport no more than once a year so her mother won't too much feel the obligation—which Tot privately thinks she never has or will. But Nola needs every illusion she can manage; he would bring her handfuls if there were a store which sold them. "You're kind not to object," she always says, making out the quarterly check when her few dividends come in. He hopes this is true; kind is her highest praise. But more likely it comes of his having been brought up to see dividends come and go. So had her siblings; she had merely been born too late for most of it.

Dawn is coming in now at the oddly high window which makes some say these houses had begun as underground-railway stations for slaves fleeing north during Civil War days. Hot as blazes already; there are beads on his lip. Never any on hers.

"I could paint, I'd paint you."

In Budge's Porsche she had been adequately pretty. Now, with a thinness like the models one glimpses undressed in Sunday shop windows—wishbone hips and an angled foot —she is bitter and beautiful. The window is part of what had charmed them into buying the place, along with the tiny, incised mantel on which he has placed the still-life, which will remain there until she has done a new painting, when it will go up the trapdoor. The walls have to be bare, or she can't work. Sometimes he thinks her whole life has to be. "Anyway, you paint better here than anywhere else in the world."

"Suppose I do. Well—"

Well—they've tried the world. Wherever the horses run, and the cousins do. This year he's working for a distant one who owns a glossy, tax-deductible publication devoted to stately homes and gardens, with racing drawn in. In a corner opposite the easel—on a small desk at which the butler at Westbury used to do his accounts, salvaged by Tot for his after-college quarters when Rootie, rather than dissolve her marriage with Wheatley had been dismantling the estate—are his clips from the local newspaper, in whose August pages the horses compete for space with their owners

—usually a dead heat. Should the archangel Gabriel decide to attend the Travers Stakes, the paper will duly report whose box he was in. And staying at whose cottage, as the largest houses are called.

"See they've published the Cottage-List after all," Nola says, grinning. The year the mayor had asked the paper not to for safety's sake, there had been an uproar from a society which would rather lose its jewels than its intercom. "I think this town is actually proud of the big burglaries it has every year. Like the locals are of which of the summer people they rent to."

The locals moving out en masse to "the lake," which means up to Lake George for the doctors and bankers renting to horse owners more for the prestige than the money, or the other lake—theirs, Lake Saratoga—if both landlord and renter are small-time. It's she who has made him see what he was never before conscious of—how too, in August, at the country club, which is left to the natives in winter, locals and incomers get to mix tangentially, or continue not to. She will draw them, then, the locals fat and empurpled with winter beef, the incomers—"visitors" is not quite the word—who if they are stylishly thin seem to keep in trim by taking over towns wherever they go. Or when fat, seem to be so from all the gross goodies of their circuit.

What he can never hope to explain to her, since she isn't interested in horses, is the wonderful layering of the world based on the sporting life, to which good blood, even if animal, brings an equality where—when a stable boy or hot-walker, a trainer or jockey may at any moment talk authoritatively to a man whose horse has just been syndicated for five million—nobody is small-time.

"Waal, no, it's the thieves' union made 'em publish that list," he says in a stable hand's drawl, which he comes by honorably from softball games played with many of those elders since he was ten—and continues now as a sacred

trust. "Talk is, they complained of not being able to keep
track of where the parties are, so's to give people the rob-
beries their station in life deserves. How are they going to
keep an eye on Bonnie Doe for instance—that choker of
egg-size ice she wore to her own vernissage?" He is proud
of that last word.

"Oh, Tot."

He has got her to laugh.

"Those postcards she drew," Nola says. "For that benefit
show. All the children in them with their backs conve-
niently turned. And practically a Winterhalter gown she
wore for it. With turquoises, those were. At four in the
afternoon, in a public park center. Oh, the thieves' union.
You're a howl."

She will gossip with no one but him. He'll look up Winterhalter later.

But she's too quick for him.

"German. Painted royal women in hoopskirts." Then she
links pinkies with him. It's going to be an all-right day. At
least, another day.

And getting on for time. "I'll take the garbage out."

Next door's cat comes nuzzling, a runt like its master, a
pecan-faced former jockey who also keeps his house open
only for the Saratoga meet. Everybody at the meet has a cat
for August, down from the thoroughbreds themselves,
where it may all begin. When people leave they turn the
cats loose, or, if they have a conscience, drop them in some
local's backyard. Nola, brought up in a house on which a
whole peninsula's cats were dumped, won't have one of her
own here, but she'll feed any stray. Venezuel, the old
jockey, off all day with his fly friends, maybe some of the
same who years ago cost him the right to ride, cannily depends on her. Tot opens his own front door and shoos the
cat in to Nola, who is already getting to her feet in her
jackknife way. Hand on the fridge, she says: "Got your
pad?"

He pats his hip pocket. His pencil is clipped to the breast pocket of his airiest shirt, an old one, loud in that refined Italian way. He's easy on his clothes and has a lot of what he calls his standing wardrobe, conventional clubhouse stuff, plus a supply of British turtlenecks and slacks, couple of velvet jackets and an extra dinner jacket, most of it descended over the years from Budge, who had also been a 42-long—with, after the crash, a final, sad increment. If they call him a clotheshorse here, that's unfair but he can understand it—they don't know what else to call him. Everybody at a meet has to be somebody, unless you're rich, which explains everything.

Out here he can barely stretch. The crazy little porch, only doormat wide, has one corner bayed out and encircled with a railing. When he writes on the pad he sits on the camp chair Nola had in mind for him the minute she saw the house; otherwise he bestrides the railing, one foot gangling, and scans left-right, sky and ground, as if the view will push open for him. The shaky title to his house, linked as it is with those on either side of it, gives it extra character. The lane is crooked, quaint and short, and so much in the right sector of town that Venezuel says all the realtors have their eye on it. He and his friends would like to buy the house on the other side of Tot and Nola's, but the retired police captain who comes up from the city every summer won't sell. Venezuel would probably like to offer for theirs, too. He wants the whole lane, or his newest friends do, three dark, silent men from the crowd who want to bring gambling back. But you two could always stay, he says slyly. Because she feeds the cat. Such good neighbors we need.

Neighbors my ass, Nola says, in exact replica of her mother's still dainty "My foot!" They won't want to tangle with your family, Tot. They're from that other racing association in town, not the N.Y.R.A., the unofficial one. They wouldn't gamble right here. Maybe in that strange villa just out of town, which pretends to be a restaurant, but doesn't like it when a customer comes. Or maybe there's where they consult about all their statewide business, from beer and soft-drink agencies to liquor franchises—and on to politics.

Venezuel himself collects poker chips from the casino days. His crowd is a sentimental one, old hands who knew the place when—which was always each man's own special "when," from those who had seen Man O'War himself and had ridden his issue, to those who had merely shaken the hand of Honey Fitz. Plus a few present-day jockeys, not the best ones, who now and then freewheel out here, hoping to raise a little hell.

Nobody's at Venezuel's now. He and his three current night owls will shortly drive in, the long limo with the black-glass side windows grooving in like on a fast curve from a good pitcher, almost without sound. Tot suspects those three never do anything with yahoo. This morning, like each, they'll have a fast change and shave, though he has never seen a shadow on their broad jaws and the clothes seem always the same; then they'll be off, first to early Mass, then to the track, not returning to sleep until maybe after the sixth, unless something in a later race interests them. What that would be he wouldn't care to think. All he actually knows is that jumpers are not their style.

Last year, the day Venezuel gleefully invited him and Nola in to view an entire set of poker chips he had picked up, one of the originals from the old Canfield Casino, now the museum—had been a day of jumpers' events only. "Nah, jumpers," Venezuel said, "women owners race them. They like those hurdles. Nah, this is the day these three catch up on their sleep." He's speaking for the three men shambling to their feet at the sight of Nola.

"How about the trotters?" Tot had said, meaning only to raise a laugh, which among flat-race people, a mention of the handsome harness track on the other side of town, middle class and unstylishly running almost all seasons, is sure to do. But not with those three staring chilly at him. What's he supposed to know and doesn't? Do they think insult is intended?

"Nah, that's another deal," Venezuel had said, swiftly pointing out a humidor-on-legs which had come from the old casino, too. He had spoken for the other three almost the whole time. "Shoo!" he said to the cat. "Shoo. You make Gargiola sneeze. And worse."

Nola had enchanted them.

What worse, she wants to know—do cats make Mr. Gargiola climb chairs? She had known a boy who did.

The three guffaw, the eldest—who must be Gargiola and is not that old, shaking his head No.

Venezuel seemed pleased, muttering "A boy, Gargiola. She thinks you're a boy."

Nola had persisted. It must have been sad for Mr. Gargiola's kids, not having cats.

The two other men burst out laughing; the younger, maybe thirty, is Mr. Gargiola's kid. The other man is Gargiola's brother-in-law. While Nola fired questions at them— yes, their daughters are pretty, and yes, the girls have made communion—Tot's flesh grew cold for fear they would see the drift. She was making them draw pictures of themselves to tally with the ones she already had in her head. And maybe they do see. Venezuel certainly had.

"Honey—" he says warningly, "hon-ey," when she says: "Dogs, then. Were your kids brought up with guard dogs?"

But the three, nodding ever faster, only slap their knees and burst into laughter.

When she leans forward to Gargiola himself, saying intently: "Bet you never bring the wife and girls to the track. Bet you keep them safe out of it. In some big house on the Island maybe—maybe Bay Shore?" their amusement is complete.

Then their silence is, regarding her.

"She's an artist is all," the old jockey said. "She knows human people."

Gargiola shook his head. Negatively, the head moved slower. "Rich girls' questions, Vennie. You never been to those parties the N.Y.R.A.?"

Now it was Nola and Tot's turn to laugh, hearing Tot's younger cousins, and some not so young, at the New York State Racing Association's mixed public entertainments, asking the arrogantly schoolgirlish questions which their nonequals don't know they might ask of anybody.

"I'm not rich," Nola said. "We're not."

The three are nodding again; they know that. Vennie brushes his sleeve.

"Stick around," Mr. Gargiola said.

The cat, in again, nudged Nola, who bent to it. Holding the cat draped in an elbow, she thanked Venezuel, shook hands with the three men. They watched that cane of hers shift from wrist to wrist like an interpreter as she managed this, and, as she walked to the door, her narrow pelvis in its box-step rocking. People watch her the way they watch strippers. Tot had stood back to let her spill the cat and negotiate the three steps down, which at Venezuel's have a modern railing. He is a past master at not helping her, using his own body-set to let others know they must not. It's no fault of his he has to stand back far enough to hear their remarks.

"Class—" Mr. Gargiola said. "Both of them. And perfect. Last thing we'd want on this road is people who'd have kids."

Whether Nola ever hears any of these remarks Tot wants never to know.

By the air wafting from the track he can tell the staff has sprayed for flies again, and incidentally for the regional mosquitoes—at which the town is grateful, as it is for so

much. The city fathers have recently learned to put out
flowers like crazy, and prices have graciously gone double
in most shops—Nola and he never arrive in time to stock
up ahead. He thinks he may know now why Gargiola dark-
ened at mention of the harness track—a matter of property,
which is the name of the game here now. Nobody uses
guns anymore except maybe the Pinkerton men who guard
the tracks and the bigger properties—and maybe not even
them.

Property is the most sinister thing going, his cousin
Wheatley says; everybody you know, or wouldn't want to
know, has a finger in it, crooked or straight. The policeman
next door has sold to Gargiola at a price. The town assumes
everybody has one. "He can retire now from being retired,"
Nola said. A stable hand has found an eight-thousand-dol-
lar watch at the Adirondack bus stop, which nobody has
come forth to claim. The busy bank, which has carved on
its north, south, and west walls respectively: SAVING IS A
GREATER ART THAN EARNING   A PENNY SAVED IS A POUND
EARNED; THE FIRST YEARS OF A MAN'S LIFE MAKE PROVISION FOR
THE LAST; FRUGALITY IS THE MOTHER OF THE VIRTUES, as you
enter to stash or cash, has a neat sign which says HAVE A
GOOD DAY AT THE TRACK, as you exit to the new parking lot.

On Sundays, all-day baroque music brawls from the museum like an antidote. Every day, the Chasidic Jews, cross-
ing from boardinghouse to park in their sable-bordered
greatcoats, look to be the coolest people, their heat being
invisible. Their boardinghouses, every year since his childhood said to dwindle, are every year still there. And here he
is, ready to list his day on the much-worn leather pad
bought for him by Nola in Florence, a habit engendered by
the first of his scattered track jobs. Inside, Nola is setting up
her paints for the afternoon. Little has changed since last
year, only the cat, which this year is brindle instead of tan.
And still not theirs.

After breakfast at the track, and after he has brought

Nola home, his first stop will be the Reading Room, next
door to the track. "Oh, a library—oh, how nice of them,"
Nola had said her first year here. It had been the first summer of their marriage, and she had been for some months
out of the rehab unit, which had among other concerns
judged her almost ready to laugh again. But when Tot explained that the broad-verandahed white clapboard house
and ample rear garden, from which members could enter
straight to the track's private rooms and boxes, was really a
kind of summer Jockey Club in which any reading matter
of note was likely to be the studbook, only her visiting
older sister, Dolly, had laughed.

"Hush, Dolly," Tot said, for they were already on the
club verandah. Too late; Walter Mallory, who has brought a
new girl to the meet every year since his heyday of the
1950s, was leaning over their table.

"How do, Tot? Tell us the joke." He is the classic sexual
playboy for each August meet and an inspiration to his
contemporaries; yesteryear is a word Walter doesn't admit.
Courtly, more informed on the general world than most of
the horse crowd, faithful to his one protégée for a season
and often keeping them as friends after, Walter is also
down to the few millions and horses which his tastes have
left him, and in these parts is therefore considered romanti-
cally poor. But, as all the men agree, what draws the
women even more than his handsomely blunted charm is
his obsessively roving eye. Women are intrigued by the naked message coming from such a gentleman—and from a
rounder who must have seen everything except the woman
he is gazing at. "Walter undresses a woman in public so
she's even proud," they say of him. "The other reason,"
Nola will say when she knows him as well as she will allow
herself to know people here, "is that he's lovable."

That day, Walter's eye had first sought out Nola; sometimes it still does. But when the joke was explained, and he
had been introduced to both girls, he bent to Dolly, inviting

her to his box. "Your time of life, don't want to keep your
nose in a book. Mine neither."

Dolly, who had been Walter's bird for that summer, no
longer visits here. Nola, watching them go, had opened her
big new handbag, in which as she said, a girl could keep her
double life.

If she has learned to laugh only with her pencil, not in
her life with him, Tot is still grateful. Though she never
laughs at him that way, sometimes he thinks she answers
him only with that pencil—though for a couple for whom
there are usually two answers, this may be natural. Anyway, he can laugh too at what comes of it, as he had at the
wash-drawings of Walter in his box, Walter donating his
trophies to the Racing Museum, and Walter at the polo
matches in a circle of the local dowagers—in each with a
naked woman at his side—and in the case of the Racing
Museum, a four-legged one.

In one of the fierce impulses which overtake Nola with
those she likes—and she likes such odd ones for her, including himself—she gave Walter all three, unsigned, and
on a promise which so far as they know he has kept, that
he hang them only in New York. "Are you surprised I did
keep my promise? No? Why not?" he had asked her every
year since, until one year she had told him: "Because
there's no better confidant than a roué."

Tot had been embarrassed, but Walter only said quietly,
"You must have a gallery by now, eh?"

"Yes, it's *my* studbook," Nola blurted, and limped away.

"She's shy about her mind," Tot said. "You know. In our
crowd." And she uses her limp to cover up, something he'd
never noticed until then. He rarely gets enough distance on
her to. Was Walter observing that? He is very grown-up
except in the one department, Nola says. Almost wise—see
how even in this crowd of hootenanny nicknames nobody
calls him "Walt." He's got a decent name, Tot had said.
What man in his right head would want to be called by the

monickers which old money with horses sticks its kids with: Oglethorpe, Peppersall—Tottenham. More often with triple-decker last names to match, which his father had at least spared him. She'd reached out to him at once, laying a hand on his cheek. He's been making her do that lately. Wondering if she noticed.

"Dolly once said—" Walter is saying.

"Yes?" They've never admitted to the fact of Dolly and him before.

"Dealer who saw Nola's paintings at your mother-in-law's house, he went for them. And some curator near Boston, too."

"The Addison, yes."

"Why won't she show? It can't be only because of—."

They had been in the garden of the house Rootie had rented that year, having drinks after Opening Day with a hundred or so, most of whom know each other well. The place had formerly been an inn. Nola goes to one of Rootie's parties a season, either at its beginning or its end. Walter spread his hands. "Because of—this?" He smiles, over his admission that anyone might not care for this hot green grass, the sail-white sky, the talk-talk between fine linen and unbecoming hats, the butlers and their familiars, the patrons—the whole horse-drawn summer, which except for his girls or any defection by death is the same as ever. The average age here must be close to sixty. Walter, whom Tot has known since his own boyhood, must be even more. Young men asked up here either rarely stay the course or are sorry specimens. Clothes are sedate at this hour, dowdy rather than sporty; Walter's own are even nondescript. Yet all the faces, many of the women's surgically kept up, many of the men's carnation with drink, are implacable in their well-being. This caravan will carry them through.

"I love it here," Tot says low. He wants at once to retract that. One should never sound hopeless at a meet.

A horned eyebrow twitches. Of course you do. But who
has to say? A hand squeezes Tot's shoulder. "Shy about her
mind, eh? I knew a girl like that. That why Nola won't
show, eh?"

"She just—doesn't want to."

Everybody knows what Nola won't do: go the calendar,
blend in—but they prefer to blame the accident, saying
Look how far she has come! They themselves keep a stolid
front toward physical ailment. The first lady of racing
drinks martinis in the wheelchair that martinis brought her
to, and from boyhood Tot has heard the elders say gently of
one or the other of them still going through the paces, and
held up by that as they all hope to be: "He's a little ga-ga
now and then."

"She—doesn't want to live," Tot said.

Whatever had possessed him, to give up Nola's secret,
unknown, she thinks, even to him? His year-by-year load
of it, of watching the bravery dole itself out like a muscle
exercise? Or Walter the trusty, who mutters Ah, now, or is
it Now, Now—and lets the crowd help ooze him and Tot
apart a few paces, from which distance he shrugs at Tot,
deprecating this—or is it a salute? As Walter turns away,
there is something infinitely sad about his haunches, maybe
the practiced way the well-worn jacket skirts the rump, as
if his tailor, measuring to there from the armpit, has said:
Now, Mr. Mallory, this measurement we have to take seri-
ously, we cannot be debonair. Suddenly, Tot sees Walter
lift his chin; two persons under forty, or who could be
taken to be, have arrived. Sisters, they are perennials here,
the elder a tiny lisping woman-girl always in pointy black,
the younger one angrily aloof, like a chaperone. They know
Walter more than well, or had once. His coat is itself again.

It's light on Tot's porch now, the leaves not yet checker-
ing the sun. The lane has a few scanty trees, many vines.

Maybe it's best to have a shallow world. Maybe that's the secret of all the meets.

For lunch, for instance, he is meeting Wheatley at the Reading Room, just as he did eight years ago to inform the uncrowned head of the family that he and Nola were thinking of marrying. That day, he had just driven up from New York, where she was still at the Rusk Institute, and he was late, partly because she had agreed at least to live with him, now that she had the walker and was "half a girl again"—and partly because it was the Saturday of the Travers Stakes, and the crowd was so great that the rookie track policeman had only halfheartedly pushed ahead this battered MG with the clubhouse sticker on it, so Tot had had to park in a public lot and walk almost a quarter of a mile. Out of this combo of excuses he had kept silent, except for a "Sorry."

Wheatley was severest with those who did not insist on the privileges due them. It was understood between him and Tot that if Tot could only learn to do this, Wheatley in turn could do more for him. Tot must learn to lean harder on what his mother's side had at least done for him by bearing him. Until then Wheatley would do only so much. Lucky he hadn't heard Tot's answer to Nola at the Rusk. "Half a girl? Well, I'm only a quarterhorse myself."

Inside, the old house, smaller than many of the cottages, had been empty, except for a group of the staff, kitchen help, waiters, and housekeepers clustered at the back, all "high type" blacks, sedate elders and matrons either brought up from Kentucky or else from families which had been here since the Civil War, some with Indian profiles. One of these came forward to meet him.

"How are you this year, Jason?"

"Fine, sir. Mr. Lanphier in the lounge."

His cousin was going over the club's accounts. Some of the better-connected Kentucky breeders, he says, men who could be invited to the inside parties, use the club for sleeping quarters while they are here. Dirt cheap, and part of its function. But they ought to bring their wives now and then, though of course not here. "Do it up right once in a while, if somebody don't invite them, then at the Gideon." Sure, all the hostesses grab for any single man, but the men shouldn't lean on that kind of bacheloring. "Or at least not do it from here."

Wheatley didn't wear wing collars, but out of his presence people were given to swearing he did. Nola had later drawn him in one, in the style of Thomas Nast's cartoons, a few originals of which her father had owned and left at Grayport. It was an era Tot could see his cousin belonged to —that huge, rubicund head and body all chest, dwindling to tiny feet which in those days might have been gaitered, and in these looked their best in the dress pumps which at night he was rarely out of. Jockey bones, he said of himself —if he could have kept to the weight, and if his father had let him. His owlish hoot always made it clear that a Wheatley's father never would have, even if of less lineage than the mother, who had been a Wheatley born. Studs could sometimes be longshots, Wheatley maintained, but never the mares. At his own stables he was even stricter. Whether or not in consequence, he never did very well there; the breeding ran out; the horses ran last.

"We'll have to let in more locals as summer members," he'd said, rising from the accounts book, his eye screwed. Nola had been right to see him as political. "Kind who'll come once, then never bother us." Tot had seen those— Albany merchants, Troy bankers, Schenectady builders and local doctors, all with timidly radiant faces. Nobody precisely cold-shouldered them, but above their heads, in continual Ping-Pong, the inbred chit-chat volleyed and was returned.

"Haven't et, have you?"

"No, but I needn't. You'll miss the first race."

"Nothing in it I'm interested in."

When Wheatley was a young man his elder brother had been ambassador to the Court of St. James's. This was said to have affected Wheatley's own character, in so far as a Philadelphian one could be. Visiting his brother in a duke's house, and seated at dinner next to a prince of the realm, Wheatley had recognized some paintings of stallions on the dining-room walls: "I see our host has some very fine Munnings," receiving the reply, "I am not interested in other people's horses." He himself had much the same attitude but until then hadn't grasped the nobility of expressing it. While, when on his return, he was asked about Churchill, then still on the scene in his last stages, he was able to reply: "He's going ga-ga like a gentleman."

Wheatley and Tot were led to one of the round tables in the garden, which in spite of the crowd even inside here on Travers day, had been kept for him. He and the waiter go through their usual dance. "Yessa, chickem salad for Mr. Laynpheah. 'Longside a mahtini very dry. Not beforehand. 'Longside."

"Matthew's our oldest waiter here, aren't you? Been here almost as long as me." When Wheatley was pleased, his mouth pursed.

"Thank you, sah. And this gemmun—I remembers. Bloody Mary and a B.L.T." It was not intended that people eat particularly well here.

"Skip the Mary," Tot said. Before Bed-Stuy he would never have seen how the black help here parodied Uncle Tom. Why, the man was fairly dancing with it.

"Well?" Wheatley said, the minute the man was gone. "What about this Nola Gray?"

Tot knew what was meant. "The house at Groton's just one of those wandering old frames, on a peninsula. It's no estate. And there's no money." No need to explain where Nola's pittance went. To Wheatley, with Rootie's millions joined to his own, no money wouldn't mean that there was none.

"Mother drinks, I hear."

Tot looked around them. The drink consumed during the meet was enormous and constant, but done by convention, as a part of the general busyness which held people up. People here rarely had to be shut away for it; they so seldom appeared personally drunk. "A little."

"And the father?"

"Dead." No need to say he had decamped.

"What was he?"

"A professor. Art historian."

That had seemed to settle it.

"You're not obleeged to marry her," Wheatley said. "You've done nothing wrong."

Just then the exodus from the verandah and the tables around them begins, their table being so centered that everyone has to troop past it. Down the steps to the private path to the track or sauntering to it from the emptying garden, his cousins are going to their boxes. There's old Gail, the only woman of them as rich as Wheatley, who when advised to sell some of a stable unprofitable for years running—and so not tax deductible—had stamped her foot: "I have spent years breeding them to this point. I will not sell off a one." Who, on being told she was winding down the family fortunes to where her grandchildren would be merely comfortable, had said: "Fine. Just so long as the horses are." The accountant informing them all of this had been shaky with admiration, and Tot proud. He and she saw eye to eye. She waves at him.

There's deadbeat Tansie, who actually rides, and as the women say, looks like a Percheron in tweeds. Here and there are the widows who take their designers and hairdressers to parties if not to bed, and the divorcées, lively or stodgy, among them Millicent, her hat so far up in back and down in front that it is a wonder she sees the two of them, but she stops and kisses. It's known that she and Wheatley have had a walk-out once—her word for it. "Hoo-oo," she whispers to Tot, "hear you're hot on someone." Wrinkles straw her mouth but she has kept her beauty pout. "Hoo-oo, hot, hot."

Longside, like Wheatley's drink, come the men, with their air of letting the women be emphatic for them, while they hold the reins. Nola says he too has a touch of it. They are known to him and to each other first by their horse commitments, after which they divide off into what they do otherwise: into committees—charity or vanity, or to offices—law or Wall Street ones, through which the trusts and the money flow toward the home and club addresses. There's Walker Watson, who claims thirty or so clubs, here and abroad.

Tot notes also the two exalted ones, in for the weekend from Wilmington and Washington, who do museums. Plus his sole contemporary and pal in circumstance, once a schoolmate at a sleazy day school where he was known as "Beaver"—whose pink-cheeked wife keeps saying to those weekend bids to Hobe Sound, Fisher's Island, Palm Beach and Cuernavaca which are a kind of underground currency here—"Leland *works.*"

Once you didn't have to, it was an easily enterable society; you could even get by without a horse. If there was an abundance of women here it was because the stage dollies who had married their bankers and polo players, or the distaff fortunes married to men who had hunted well, had outlasted all of them. Heiress was a word the local paper loved, confidently first-naming them, and often allotting them their brand names.

Here comes the Mary Pickford of their set, a tiny, girlish eighty, with knuckle-duster rings, who has appeared every season of Tot's life as faithfully as a biddy on a cuckoo-clock—had she been Ralston, or Quaker Oats? Lumbering on alone is the huge, dazed woman who has had the ill luck to be the ball-bearings girl. Always good for a last-minute contribution for a charity gala's decorations, Rootie says—

and always came. He spots the mouthwash heiress, a blond zinger from Chicago, and Baldwin Locomotive, ancient money now. For in time the brands fade, or mingle so with other bloods or moneys that they are lost. Or doughtiest of all, earn their honor in the right way, with the thorough-breds. Who, watching Alydar run under the Calumet colors can care that Calumet was known best as a baking powder once?

After the horses, he really prefers those regulars who earn their characters by being here, each year becoming more genuine. He searches for the smart, unservile, elderly hat manufacturer who humorously enjoys what he sells and can couple his rise with Saratoga history. Tony, the Long Island trainer who each year used to invite Tot for lasagna and clams Positano in his cottage—five rooms and a Pullman kitchen, that he and his girl used to share with another trainer—may not be here ever again. No lucky horses, three years running. So, no more horses to train. "The owners—" Tony said last summer, discarding the clams which roasting hadn't opened, "they can shut their faces like these here clams." His girl had quit her job as assistant buyer in a big store to be a hot-walker for Tony's horses—"Jesus, I started out, I thought a hot-walker had something to do with sex and old guys." Since then they had been all over the map; Tony's horses had been highfli-ers then. She and Nola would get on. They had both been to Yucatán.

"Ever been to Yucatán, Wheatley?"

His cousin, busy with the extra half portion of salad brought him without his having to order it, raises his head to stare at him, as if investigating him for loose parts. "Why?" He considers. "We have Nassau."

Nola's own crowd never hit the Caribbean. They went to unstable countries only, usually by backpack; "Hoping to stabilize ourselves," she'd said with a grin, that night in the front seat of the Porsche. "Like coming here to Bed-Stuy.

Not slumming. But you know." She'd had a pert way of talking then—light. But the seriousness had been there. "I was at loose ends for Easter," he'd told her. "And I knew Chop." Chop had been the candidate's son, otherwise not motivated. "Oh, I see—" she'd said, and he could see that she did, even perhaps that his only travel souvenirs were the lederhosen and Alpine skis loaned by Budge when they skied in Vermont. Swarthmore do-gooder or not, he already liked her. She spoke to him as if he were grown. When your main interest was horses, lots wouldn't. "Well, at least you're not Bryn Mawr," he'd said. To his surprise she'd kissed him—though when they were hit they were sitting quite straight. He wonders whether it would help any to tell Wheatley that.

It hurts him that she will never again be able to backpack.

Back there in the Reading Room's garden, it's a blue-chip day. Each week in the Occupational Therapy room of the hospital, where by God they have her not only painting with her arm in a splint but instructing, he tells her how much of a watching game racing really is, yet how it keeps you moving. She smiles when he tells her how painterly horses are. Ach, your pictures are so painterly, the German woman who is head therapist says, coming up to them, and can't understand why they laugh. Each day the nurses tie Nola's hair back with a ribbon. Each time he comes, she asks him to remove it. "But the people at the track—" Nola says. "You never tell me about them."

Down the path they come now, in twos because it is narrow, but not necessarily in pairs, though of course they all know one another, those silver-crested heads and blazered bellies, the unisex canes, froggy chins and swooping, shadowy hats. Of course they are not all strictly his cousins, or each other's, except as they have all become related here, working so hard at their idleness. Outside, beyond the clubhouse and above the boxes, is that grand-

stand they never really see, except as it frames that mile-
and-a-half oval in whose center the trees rise etched in
another air. When he was a kid here, some stable hand told
him that running horses make a magic circle; those elms
would never die. Now he is not so sure they are elms.

Nola had given him a painting of hers for his twenty-
fifth birthday. He'd been twenty-two when they met. In
the interim he has had a standing arrangement, not an affair
really, with one of Walter's former girls. He knows about
the married older man who keeps her lovelorn. And everybody here knows about all of it. Walter hadn't minded
about the girl; as the notches slip by here, he'll move on,
the girl will, and Tot would; it's protocol.

Except for Nola. Who stays where she is. It's no system
of hers.

He had her painting upstairs there with him, in the Club
bedroom he would occupy all summer, flying down to New
York to see her as he could. On the first day of racing, going
back to his room for his binoculars, he'd found the second
housekeeper, a severe auntie-type, standing in front of it,
laughing fit to kill. Hand over her mouth, she apologized.
"My girl did it," he told her. "You know—the one in the
hospital." The woman nodded. They too knew everything.

He had put the picture, which was unsigned, on a stand
he bought for it in the art-supply store in town. Though
not large, its upper half is all taken up by a grandstand
seemingly dotted with onlookers. The bottom half is the
Saratoga oval exactly, except that the entries are some of
them still at the starting post, some already galloping down
the fairway and some bearing in for the finish—which of
course could never happen. A few are even scattered between, loping lone. One and all, their heads are albumed
flat with the canvas. They are people. Up above, the dots
are then identifiable: everybody in the grandstand is a
horse.

She'd never been to a track, he'd told the housekeeper; he'd only described it. Hadn't she though, the woman said.

It's now almost one o'clock. Down the path come three stragglers. One of them is Wheatley Junior, who has been politicking inside. A blond boar of a man, he has a small version of his mother's face embedded in his flesh. The tailor who keeps all that lard in is talented. Since his elder brother Budge died, Wheatley Junior and his family have not been in tune. The family trusts, as set up by the founder, go sideways, sibling to sibling, in a kind of primogeniture which may be the one British idea of which Wheatley Senior does not approve. Rootie is not here this season. She had spent the previous August saying to all and sundry: "Going to England next, are you?" and if the answer was a Yes, crying—"So am I! For the backgammon!"— and has since not returned.

Wheatley Junior's wife is probably in their box, with their two lacy little girls pinned to her side. At Junior's side is Mary Angela McRooney, who after her marriage to a French count was annulled, changed her name to Marie-Ange. On her other side, but only because he too is late, is a character so genuine that nobody remembers his real name, which doesn't matter, since though he is spoken fondly of to strangers, nobody introduces him. He is called Liver Lips.

Father and son nod. Marie-Ange pecks at Tot. "Hah you, *cheri?* Hear things about *toi.*" She leans to his farther lapel, flicking that year's job insignia, which is to get him past the guards who don't know him. "Heav-vee." She and Wheatley Junior pass on. From behind, the two of them appear to be traveling in the cloud of her hair, to each tendril of which one may fancy a conquest attached. Liver Lips has already gone on to the betting windows, a clutch of greenbacks in his fist. Because of this habit, it has sometimes been falsely rumored that he makes book.

For a moment all is warm sun, with the waiters tidying in the background, from which one can hear the track's dis-

tant hurrah. After tonight, though there'll be another week
to the meet, the vans will start going home. Except for a last
trickle of sales in the shops, empty seats in the restaurants
which have flashed open for the season, and love affairs
either looking ahead to the next meet or going through the
last throes—it's over. Next week, as they say here, you'll be
able to shoot a cannon down Union Avenue and hit nobody
but a local. Which is the soul of Saratoga, Tot thinks—them
or us?

Until that day Tot had never thought of such a thing.
Though Wheatley might get notices of some extra-schedule
N.Y.R.A. committee meeting, or of a yearling sale at Fasig-
Tipton, the auctioneers, he never comes; far as he is concerned, as with most of the others, until next August the
town sleeps. He hadn't liked Rootie's selling the house,
which was her inheritance, not his. Though their families
never come up except for this month, they have been doing
that since the turn of the century.

Back there, interviewing Tot, Wheatley doesn't yet know
that in the next year's election of the Racing Association
president, his own son will nose him out by a hair. Or that
in compensation, he himself will take over Marie-Ange.
While Rootie, living in London with a lover called Alastair,
and shortly to leave for a fat-farm in Buckinghamshire, will
return from there to find all her orientals and silver and
other goods, including Alastair, vanished, along with her
fat—and will then more or less come back to him.

While Tot, back there, doesn't yet know that he will fall
pathetically ill with hepatitis, with not a soul to visit him,
and that—almost as a consequence the doctors will say,
Nola will propel herself free of the apparatus which tethers
her to the hospital, into a wheelchair, and toward the first
wedding ever in the refurbished Canfield gambling hall.
Everybody will hear it was charming, with a string ensemble from Swarthmore, a band provided by Chop, the best
man, the wheels of the chair strung with satin ribbon, and a

makeshift pulpit made of a chest said to have once held croupiers' gloves and almost hidden by a hill of white roses —though nobody from here will come.

All Tot knows just then is that everybody here seems to him to be running, even to that New York tailor who has had to make Wheatley Junior's suit, and is yet to be paid for it.

"Eh, eh?" Wheatley says. His jaw snaps shut, recollecting what he and this uselessly good-looking young squirt, in shabby whites and loafers but thank God wearing a decent blazer and tie—are there for. If he would only use those good looks of his, the jaw says. With what the family could do for him then, a mouthwash heiress should be bearable. "I told you. I shan't tell you again. Making a three-year-long ass of yourself. You don't have to do—any of it."

The sound which Tot makes is unusual for that garden. As Nola will one day note, there are no agonies here.

"I *want* to. I want to do *something* wrong."

On his own porch, Tot puts down the scratch pad, gets to his feet and straddles the railing, facing west. He does this each morning, once his list is done. Today will be as uneasy as any other but these small acts smooth. Six o'clock, and a red sun coming up. Though he can see only down to the scraggle of bushes where the cars enter the lane, all Saratoga is before him, in its spruce time. Resort colors flock streets which have mustered a late-Victorian smile. The bank is Mecca. In cool niches, under the 1930s WPA murals, the Post Office is unwittingly selling more than stamps. For a month, get anything you want in this town and gamble for anything—except with chips. In the refurbished lobby of the Hotel Adelphi, the mahogany-and-gilt plastrons, epergnes of pastry and frilled young waitresses look ready for a sex farce, or else for a scene out of that movie he and his crowd loved so once—*Elvira Madigan*. A hit man was apprehended there yesterday. The man's picture did not appear in the paper. This may be an upstate town, but it knows what it is doing. The sins of a racing season are like vaudeville. They too move on.

It's time. They both like to get there early. He pokes his head in. "Ready?"

"Ready." She has on her drawing hat, a childish white cotton beach hat with a short sloppy brim that buttons on. The longish, crushy jumper and skirt hide the assymmetric hip and orthopedic shoe. It just happens—or does it?—that her pale colors and fallaway figure make her seem very much the girl of the moment, and at thirty not old for it. Only the wrong women at the track are ever stylish, but this is not that. The bag is what touches him most. In it she keeps her supplies: pencils, sticks of charcoal, paper, and a spray can of fixative, aspirin and a stronger compound for the end-of-day pain which comes of a rocking walk. But her arm alone will not support even that light a pouch— woven for her once by another patient, from cotton-string the several colors of therapy. So after all, the bag is a backpack.

Left behind is her own easel, one of normal size, on it a blank canvas he had stretched for her the night before. Once he returns her home she'll paint for hours, getting her own meals until he comes in, very late. There are as many parties and other events here as there are minutes, and the paper wants him at all of them. In the beginning this was because he has what they call the "entrée," but now, though he doesn't write well and a reporter often mocks it up for him, they like what he talks about. Two fashion magazines have asked him for articles. What he likes is to put in some old track lore, so that nobody will think that what's going on is new. He even knows who's who in those old bronzed pics called rotogravure.

All I do, he said to the young editor who asked him—is to go back in my head to the library in Old Westbury. Public library? she'd said; he could see that dampened her.

No, old Elmo Wheatley's house, gone now except from a few people's heads. Oh, I know, she'd said with passion; it's only your life. She could ask him questions about it, if that would help. He'd liked her at first, so young and eager, and straight of spine. There would have to be a lot about horses, he said. Oh, put in some withers and fetlocks, she'd said. And you on a horse. You'll photograph so well.

The cat is still nuzzling and prowling. "It likes sticky buns, what do you know?" Nola says, and holds out her hand for his list, which says, after the Reading Room: "Fourth and Sixth Race. Polo Field at Five. Racing Museum —Champagne Party for Presentation of Duveney Cups. Rootie's party at Surrey Inn."

He would come back in between, sometimes twice, either to change or to check her and the house, as he always says. But also to catch a glimpse of her in her working calm. He may even be jealous of that. There's a certain hour at the stables when the horses are being ministered to and the hands fall silent, everything clues in, and all vanities stop.

"Funny—" he says. "You don't like cats that much. And I don't scarcely get near a horse. And yet—"

"And yet what?"

Neither of them knows.

Yet together they both do. They go on with what's here.

They close the door behind them. Nola's never for locking, but he always finds some excuse. Though it mortifies him, his clothes are crucial here. And the rich don't pay him any sooner than they do the shops. "Who knows but somebody might think we have diamonds, too." He locks up. Dawn is over.

"Jesus, it's hot," he says. She never feels it. But at least it's always the present, here in their lane. They won't reach the past until they get to the track.

She takes his arm this once per day. The steps are too old and uneven. Going down them, the one railing is on the wrong side for her to manage the cane as well. End of sum-

mer, when the checks come in, he'll replace the steps and
put in proper railings; he already has the estimate. Twelve
hundred is what he will get for his duties at the Polo Field
as steward and general soother of visiting jocks and wom-
en's committees. It's not fair for her to be stuck inside all
day while he eats fancy food.

Though he'll miss having her on his arm like this. Leaning on a husband is not the same for her as for other
women; it's a confession, of what she will never confess.
What is it he yearns for her to confess?

Watch out!—he has no chance to say it. The cat is caught
in her long furling skirt; she's stumbled. But Tot has caught
her.

Is that why the heavy orthopedic shoe shoves out in re-
flex? Hitting the cat, just as one of the sharpy cars which
buzz the lane tooting at Venezuel's house, guns on through
—the cat's short, snarling parabola meeting it slap under
the wheel.

The car had not stopped. Cats can be surprised, then? By
death only, maybe. He can't see for sure. Nola is bearing all
her weight on him.

Just then the long, blacked-out limo grooves slowly in,
pulling up short of the brindled spot on the road. Gargiola
gets out, Venezuel after him. Gargiola peers down the end
of the lane where the other car went. "Who was that." He
sounds as if he knows.

"Issy and Marco," Venezuel says it reluctantly.

"They never to drive through here again, understand?"

When the old jockey nods, his dewlap wobbles like a
bird's.

"Penalty, they ever forget." Gargiola's shoe tip lifts the
cat, drops it back. His left thumb directs Venezuel to take it
away. He looks up at Nola in his slow, heavy-browed way.
"Sorry, missy."

As Venezuel bends to the cat, its hind leg moves, high

and wavering, the arched body lying where it is, and the head. He cranes at Gargiola. "I don't got a gun."

"Who needs a gun? That ain't a horse." Gargiola's thumb flicks again. Under Venezuel's porch, next to the corrugated-tin trash can with his name on it, is a small neat woodpile. Venezuel squats to it. In his worn habit and boots, in outline he could be that younger track hero pictured at the time of his scandal, crouched over his mount the way men of his continent rode—but secretly ready to take a fall. When he stands up, hefting a log from the pile, the seamed phiz is a shock. He's chosen a log with a narrow end. His hands were famous.

Tot finds his voice. "Let us take it to a vet."

"A vet?" Gargiola says, almost dreamy. "Right. A vet."

"A vet?" Venezuel has false teeth. When he smiles the lowers jut. "Sure, maybe Doc McKinnon at the track? Same one who's minding on that colt they're keeping under wraps for the Triple Crown. And I come up with this job."

"There's a dog vet on Route 9." He had dosed Rootie's pug. "I'll take it." If Nola will loosen her grip on him.

"Excuse me. You are good neighbor. But it is my cat."

Its eyes are glazing. But when Venezuel advances on it the pink gums snarl.

"Take your wife inside, better," Gargiola says low.

Making a sharp noise, not a scream, she has let go Tot's arm. Brushing him aside, she grasps the railing with both hands. This means swinging the inert leg with the big shoe as a separate weight, which he has never seen her do upright. He knows better than to help. She does not drop the cane.

So she negotiates the first step. The second step creaks as she lowers herself on it, between cane and railing. That movement, with him ready, she has sometimes done. For the last step, using the cane and a balancing talked of but never dared, she brings herself to the ground. He has no more breath. Two ordinary paces with the cane bring her

where she wants to be. She holds out her hand for
Venezuel's log.

Venezuel stiffens. He's South American, maybe Indian
and Catholic, too—what does she expect?

"Sure it's yours. But I feed it. And I kicked it."

Venezuel doesn't move.

"Tot? Bring me a log."

In the silence he wishes Issy and Marco would come
back, gunning their tires over the sunlit green. Then he
walks over to his own woodpile and hands her one.

"Jesus," Gargiola says.

They don't know how powerful those thin arms are,
from wheelchairs and walkers, crutches and canes. She
brings the log down. The cat's wavering leg stops. Then she
reaches behind her to their own washline, where hang her
prized kitchen towels, the old Irish linen ones the handlers
used to use for rubdowns, marked with a woven-in STABLE
RUBBER on a red stripe. She drops one over the caved-in
head.

Tot has stepped back. The cane, that fulcrum ever between them, is on the ground. She takes two steps toward
him, a third tottering one. He receives her on his chest.

"Drive me to the track."

He has to help her as usual into their old Volvo. The
black limo has to be shifted in order to let them out, and it
is. They do not look back.

They're late for the trials but take a table anyway. She
does not draw. Most of the people have gone on anyway.
She seems to want to look and look at the day itself, at the
porous turf, raked to a brown crepe paper, on which the
horses have been running, and at the grandstand of cloud
in the very blue August sky. There's a breeze now; it's going to be one of the priceless days.

"Everything smells of patent leather."

From sister talk between her and Dolly, he knows she is

thinking of the shiny strapped shoes small girls wear for best. They do not speak of what she has done.

But when he is ready to take her home, she says she will stay for the day. "For all your list."

While he drops in at the paper, he leaves her at the Reading Room, where the black staff make a nice fuss over her. When he comes back he finds he and she have been commanded to lunch by Wheatley, who had noted her. Wheatley's table today is on the porch; since his young days in England, he cannot abide this Hudson Valley heat. He is courtly to Nola in his best British style—making an effort for the ladies as it were, though in from brusquer affairs. "It's no wonder the British couldn't survive India. Don't let them tell you it was Gandhi, my dear. Sweat. Plain sweat."

"Oh, I won't," she says. "Let them tell me. But is this—the Hudson Valley?"

"River's not ten miles from here. Over at Schuylerville. Nice little stream by then. But not so unnavigable a friend of mine can't come up from New York Harbor every summer in her boat."

Which Tot has been on—a small yacht with a deeply mahogany boudoir and lemon-striped beach chairs, where the friend and Wheatley have a deliciously navigable affair, nipping off bits of the packed days—before polo, after parties, as a clubman can. While the "captain"—some young midshipman earning his summer dollar, keeps watch.

"It *is* rather like the British Raj from this porch," Nola says. "They could make a movie. Outside the hedge there, all those hawkers, and hoi-polloi. Up here all the linen and the white hats. And the tall glasses."

"Oh, you Swarthmore—" Wheatley says. "You girls never get over your colleges."

"Chickem salad for the lady?" the waiter says. "Go-ood morning, suh. And a Bloody Mary for this gemmun?"

"Champagne," Tot says. "For us all."

Wheatley's collar twitches. "Hope you can pay for it."

"Shut up, Wheatley. Just drink to the lady."

When the bottle comes, Wheatley waits to be enlightened, finally drinks. Their table is being noticed. Porches creak with gossip anywhere, but on days like this the fine tweak of it is irresistible. Such blood-unities are here; in the very air one hears the fine tinkering of the past. Underneath, what's that vascular pumping? The present, eddying at everyone's mouth.

Nola arches her chin. The day has grown beyond even her drawing board. But she is smiling; she'll catch it.

"You come into money, I could let you in on a colt," Wheatley says to her. "Some of Secretariat's haven't panned out, but there's one—"

"Oh, I'd want a mare. I mean—a filly." She holds out her glass for more. "How does a foal get its name, anyway? I've always wondered."

"Ah. So that's it. Why you so shiny-eyed." Wheatley casts her narrow waist a squire's look of disbelief. "Well, well. Never too soon to begin a family." He glances with morose pride at the table presided over by Wheatley Junior, who had never quite got through—or over—Yale. He stands up, pinching her cheek. Always royally without paraphernalia of any kind, field glasses or cigars or wallets, Wheatley's hands are always free for the pinch. "Very glad to hear it. Rootie be calling you. Well, see you at the paddock." He leaves the bill.

As she and Tot go down the steps, Nola this time rocking between the cane and his arm, the air behind them is very quiet, then murmurs again in little keyholes of talk.

"Paddock's grassy," Tot says. "Come."

They stand watching the entries stepping imperially toward the track. A jockey's outline, hip-welded to the moving horse, has a kind of cherub confidence, no matter how worldly the face above. Some horses are being circled in front of owners, others led by handlers who clomp ahead like Tin Woodmen.

Tot has stationed himself a couple of feet from Nola, hands at his sides. He turns up his palms. "Come."

The cane hangs on her left wrist. About to fling it to the ground, she remembers its other capacity and jams its steel-tipped ferrule into the grass almost upright. It stays. One hand is on her nerveless hip, one at her breast. Her thin-skinned collarbones move with her breath. His stare says he hopes to move her toward him, with its force.

She rocks toward him, once, twice, landing each time with the heavier shoe. A third step and she is within touch of his hands. This time she does not cave toward him. She stands, and stands on her own feet, eye to eye. No one notices, or hears Tot's gulped sob. "How?" he whispers. "How do you do it?"

"I think . . . cane. I image it." She too is whispering. "And it's like it's there."

She takes his arm, but almost like any woman. "A house is so—static. Any house. Here—everything moves."

They ooze with the crowd, aiming for Walter's box. In the boxes the women sit like flowers planted for the after-noon. The men are shifting, active, as on a stock-market floor, often not talking of what's around them. Few in the boxes go downstairs to the betting windows to place even the small ceremonial bets, which would not cover a thoroughbred's weekly feed. Their gamble began a long way back. During the race itself, while the grandstand shouts and rises, these owners of strings of stallions and brood mares, who maybe last week at the sales purchased a two-hundred-thousand-dollar horse singly, or joined some syndicate for millions, will sit immobile. They look bored.

Tot has to go downstairs for the paper. He leaves her in Walter's empty box.

Downstairs is a different world. Tipsheets are being car-ried underarm, binoculars leased at a stall. Women wear

every kind of costume, from showgirl outfits to grocery-
vendor sweaters and splat shoes. Knowledgeableness runs
the ranks like fever. Some are solemn with it, as if just now
anointed by a hot tip from a private demon. Others holler
and jostle and trample from the gambling excitability inside
them; win or lose, you have had this.

He has a moment's ache to be one of the lower classes,
jolly and anonymous, though he knows better than to believe that upstairs is only power, downstairs is only joy.
But here, too, they are visiting deep summer, if only for a
day's outing. Mornings, the longer-term old geezers—who
will later fill the porches all the way from the rackety
Broadway hotels to the Gideon—which sits poshly in
Franklin Roosevelt's Works Progress–built park and in August will not take just anybody—will cluster all together at
daffy-shaped pergolas to take the corrective waters. Now it
is chance-taking time all over. Night lies ahead like a separate resort. Then toughs from Albany and Schenectady will
crowd in, to broach the honeysuckle lights on upper Broadway, or to gawp at some tent left over from a last night's
soirée. Under cover of those a college rapist will ply the
wooded campus, though he may not make the local paper,
should he succeed. That same night, four high school girls
will pledge their troth while thipping thodas at Mc-
Donald's, and this the newspaper will record.

Meanwhile, in a twenty-room cottage that a genteel
Catholic lady last year left to her church, which then sold
it, the new owner, who has auctioned off the Tiffany votive
window for enough to re-cover the entire downstairs walls,
including the library's shelves, with leopard-spotted suede
—is having a housewarming. There, on a sofa stacked with
pillows fashionably on end like after-dinner mints, Marie-
Ange will change her bed allegiance, as she does in August
of every year. Men will dally with her or avoid her, all that
long night. She, whose presence makes some parties, de-
stroys others, will be dressed as Queen Mab.

What can't happen at a spa—where Midsummer's Eve is on three separate days of one week claimed by three different hostesses?

Or where on an obscure lane, a girl who in the morning will regain the power to walk alone—or to take three free steps, may lose that power—or the need—by dark. It can happen. As happened in the dining room at Grayport, to a back wall of which she had tottered once, landing with her arms spread butterfly, the cane dangling or seeming to. "Saw her father behind the swing door maybe," that coarse, tenacious woman her mother said afterward, winking. "He used to measure her growth on that wall." The breakfast table had smelled of her spirits. He had picked Nola from the wall like one did a flattened moth, before she had slid down it all the way. Had she or had she not taken a step or two to it? The use of a cane is a subtle thing. The growth marks were still on the wall.

They hadn't spoken of her mishap until a day later, lying in deck chairs on the lawn of the Block Island hotel they had fled to, which her younger sister, the one who also helped fund their mother, was that summer helping to run. In the foreground an iron dog looked out to sea.

"I just fell," she said. "I used to fall toward him. We had a game."

Maybe you still are—her mother had said, as they packed up to leave. Falling toward your father. Maybe that accident of yours only clinched it.

"She's smart when she's drunk," Nola said.

"Crap." Broken bone is broken bone. He didn't want to say that. "She's the one still falling toward him, don't you see?"

He'd surprised them both. Dr. Tot. Who would have thought him capable of it?

"Maybe if you image yourself—" he'd said. "Walking." The way the therapists had taught her to image a particular muscle move.

A rehab unit is so enclosed. In salt air its language can sound false.

"Oh, I am—" she had said. "Right now I'm imaging myself toward that dog."

Downstairs in the men's room he meets Gargiola, who beckons him. "Like to talk to you."

"Sure. Come along. I have to check the size of the gate."

Biggest gate of the season so far, the man in charge tells them. Tot writes the numbers down.

"You have a betting system based on how many at the gate?" Gargiola says.

"Christ, no. It's for my job."

"You have a job?"

"Of sorts. I always do."

"I didn't know."

A gray-haired woman passes, the former state governor's right hand. "Hi, Tot."

"Hi. Didn't know for sure whether you'd be back or not."

"A Guv is a Guv." She hurries on.

"She's got it right," Gargiola says. "But how does she know?" He listens to Tot's explanation with his head cocked. "Like your job, don't you."

Tot laughs. "It's here."

"Like it here, huh?"

"Yes," Tot says. "I like it here. Don't you?"

"Like the palaver behind it. And out Union Avenue, day like today, you can see clear to Vermont."

"Vermont?"

"They have horses too now. I own part a track, the Green Mountains. Not exactly thoroughbreds out there, though, ha?"

"No." As the thoroughbreds, if they could know their own exactitude, would likely agree. "But a horse is a horse."

"Not here. God should strike you dead, saying a thing like that. Say, listen. Want to ask you——."

A man eyeing them greets Tot. "Your wife admires our cannas—talked to her just now. Send her some, anytime." He passes on.

"Who he?"

"Buck Slater. Head of the track."

"Owns it? When'd he buy?"

"Lord no. Runs it. For the Racing Association."

"Ha, just an employee."

"Don't tell him that."

"He an employee, he knows."

"Yes," Tot says. "You wanted to ask me——?"

"First, I want to say sorry. About this morning."

"Couldn't be helped."

"Your wife takes things hard, don't she."

"She's had to."

"That Venezuel. He don't like women, you know."

"I didn't."

"Yah, one of those. But he likes her."

"Well. Well, I better be getting back to her." But he finds himself liking Gargiola. The man is probably a character. "She tries it every year. To go through one whole day on the job with me. And night."

"Never gives a scream, does she?" Gargiola says. "Next door, we never hear a thing."

"Well, I don't beat her," Tot says lightly.

"That's for sure." Gargiola squints up at him. "Not that thoroughbred . . . Hey. What's the grin?"

"Only, that when they say that about a woman here—and they say it a lot—the joke is, who are they complimenting—the woman or the horses?"

"Jesus," Gargiola says. "If that ain't crude." He snicks the handkerchief folded to a point in his breast pocket; it matches his tie. The suit is a beaut, but for business, a city suit. "Even men like your cousin?"

"My cousin?" It wouldn't do to ask which one.

"Wheatley Whatsis. The guy with the—." Gargiola pokes his own buttonhole. Wheatley always sports what he calls a posy, provided by Rootie when she is home, even when she is not speaking to him. Gargiola flashes a smile. "Why I'm hanging you up—I been offered membership, the Reading Room. Buzz me straight—should I join?"

His teeth aren't white but are real. His hair, cut straight up, is still dark. Some of the women will call him virile among themselves, and smell venture capital. The men will sense money maybe freshly laundered and new in the pocket, though there isn't a bulge in that suit. Such women will talk past Gargiola in the Reading Room, to such men.

The eyes are not just a character's.

"Only if you use it," Tot said.

Gargiola roars silently. Tot's hands are seized, fisted in his, then shaken loose. "Go in peace."

As Tot starts to turn away, one of the flexible hands takes him by the shoulder and turns him back again to be stared at, the way a man does when he's putting it to you. "Women had ought to scream. My girls scream at any little thing."

Upstairs, he sees a clump of people surrounding Walter's box. He rushes there, finding Nola calm in its center. The new governor, passing with his daughter, who remembers Nola from the time they both worked for the party's head candidate, has stopped there, a retinue forming behind.

The daughter is plump and plain, and gawkily relieved to find someone here to know socially. Nola meanwhile gives him that certain look. Bathrooms are a problem here, because of all the steps. She can't be whisked away, but a cripple can always leave without excuse. Only at such times does that harsh word shadow him. Under the short brim of her hat he whispers One-two-three-*Scram*. Behind them, the governor's daughter, squealing "Bye-bye!" adds tactfully, "What a cute bag."

In the patron's room at the track they have Virgin Marys
and crackers after she emerges from the john, and go on.
On this day, because of all the logistics, they eat fully only
at home. Outside in the patron's parking lot they pick up
the Volvo from between a Mercedes coupe and that coffee-
colored Rolls which comes every year from Wilmington.

The polo field is a scraggly local meadow redeemed by
contributions from the August people, though its marquee
still looks odd. Picked locals, prodded to recall that native
polo began in these parts, are pleased to serve on working
committees, and as part audience to a sport so elegantly for
the few. The August set supplies the players and mounts.

There's no match today, only a committee of women under the marquee, fussing over tomorrow's refreshment
plans. The seats in the stands are unshaded and hard. He
leaves Nola in the car, backing it up for what shade it can
get under a hedge planted as encirclement. The hedge, facing the highway behind the field's farther edge, still looks
tentative, but he will lay no bets against the field and its
backers.

Lord Monsey is waiting for Tot with the famous polo
pony, of Indian ancestry, which he hopes to have Tot ride
in a match or two. Rootie's party this evening is in honor of
Monsey and his lady, houseguests whom she has enticed
over the water. If she cannot have England she will borrow
it.

Monsey, a newspaper owner given an earldom, is long-
boned, solemn and sixtyish heavy; if he ever rode competi-
tively he is certainly past it. "Here's the nag."

The small horse standing in its makeshift loosebox is a
horse in a fairy tale. Tot had once seen a royal consort
emerge from a visit to a banking house in Wall Street, his
silkily valeted figure and brushed hair unearthly under that
frayed financial sunlight. The pony, aloof on this tough,
yellowing turf it has been brought to out of its own moist
midsummer, has the same pedigreed gloss.

"Won't you ride him for us? Be honored."

"Thanks." He chooses the easiest beg-off. "No kit."

"No problem."

No, of course. Some one of them here will have everything, or they will provide. His own gear lies in the vanished tack room at Westbury, along with a polo mallet and scarred ball from the last chukker of his final game, after which his teammates tossed him in the air. He can feel that rough, repeated landing, lying in those arms for a minute each time like a babe in its crib. "Thanks. Much too rusty."

"Oh, not tomorrow, m'boy. Next week's match. Brush up with the teams in between."

Even Rootie has urged it. It's not like borrowing money, Tot—which they both know she will never lend. It's done, Tot, I assure you. In England anybody might borrow a mount . . . Anybody who rides like you. Maybe she's forgotten how, early in his marriage, a tumble had laid him up for months. Leaving Nola to the mercies of Grayport—a practical nurse who ended up tippling with her ma. Or else Rootie, given to urging divorce as proper for the early mated and maybe mismated young, has not at all forgotten.

Tot touches the pony's flank. It stamps a hoof. Look at those hindquarters. He can feel his own astride them, as he angles down for the long scoop. A royal mount can be a worker, too. There's a twitch of the hide, a nosing, an *augh-h*. Tot laughs aloud with pleasure. The horse knows it's admired. "Look at that eye."

Monsey's own, as smart as his beast's and a little like them, regards him. "Why not, then?"

"Thank you, but I can't risk it. Family matter."

"Ah. Wife won't let you ride."

"Oh no, she'd rather I would. Loves to watch."

"Ha. Sporting gal, eh?"

Tot sneaks a glance at the Volvo, its blunt, faded shape iridescent with heat. He can just glimpse the white blur of hat. "Very." He turns to go. They shake hands. He takes a last look at the horse. His dead cousin Budge never played polo. That gear left at the Westbury house had been bought on its own.

"Offer stands. Anytime." The Englishman looks puzzled. He, too, has caught sight of the hat. "Two of you care to?" He gestures to the marquee. "Sun is broiling."

"She's very tired," Tot says. He cannot say she is an invalid. He has never known how to say it. Rootie must not have told the Monseys in advance. "Tonight." He's suddenly so tired he can barely get it out. "You'll meet her tonight."

In the car, asleep with her head back, she looks like tired marble, like that bust at Grayport attributed to St. Gaudens but not accredited, which her mother has never been able to sell. Marble too can grow fretful over the years. His wife's not that yet. Looking down at her, the stick, the hat, the bag, he can feel her weariness in his bones.

But over a supper heated by him from the freezer, and with her wide awake, they are themselves again. If an image hangs before both of them, they do not speak of it. Only of the party—does she still think of going to it? She does: after all, isn't this the one day? Well then, he has a surprise.

For the last few years she has had only a single evening dress, a shepherdess pink-and-green, charming, but always the same. The dress he brings out was once immured in what at Grayport is called the Goody Closet, almost empty now. "Your sister sent it back." Not the helping sister, not Dolly either, but on application the dress had been sent. "I had it washed by that old woman out the peninsula used to work for you all. She said she recognized it. Your great-grandmother's wedding dress."

"Great-great-aunt." It had belonged to the marble bust.

Rootie's evening party, like most of her crowd's, is set early. Morning horse-reasons are alleged by some, and are real enough. But the other truth about parties here, which

are for the middle-aged who have no other entertainment
but themselves, is that nobody can wait to get to them.

When Nola comes out of the bedroom, all antique white
and lace-chokered, he is sobered, even before he turns her
around to button up her back. And turns her around again.
The dress, austere with lace at the top, wild with it below,
nestles the long neck, pointed chin and piled hair just as he
expected; the skirt hides as he had hoped. But there's no
hiding what her indented mouth says to him as his brushes
her hand. "Smashing," he says, and she is. No one nowadays has that small a waist, no matter the reason for it. But
the dress is after all a wedding one, with that double effect
—when used for other occasions, which such dresses bring.
As a sometimes exacting painter of herself, she will have
seen that she is aged by wearing it. Yet can she see how
behind that double-edged veil the thirties casts, he can still
see the girl, in flawed outline?

From behind his back he hands her his second surprise.

"Wherever did you—" she says.

"Day I drove Wheatley to Wall Street and back." In the
Bentley, until then trusted only to the chauffeur, who had
had a coronary. For which odd jobs Tot gets payment in
kind, of the sort designed to help him keep afloat here:
tickets to the Museum Ball, to which no one gets in free—
value four hundred dollars, or his club memberships paid.
"Saw it in a shop on Madison Avenue"—which specialized
in romantic maternity clothes. The article he bought had
been crooked shepherdess-style on the arm of a window
model with a sensitively curved stomach. But this he does
not say. Oh, she'll love it, the pregnant salesgirl said. Kind
of a fun accessory. I have one myself.

A slender, cream-colored Parisian walking-stick dating
from the twenties, here and there gilded just enough not to
have its owner mistaken for blind, it is strong enough, too;
he has tested it. Use me or not, it says to her; whatever
happens, you are not to blame.

"Couldn't stand that old brown one of yours any longer."

"I knew you couldn't," she said.

Rootie's front lawn, ablaze with floodlights and uniformed Pinkerton guards, looks as if a small-scale revolution may be in progress, but it is merely that all the ladies have been to the bank.

"Evening, sir, madam—er, miss," the surrogate butler says, and the stutter pleases Tot; the man even tries to take the cane. This former inn which Rootie has rented is barewalled, and furnished with nullities of which there are scarcely enough, but everybody is here, the women in the sequin-struck yardage they're used to, the men also very correct, no fey shirts or cummerbunds; a colored dinnerjacket might even get the back door.

Most correct are the two pallid sprigs who here represent male youth. They are not particularly pimpled, but afterward one tends to recall them as so, with small heads of indeterminate jaw. Being foaled has been the main thing with them, and the blood has run out, the brains too. They will have been to the small, select schools which still teach the attenuated manner, and to the less distinguished colleges. For sheer want of personality they will sometimes procure for themselves a bad name. One of them, Hardingham Biss, who is Tot's distant relative, flounders around the girls of the New York City Ballet during its season here, and is known as a brutal one-night stand with the more naïve collegers. He has better-grade siblings who never pay their devotions here, as Tot is sure he will do all his lucky life. His pal is a puffier example. A family chauffeur once summed them up: "Oh, Dingy and his pal, they just got no physique."

They scarcely nod at Tot and Nola, who do not count. They will do the same to Lord Monsey, since he does. Though right now everyone, including Monsey, is looking at Marie-Ange, who every night of this important week will break out in one of her "newies" from Paris. Tonight's is a black lace jumpsuit with slits easy to follow. She has been to the Golden Door spa to prepare for it. Everett Salls, the crowd's wit, is heard to say from his wheelchair: "The ass is the newest of all."

They eat at long trestle tables and board benches set up by the caterer from Albany, whose much decorated food is often hard to identify, what with so many yellowish sauces, noodle-cut greens, and a dessert half cardboard marquetry and flying a Union Jack. But the wine is a Mouton Rothschild; there they buy the best, though often supping it down with potato chips. In the beginning Nola asked him how it was the sporting rich got so little for their money—or was it only up here? *That* he could answer. "On the move as they generally are, it's usually the same everywhere." Do they like it all right that way—she persisted—the expensively bad food and dress? Or is it they just don't know? He isn't sure. The people she calls "they" have so recently been "us." But she has cherished his reply, now a byword between them: "They have so much else on their minds."

Down at a table's end, Rootie, signaling to rise, shaking high a wristlet of square diamonds pure enough to drink, is fending off compliments. *"Nouvelle cuisine.* At least that's what they bill me for."

As they move to other downstairs rooms which give on the entry, Bonnie Doe breezes in from a party on the opposite side of Broadway, shrugging it behind her, her white hoopskirts and scarlet sash billowing. "A tent! On a night like this. And with tomorrow's tent coming." That will be the Museum Ball's tent, already set up on the museum's grounds, whose canvas walls will tomorrow swell and depress to such a bladdery motion that cars passing by on Union Avenue will pause to watch. She flicks out her crotch-length string of pearls the size of sourballs, which are generally conceded to be real at all times, since Bonnie Doe, once a small-time singer, is not well-born enough to be comfortable with paste. "I've had it with tents. Had one last year. Only so much you can do in a tent."

Her husband, Button, who it is admitted may be the best-tended eighty-five-year-old anywhere, knows this already and has delayed at home, just now following her through the door, worshipfully. He is a mild man with only one vice. In his case the borderline between sweetness of temper and senility is close, but given his pedigreed millions, which are impressive even here, nobody is about to examine that.

"Button's been looking at movies of the Duchy," Bonnie Doe says, flinging her arms toward one and all. Button, named for that ancestor whose signature on the Declaration of Independence is the rarest, has no further ambitions, but she would like him to be an ambassador to somewhere, because she could be such a good one. To that end they have to date bought anticipatory houses in five countries, each time letting the current Administration know. Where appropriate—though Bonnie Doe complains that such countries get fewer, they build a religious chapel to match. "And whey-ah," she now says, "—are the guests of honnah?" She is not Southern, but with costume can become so.

Lady Monsey is just at her elbow, an austere, frankly middle-aged woman in what Tot's mother would have called an afternoon dress, of navy blue. Monsey himself, after one quiet look at Nola being helped up from her board bench, has brought his wife across the room to meet her. To a murmur from Rootie, trailing behind them, of how democratic Lady Monsey is. "Served us tea at the castle with her own hands." And they had really bought the castle only because of its stables.

Bonnie Doe, presented, bows straight-backed enough for

independence but deep enough to allow her curls to fall forward.

"Duchy?" Lady Monsey says to Button. "Yaws?"

Bonnie Doe usually speaks for him. Otherwise he may without preamble begin one of his jokes, which are vintage, but not rare. "No-oo," she silvers out. "Not all ours. But kind of a chunk of it. Being the size Liechtenstein is."

"Speaking of sizes—" Button says to Lady Monsey. "And duchesses. Know the one about 'Me compliments to the juke'?"

"She's not a duchess, Butty," Rootie says, giggling. "Doesn't want to be, do you, Leda?"

"Well, in this one she is. Visiting a military hospital. Leans over the bed a wounded soldier, and she says: 'My good man, where were you wounded?' And he says—"

"Admire your dress," Monsey is saying to Nola. "London—all my daughter's friends are wearing them. If they have the luck to have them."

Rootie, to whom the dress a minute ago was what you wear if you can't afford to buy, says: "Why, Nola. Didn't you get that from our side?"

"No," Tot says. "You gave her that big easel came out of the family bank, remember? She hasn't yet painted anything big enough for it. But she will."

"And the soldier says, 'Ma'am, all I can say is, if the juke was wounded where I be, you'd be a very un'appy duchess.' And the duchess says—"

"Ah, you paint," Monsey says. "All you busy girls. My own daughter's working as a reporter."

"See?" Rootie breathes to a bystander. "Their daughter works."

Butty is used to his words being hung on. Where they aren't, he and Bonnie Doe don't go. "And the duchess says, 'My poor man, is the bone broken?' " He puts a hand on Monsey's arm. "The bone. Heh-heh. And the soldier says —heh, 'Me compliments to the—.' Ah-hah. Heh."

"Oh you—" Bonnie Doe says fondly. "You. Isn't he dev-ilish?" She really does think so. All their life together that has been enough for them.

"Tot's a reporter," Nola says to Monsey. Lifting her face to him, she adds low: "I saw that pony. Make him ride it."

"Oh yes, Tot," Bonnie Doe says, "but in London they wo-ork at it." Bonnie Doe is seldom mean. Where they go, people give them so little reason for it. But Nola's dress is too much what hers was meant to be. "Hear that, Butty? Lady Monsey's daughter is a writer."

"That so? That so." Button has one topic—his life— which supersedes even his jokes. "Now Bonnie Doe and I are just looking for a writer. To do our autobiography."

Monsey has had to turn away. The English, when they finally laugh, really crimson up a job. "Have they only the one?" he mutters to Tot.

"Now, Button. She wouldn't want to do us." Though on the peaks she and Butty inhabit, this is one of the things Bonnie Doe does not really believe. She lifts her pearls to-ward Lady Monsey. "What paper's she on?"

Lady Monsey, inspecting her own blunt nails—gardens, no doubt, is surprised, but her eyebrows are equal to it. What other paper could it be? *"Ahs."*

At that point, plumb in Lady Monsey's vision also, is Marie-Ange. She is waving her finny behind in search of a sofa, the two spriggy young men following, but no sofa seems to have been provided. And where is Wheatley Se-nior? Sometimes in August a host is not at his own party, but that is not Wheatley's way; he is the main cousin to too much. Perhaps that affair on the little yacht in Schuylerville hasn't yet foundered—or was that another year? Events here are crushed so close, like rose leaves all in the same bowl, that if properly attending all as ordered, one may see the progress of any affair in perfect focus; in fact, this is what most people do for reading matter here, and as the

most respectable of pursuits. What's wrong with a world
where people are sportsmen and -women to the end?

No, Wheatley is here, and has discovered a sofa for
Marie-Ange. And who is he leading up to join her, brushing an heiress or two on the way? A good heir, like a good
man, is so hard to find, yet in the nature of human account-
keeping they too must exist. Why, it's Lord Monsey, his
soft brown pony-eyes almost preceding him, his long-
chinned complexion returned almost to norm.

At Tot's side, is his cousin Rootie about to send up a cry?
Her skinny, waistless, red-lipped style, with those pointed
cheek-wings of black hair, has returned twice since she first
copied it from an elder sister. Didn't it come back in the
1950s? And now once again it is the very thing. The cry
spins from her, imprinted upward by that flung diamond
wrist: "Oh, are you going to England next month, too?"
But to whom is she saying it? Walter Mallory, devotedly
interested in Nola's cane? Or Bonnie Doe's back? In this
crush it might be addressed to anyone, and was it a cry or a
wail?

"So am I," she says in the harsh voice roughened with
cigarettes or alcohol, or maybe only with the stinginess so
often carried in the sporting blood like a guardian white
cell. "So am I. For the backgammon."

Out on the Surrey Inn's doorstep, Tot and Nola are leaving early, as they do everywhere, yet he has a feeling the
party has not yet done with him. He had the same feeling
after last year's party.

Behind them, the door opens narrowly. A man's hand,
gold links shining on the cuff, thrusts a white card into
Tot's. The door closes.

Tot still seems to be standing in that brief shaft of light.
He has remembered what he has forgot, though not precisely which. The gilt-bordered invitation, on the stiffest
pasteboard, means that it was one of the power rituals of

the month—why must his dingbat subconscious always pick those? The card will merely give him the new name or names attached to said ritual. Before he has a chance to look, the door opens again—though a host's time is valuable. "Where were you, you squirt—when they gave out the Duveney Cups?"

In the Volvo, he and Nola grimace at each other like truants, then begin to laugh. The car is facing north toward other one-month-inhabited so-called cottages on either side. Norman-style villas or American gothics or other survivals, they are only a patch of enclave now, rising perennial after a winter of solitary porchlights. Tonight they are awninged and floodlit, or red-shaded from within to set the Tiffany oriels glowing, or rearing porticoed pillars thicker and higher than any Greek Revival house ever had a right to.

Ahead, the dark cone at the end of the street called Broadway seems still to lead to what his mother used to call "the Lake Georgic silence," where her grandparents had had a rambling way station of a summerhouse, and then on to the stony, moose-hung Adirondack retreats with ten-mile-long driveways, where, sitting upright on the gnarls of rustic furniture, eating quail and deer shot on their land and splashing in icy natural tarns, the children of that generation had been tutored in vain toward the simple life. As he and Nola swing away, the festive yellow from the tent party across the way slides behind them. They face the remains of the old town now, and beyond it to the south the other highway, scabbed with fast-food huts all grimly together, lit up like the fun palaces these want to be.

Their own lane, as they turn into it, no longer depresses him. Homecoming has all his life had certain heart-sinkings before he goes in to the always positive joys of one kind or another. Today has merely been one of those days, or lists, during which you never have a full meal or drink, only the constant social sips that leave you nervously keyed up—

but for what? Here what gets him is those steps. He solves
this by lifting Nola in his arms, to carry her inside. Did he
do that last year, too?

At the top he almost stumbles, the way you do when the
known space isn't the same. Bat-sense. The air is thick,
silent with objects he can't quite see. He and she never
leave the porchlight on, that surest sign you're out—only
the one in the bathroom at the back, and an attic bulb
which shines eternally for the paintings stacked there,
though who knows whether that's better for them than the
damp?

"Have to put you down a sec."

"I'm no bride." She hangs onto the porch railing. He
reaches across what should be a balcony-size deck with a
small chair. Before he fumbles the light on he's smelling
lush green and mingled scent. Flowers. But not cut stuff.
His porch has been planted. Window boxes, spilling vines
and pink-purple trumpet shapes, the boxes clamped to the
rail. Hanging baskets of fuchsia. Urns of prim yellow-and-
orange line the house wall; side blankets of fern mask
Venezuel's on one side and the police captain's on the other.
What makes him laugh out loud is the tall dracaena, bent
solicitously over his chair, like a barber. "Look at that. My
chair will never be the same."

Local taste, all right. In August the nurseries and flower
shops glory, and winter in Florida on the proceeds. Bonnie
Doe, leading all the rest, had once spent thirty thou lining
one of the huge old drink halls at the spa with roses for
Button's birthday, though gently dividing her custom
among all the town's florists, and "not to look snooty,"
serving hamburgers with the champagne.

"She must have had a crew here," he said.

"Who?"

"Rootie. Who else?"

"She usually sends roses."

"Maybe none left."

Strange plagues of want strike the temporarily gilded town—dearths of frozen raspberries that year the hired cooks were all on the same recipe, or of bottled water, or real butter. Meanwhile, a too-obliging liquor store might be left with a load of vintages the winter town will never buy.

"Look down there," he says. "The top of the cistern. They even did that." He trains the flashlight he always brings from the car. "Are those dwarf roses?" The tight-closed buds tremble as if on trial.

She stares at them a long time. "Portulaca. We had them once, at Grayport."

As he lifts her up again, a coral fuchsia brushes his ear like a mouth and he guesses what Rootie must think she has done this for. How would Wheatley have told her? When talking of women, or sometimes to them, he likes to affect the coarse squire. "What do you know"—would he have said?—"that girl of Tot's is in foal."

No matter. Once inside the house she is clearly making the little signs women do when they are going to sleep with you—hair let onto the shoulders or the neck arching it back, a veiling of the eyes. Though she slips into the bedroom to change, he waits here; to her the actions she must go through are not seductive; she will not believe him when he says all women have certain routines they rate as ugly and often wrongly hide. Sometimes, slipping out of a T-shirt under her eyes, he feels guilty of his own body. It has not yet begun to lie to him. Maybe she is silently drawing it in all its easy articulation.

In the small bedroom, really her dressing room and just big enough for a double bed, they sleep instead, by her insistence, on separate, less than twin-width beds, since she may wake at any time for a pain pill, or to do her ever-remedial exercises. At the outset he demanded a double bed; now he no longer pretends he prefers it. The truth is, he needs his sleep. Tonight, though, they are going to stay here in the room which is studio, dining room, and sitting room all in one, as their life is, and they will fall asleep on that broad couch, backed with her books and sewing kit and their tea set, on which, as she has said, they conduct their mental life. Her "they" is kind, ignoring his porch. Living in one or two rooms, as they usually must the rest of the year, and this the largest, they have reticences—nothing to do with sexuality or nudity, or even bathrooms. His comes from having grown up in other people's houses, hers from bundling with sisters who nightly told everything.

He hangs the new cane on one of several hooks near the couch. There are similar hooks near stove and fridge, table, door, and work corner. She uses them as unconsciously as any workman might trip a mechanism in everyday use, translating her cane from hand to hand to wall and back, quicker than the eye. Though he has tried to make the hooks of equal height, a rhythm remains in her progression around the room, one as hard to pin down as which two of a horse's legs are in synchrony—yet when he and she are apart this is the rhythm he visualizes her in, and would, were she to die.

"No, give it here," she says from the couch.

He brings the cane and himself, in a rhythm too.

The cane twirls in her hand, sparks light. "Too pretty to throw away. But I'll try."

He gathers her in his arms, to squeeze her until she cries out, like any normal girl. They kiss, are moving, entwining, like other people. Far back in the mind of each, only a pinpoint, is the fact that they are. When a man must lift a dead limb, must feel the sharp of a hip not all flesh against his own, when a woman cannot turn to tease with breast and buttock—then you do mark it. When a couple cannot twist, roll, jackknife, splay—and fall.

"Good?" he says, yearning into her.

"Love . . . ly."

Is that so because they don't do this too often, so many details having to be right for it?—or because of all the friendship time in between? Would it be even better if they went on more regularly, or tried? Since the beginning they have asked themselves many things. They are grateful she wasn't a virgin when they met; with her as she is, they couldn't have coped with her being a virgin as well. The physical risks, the freakish solutions for it, are seductive enough—even if you would give anything not to have it so. And the comedy—she said. Like riding a bike with one leg, isn't it, for you? The cleanest answer always goes down best with her. And for you, he'd said. "Who knows what a regular couple is? We aren't."

At times he does think of other women, healthy girls you might bat and scrap with, and rowel until they shrieked— and go pinky-linked with to the deli for sandwiches after- ward. And home to do it all over again. As for her, who knows what she thinks?

He does. Wouldn't it be best for you—she'd said early on, to have some other, someone who—you know. He's not smart her way. But he knows when to slap the ones who are. "You want to deny you exist. You want to deny me— the satisfaction I get from it." Her face had stung with plea- sure—that he could slap.

But that was early on. You slap a child to make it breathe, not thinking of all the pain in store for it. He couldn't do it now.

Isn't it enough that both lie there on the old paisley throw that by now has as much mend as pattern? She keeps sewing the holes together as if it's her map of the world— the one they come back to. It's enough that both their faces are wet, no matter who has wept for what.

Sometimes she falls asleep then, which completes his pleasure. He imagines her body for this one night swung in the easy hammock of the norm. Or he will go over his own accounts—mostly that attic treasure for which he wants first safety, then for it to be in sight of the world. Or, pretending that he is doing what others do when they count sheep, he sets himself to sewing a sail.

Once, when she was in the hospital at New Haven, to save money he had lived at Grayport. In order to get away from the house during the day he had apprenticed himself to three elderly brothers who still made sails in a wharf-side loft halfway between. "Ever been to sea?" the senior brother asked, squinting in that airy light.

Though Tot had crewed a few times on the Sound on a friend's Star, the phrase had been of such formality that he'd felt obliged to say no, which appeared to give satisfaction, along with the second brother's verdict: He ain't no hippie. The third brother nodding, they took Tot on for the novelty of it; nobody apprenticed now unless you could rope in a son or nephew, of which they had none.

Sailmakers don't like to give up their secrets. Each of the brothers had been apprenticed by their canny father to a separate firm, and all the long day their rivalry crisscrossed the shop the way the stitching Tot was being taught zig-zagged the pennant of duck he had been given to work on. Even though palm-and-needle was impractical for the small sails they now made, he had to learn it before he was allowed on the machine. Brother Dick, late of Ratsey and Lapham, City Island, had seen sail made by Ratsey of Cowes in which this stitch was inside the edge of the seam only. From Silas, once of Cousens and Pratt, Boston, he'd learned that hemp rope, when stretched, retracts fast, which is helpful in finishing off a cringle in a sail's tack. Have to shrink the thimble in, not hammer it. Ben was the one who knew all the bad stories, of amateurs who tried to sew cotton sail with linen thread, or set a new jib to dry without the sheets attached, so that the slapping of the clew punched holes in it. Ben had been trained in the mur-deress Lizzie Borden's town, Fall River, the two others joked, so his view of life was extra dark.

In Tot's half dream he is sitting at a bench of his own,

bench hook fast to his right-hand end, where are the big pointed wooden spikes called fids. He has already done his laying out. It is his fifth sail and he has managed to get fifty square feet out of seven-and-a-half yards of yacht-grade duck. Even Ben has approved of its outer curve. "For once your roach ain't nigger-heeled."

Tot has chosen oak, faced with brass instead of aluminum—for wherever weight won't count, stainless steel wire over galvanized, and has numbered his cloths, meanwhile borrowing a needle for luck from brother Dick, the kindest. Beeswax and pricker are ready. Once he has finished that sail, his first marketable one, and takes his leave, he will learn the secret of his qualifications, and of their scorn of the modern sailor. None of the three has ever been to sea any nearer than the christening of a sloop. But right now, he is about to begin.

But he can feel her mind burning on beside him. Opening his eyes, he sees hers are wide. Outside, a car door is slammed; somebody at Venezuel's has come home. They listen for his door, which is creaky. How small-scale life here is. Does the fastest mile at the track make up for that? Water and sail—are they really another life? What is?

She sits up, using a hook, her fine hair in damp halo. Does that flower-fume from the porch cool the heat or heighten it? This is the wishbone hour of the night, when perception goes either way, and he trusts most the retinal images which have been on the inner eyelid since childhood.

"Tot. Rootie didn't do up that porch."

"Then who?" He closes his eyes for the answer. That loft, so airy. Sewing the sun to cloth so easy. Float away. Leave even her who is anchored at his side.

"Gargiola. I think he's standing outside."

"Has a right to." Maybe his left foot is a little closer to Venezuel's garbage pail than to ours.

"Outside us."

"Isn't everybody?"

His own echo wakes him. He sits up, unguarded still. What did he just say? "Flowers make me groggy." He snaps his fingers, a falsity he despises in others. "Right. The window." He pads to it.

"He there?"

"He is." Standing in the light of his hired limo. Not many of those up here. They mean New York, or Jersey, and men dressed for business, not lounging toward it, like here. Though by the glare on a white jacket he can see Gargiola must have somewhere along the line changed clothes.

"He looking up here?"

"Might be."

King of the mountain, in a white suit. Gargiola isn't smoking a cigar, but he has that air of self-appreciation a cigar gives. Yet the night makes him look small—even on this lane.

He hears her percuss across the floor, the swish of a dressing gown plucked from the wall. The tiny dice-shaped house has its own sympathetic creaks. She stands beside him at the window.

"Why would he do it?" Tot mutters.

By her sigh, so seldom escaped, he can tell he should know.

"Because of the cat."

He turns on the light.

"Oh, don't. He'll think we think he's a prowler."

"He is. He's stolen your sleep."

Out there Gargiola is looking up, dazed or hopeful. His feet are on his own land—or Venezuel's.

"Now we'll have to ask him in," Nola said.

At their signal Gargiola throws up his hands gaily. He had expected it.

As he enters their door he bends deep, a man not too tall for it but acknowledging he brings in the night, and a life other than theirs.

No, he wants no drink but he'll have a seat. The heat has not blurred him but has maybe softened his voice. Choosing an iron garden seat, cracked, he sits, looking around him. "Nice. Venezuel said. I like a crowded house."

"And porch?"

"Hah?" He catches her smile. "Oh. Oh yeah." He can't pretend not to know her meaning. He doesn't. But he dismisses it.

"But—thanks. Really, thanks."

"You're welcome," Gargiola says broadly. Clearly it was one of the things one does for women, and a gesture gone with the day. "But—listen." He lightly touches Tot's knee. "You have wine, I'll take a glass. I don't whiskey." When the wine comes, he sips, his eyes creasing. "White wine. Very *in,* Pa, my girls say. Oh, Pa, don't drink no more that Dago red."

Those tawny eye-creases hoard shadow. Maybe these two on the couch can sense the held-in resource of a man whose knowledge is wider than grammar. He clinks his glass with both of theirs, "Lissen." His idle hand grasps the chair arm, knuckles high. There are no rings on it. "Lissen, I joined." He leans back, twirling the glass. It is one of the blue ones. Tot, watching that grasp, is not worried. "Phoned my three girls all down Long Island. 'Your pa's joined up.' Gloria, that's my youngest—'What, Pa—the Army?' 'No,' I say, 'I joined a Reading Club.' "

For a second that gets past them. Gargiola has meant it to. The crinkled eyelids expect it, the hand on the chair as well. Then—who knows who starts it?—they all three begin to laugh—and they all know why, though it would take a month of Sundays to say.

When it dies away, Nola says: "You dog."

He and Nola smile at each other like cronies.

"You girls—Gloria said 'You devil.' " Gargiola clicks his tongue for his girls' manners. "Only the boys grew up their mother. So those girls think they're all mine or I'm all theirs, know how it is?"

Of course they do. Tot the fatherless has maybe learned such things best, from those most consistent educators, the long line of house-and-stable underlings—vaqueros from the Argentine, nannies from the Midlands, trainers from Palermo, and Indian-profiled blacks from Saratoga itself—to whose spiritual care he had been left since he was born. The nannies were never his own nor the stables either, and the only help he could lay claim to personally were "the couple"—a terrifying Finnish pair his mother had briefly been able to afford, and the Scottish gardener at the one school where Tot had not been a day boy—and that man only because Tot had picked up from some other servitor what the game of curling was, and would listen to talk of it. Such people like you to be lorn or out of place; it makes them feel safer. Nola, too, had had them, in the people on the peninsula who had cleaned and repaired the old house, sold it eggs, and remembered its ancestral dresses.

Meanwhile you learn from them what your own family will not supply. Generally they adhered to strict churchgoing but did not always go—these nurses who at home had played the pools but here might gamble on something more foolish, these chauffeurs who disapproved of your mother's divorces but lost their jobs because of drink, or light-fingeredness. A low-grade criminality affected them—or their relatives—like an expected disease. Sex might come in any variation but was never described in words. Mothers died early, and the girls did or did not take care of their pa's, or ran off with the boys who had run off early.

It was a code of conduct like any other, leading to the strengths a code can lead to, when like Gargiola, whose nose now lofts proudly, one has done well by it. "So from now on I stay at the Club, I tell them. Now the boys gone home, don't look good your pa bunk with Vennie." He chuckles, easing back in the iron chair. "People might talk."

But his smile, finding a horizon even in this tiny room, is not for that.

"Why?" At times Nola has the cripple's naïveté. It's the constant removal from so much.

"He's gay, Nola."

"Nah, nah," Gargiola's hand fans stiffly, meaning that's not the way to say it. "The girls know him since kids. He was barred from the track that time, he cooked house for us."

"Oh, of course; why didn't I—" She gazes into space with the cartoonist's squint. "He's always munching those liqueur chocolates. And those goons in that orange car, are they that way too?"

Gargiola gives a blurt. "Don't never offer them no chocolates. Anyway, they don't come this way again."

"Yes, I heard," Nola says. "Penalty. What's a penalty, Mr. Gargiola?"

He leans forward to pat. Men on the knee, women on the hand. "Nothing you'll ever have to pay." He stands up. "Thanks. Lose my only horse, get a bid to join the bigs. Been a day."

"You lost a horse?" Tot says.

"You weren't there for the seventh? She broke a leg, had to be put down."

"My God—Straightaway?" Syndicated for three million —and the two-year-old hope of the year. "Straightaway was your horse?"

"Me and two Japs not here. So the trainer gets me down from the stands. And when it's over, who should come by but your uncle Wheatley?"

"Cousin."

"Cousin. Extends me his sympathy, the horse. Insists me back to his box. And by the way, why ain't I a member that Club? So I say, 'Funny, I been tipped off this very day I should be'—and slip him a check then and there, ten times the hunner-dollar membership—Jesus, you guys keep it

piker. And then I say, 'And you won't find me no no-show,
Mr. Wheatley. You kindly tip the steward I'm a member,
I'll stay there this very night.'" Gargiola's eyes, slitted almost closed, opened wide. "He goes that dark shade pork—
he do that regular? He better watch his pressure. Hold the
breath like that, you could pop a vein."

"Oh, he would never say anything," Tot says. "Anything
wrong."

"Not him. Only that Wheatley ain't his last name, he
says. And would I kindly not call the place the Club."

"But what were you doing in the stands?" Nola cries.
"Owning a horse like that."

"I come from there." Gargiola's voice is colorless; it has
given this explanation before. "My old man's dad worked a
track. Goshen. You know Goshen, huh? But he always bet
our money here."

"Why don't your girls come here, take care of you?"

At times Nola has a certain Grayport arrogance herself,
which abashes Tot, but only because he wants people to see
through it to the purity.

Gargiola is not bothered. "They say, 'Pa, build us a
showcase house, buy us a box.' I say"—his head moves side
to side; he has the habit of audience—" 'You're us, you're
smarter you don't buy no box. You do something you get
offered it.'" The head seeks Tot. "What do you say?"

Tot hesitates. "Will you buy more horses?"

"If you say to."

Tot knows that this is so. He shivers. But will you love
them?

"Just say the word."

It could happen. From this small house, spiraling out of
its one-flue chimney, a new syndicate. Meanwhile, the
pliant old framework of this city gives a little, as it always
has, like the plushy sofas of its heyday. That savvy August
calendar, never too discriminating where there's dash and
funds to nudge it, unrolls for Gargiola's girls. Some circles

they'll never get to, of course, never even know about. Except for those, aren't there invitations enough for everybody?

But not enough for this man. Not far enough.

"There's a couple here," Tot says. "Big politico from New York State. Member of the Commission, natch, a box. Stay at the Gideon, though, don't own a house. No horses of their own. After ten years, last year they build one. Right in the district, next door to all the parties. Finish it last June–July, just in time. Give a housewarming. For the hundred fifty people they thought they knew."

"Yeah?" Gargiola says, his face alight. "Yeah, what?"

"Twenty-five came."

"Jesus. A closed shop, huh."

"Not at all." To the end of her life that woman would consider herself done in by the merciless calendar and its hostesses. Or blame it on her being Italian or Jewish or even Democrat, or whatever they happen to be. But the prejudice goes deeper. Or the religion does.

"So, what's the answer?"

Can't the man see? What do the owners talk about in those early-morning trials—will talk about with anybody in their same fix-mix of hard cash and sentiment? A syndicate is one thing, a stable another—and horseflesh a stricter calendar.

"Somebody here run that end, too, huh?" Gargiola whispers.

Tot can only nod.

"Name of?"

Man O'War, Citation, Seattle Slew, Alydar, Affirmed, Secretariat. But not only them, and their kind—with here the white blaze held high as a tiara on some noble head on canvas in the Museum, there the red dapple that was Secretariat even on the day he lost to Onion—each shining without need of studbook, in the eyes of somebody who has an operation of his own going. After them, why, all the pos-

sibles, the no-names or nearly, slogging the Exactas, the
Electas—and always that twenty-to-one dark creature, who
might end up a Triple Crown.

Some owners are more devotional than others. Some are
monstrous people, or ridiculous. A horse doesn't necessarily dignify. Nor do you need to love them at the start, or
even later. Some owners never come to it, only loving the
gamble or what it can get you—a guest list, girls. Whatever
—have to fly your own colors, if you want the full, mul-
ticolored return. Gargiola won't have figured that out yet.
Some of the smartest never do, especially those who will
gamble on anything.

"Pay you twenty thousand for that answer."

Tot stands very still.

"Oh dear"—Nola says—"now he can't answer you, you
stupid man."

Gargiola whitens. "I'm good for it."

"Oh dear, oh dear." She plucks a cane from the wall and
rocks toward him. "I'll give it you for free. Or almost." She
places her hand, the drawing one, on his lapel. She's liking
him but watching him, too—he's a good subject. Drawing
them is understanding them. She always likes them during
it, and sometimes after. "You tell Gloria—" she says, and
Gargiola at once smiles, relaxes. "Tell her—here you build
the barn before you build the house."

Gargiola freezes, head cocked—a man who is learning
something. He is not stupid. "You're—a doll." Quickly, he
kisses her. Poking a mischievous glance at Tot, he steps
back. Behind him, the rickety end table from Rootie's servants' wing falls over. The crash is blue.

Gargiola stares down at the iridescence on the floor. " 'S
late, isn't it? And I've done it. And I'm sorry. Too late." He
gathers up the shards in his handkerchief. "Where can I
replace?" He sees in their faces that he cannot.

"It's all right," Nola says carefully, "I have more." Involuntarily she and Tot glance at the still life on the mantel. All three look at it.

"I heard," Gargiola says huskily, "I heard she paints art."

Tot silently brings him a wastebasket. He drops in the handkerchief, still gazing at the painting. "So you have them. What a girl." He turns to Tot. "And you—you work." It's their turn to stand dumb. He sighs. "I wouldn't offer you no job of mine. All on the level, don't worry. But you wouldn't take it. And she—she'll want that picture. But Venezuel says she does them all day long. So tomorrow, I come around, eh, look at the stock. Pick a couple or more. Any price. Preferred high." He bows. "So, *buono notte.* Good night."

"No," Nola says, turning away. "But thanks."

Again that alarming clench at the man's nostrils. What has that other white-clapboard side of summer here, of Main Liners and Marylanders and Kentuckians, taken to its iron-railinged, one-month-a-year heart? "My girls have lovely dining rooms."

"She doesn't do that," Tot says. "Sell to anyone."

"Never? You swear?"

"Not so far." Tot notes his own feet are in running shoes; when did he do that? "Galleries have asked. And worry not. The price would be high."

The man is surveying the room again. "You two could sure use it."

Tot begins to laugh. "We sure could."

Nola swivels at this betrayal. Lovemaking has made her face supple, though. It could pass again for a bride's.

Gargiola takes no notice of that. He may be one of those men who love regularly, without much regard for the personal. Or equally one of those who love once. He towers over her as if she's a kid. "Why the hell not? You keep them all? Where are they then? . . . Up there? . . . You making an estate your fourteen children, no? Huh." His anger is more than financial. He's assessing her the way an oculist does, with the speculum between his eye and yours, right-left, left-right.

Nola, studying him too, is already drawing him in her mind's eye, maybe paying him for his flowers, or making him pay for them. He won't know which until it's done.

But he knows something—after all, three daughters. He smiles at her, one end of his mouth up. Yes, the women will go for him, the younger ones even, doomed to their pallid or fat-boy specimens. "What's the crap?"

She's studying her stick. The old trusty that takes her between stove and fridge. "Because I can just barely"—it comes out a whisper. "Afford to give."

Or did she say—to live. No, that's his own nightmare, true as it might be.

It's finally cool. Gargiola looks at his watch—almost time for Venezuel to drive in. The air's bestirring itself, getting ready for the push toward razors, and other penalties of the morning. Gargiola looks tired; maybe his own three are not all paragons. "So you keep your foot on your husband's neck, huh? Better you scream."

She is already coming toward him. Dropping the stick to the floor, she has lifted the stoutly framed still life from the mantel and clasped it in front of her, like those men who walk the streets with signs hung on them fore and aft by straps over their shoulders. Tot himself sometimes forgets how strong her forearms are. There are no straps. And there is no cane. He holds his breath. Maybe he will die of it. Leaning on the picture as if it is not in midair and held by herself, she is walking toward that man—not to Tot. Does that make it easier?

Gargiola, across the room from her, doesn't move. He has caught the image.

Hayfoot, strawfoot, she reaches him. "Here."

If the man takes it, will she fall?

He takes it.

Now she will fall forward on him.

She stands.

Tot stands alone, under the shadow of the big easel. It's a peculiar thrill, naked and cool along the backs of the hands, this feeling of separateness. All these years the easel's high triangle has kept this waiting for him. He thinks now of its front side, of jumping up, light as a cat, to poise there, a foot on each of its oaken joints, his head at the peak, hands at his sides. Man on Easel, Alone.

"You knew I wouldn't catch you, missy, didn't you? They always knew when, my kids." Gargiola crosses the room in two strides, picks up her cane. Straightening up, his head bumps the mantel. Rubbing his crown, he sees the picture concealed until now by the other. "What's this one?"

"She gave it to me. One birthday."

People need a minute to decipher it. But only a minute. That's what's wrong with it, she says of the picture now. Cruelty, to be worth anyone's time and study, ought to take longer than that. But when you painted that, you'd never seen the place—he always answers, hoping to let the matter rest. She never will see it, that lovely, shallow spa which for a month hovers never-never, as real as you and me and the postman, over the locals' church suppers and death notices. She wants the deeps.

"Haw. Haw. Haw haw haw." Gargiola laughs with no mouth-stretch, a rumble like a command. "Blow that up a photo-mural, I got just the wall for it. Out Lake Desolation, that old-style nightclub, dates from the early days. We renovating. Got no plans to open yet. See what comes." He says this last with dreamy authority. "We got a new governor." He shrugs. About to hand her the cane, he says: "Or maybe you want that other one on the hook there."

She accepts the old trusty. "Notice everything, don't you."

He regards her, a muscle in one cheek winking. "I was a kid, we had a large family. Healthy but also invalids all ages. Trusses, walkers, crutches. Field-pickers from the old country, have to walk looking their knees. One granddaddy with a stroke, sits all day on a seat with a hole. Two my cousins, TB-ers, headed for the coffin early but meanwhile pretty spry. Nobody in a home. People wear out, you keep them with you. My own mother wore a breast."

At the door he says: "She could paint that wall herself, out Desolation. Any subject she wants, so long it's Saratoga. Fix her a chair with a hoist, no problem. Don't mind offering *her* a job."

He peers back to where Tot is. "Or she could paint my dead horse got shot, to fit on that thing. Human size."

He pats the still life under his arm. "Thanks, I appreciate. But I got two more dining rooms to supply. Nobody takes care me, see? Without I take care them. So I come back tomorrow, after the seventh. And this time—I buy."

He points a finger at Nola. "She don't offer people no leeway. That ain't safe."

Tot is in his favorite summer-night place, on his own roof, his back against his brick chimney, never pointed up since built and not yet needing it, an arm negligently around the much newer turn-of-the century housing for the bathroom vent. Porches, no matter how amiable, are for display. If he falls, it will be onto the mock-orange, and soft turf. It is long before dawn; even the birds have not begun. Nola took a pill, then another one. She sleeps. He can smell the alien note of the gift flowers. The porch is no longer his only, and he is glad. He will nurture that new setup like a father.

After the first pill didn't put her under, Nola said from the other bed: "My father was a gambler, too. Sure he was. Didn't we live for years after he left, on the art he'd collected? He used to send us instructions on what and where to sell next, and for how much. He never lost." Then no more letters came, and they surmised he finally had.

"What'll you sell?"

He has actually said it.

"What did he mean," she says, "that it isn't safe."

"He doesn't like to owe."

"I can understand that. But I go on doing it."

"He"—he lets the long breath ride—"doesn't have to."

After a while she says: "What can he do to us?"

"Squeeze us out."

"He wouldn't!"

"No. Some lawyer."

At this hour the small nesting house is at its best. A lane, a porch—even a swamped one, a door, a couch. And a roof. Even if the title to all this has never been properly searched.

"He has a—kind of dignity," she says. "What he said when he broke those glasses. Like a verdict. I admired that."

"It won't do—to like him. Yet that's part of why one does." Tot feels a certain kinship. That may be just what the cousins say of him.

"Tot—." She is rolling the pill bottle on her bedspread. "I don't give you much leeway. Do I."

When he is unable to deny this, she takes the second pill. Quickly it makes her dreamy, even giggly, as a release from pain can. The pill is not just for sleep.

"I'll invite him for tea," she says. "With the governor's daughter."

"Wrong governor."

"So he is." Her profile is calm but looks its marble age again. He supposes that this alternation will go on recurring. And he will go on noticing.

"Lake Desolation," she says. "What a name for a gambling joint."

"Some priest was martyred there. Indians."

"Tomahawks—" she says. "If you make too much moola off the house." They should laugh at that but don't. "You think he and his crowd could bring gambling back?"

"If he has a crowd. Or—" He won't say it.

She does. "Or if Wheatley's crowd becomes part of it."
Her lids droop. "He's so old-fashioned," she says, slurred.

"Who?" His cousin?

"Gargiola."

"So's Saratoga—or that's its pitch. And he comes from
Goshen."

"Wha-ts—that mean?"

"Trotters. Famous once. But he wants to make his stand
here."

"With the thoroughbreds. And Gloria meeting them . . .
Like to . . . meet Gloria." She is almost asleep. "Hope she
likes . . . picture." Her eyes open, wide.

Now they're coming to it. In their routine, always year
by year the hardest for her to ask and him to answer. Did
she—really get out of the wheelchair, yesterday? Leave that
walker at the Salvation Army? Let the cane drop?

This time he cannot bear it. Because they are coming to
the end of it. "Go back to sleep."

She sits up, hair wild, eyes too. He never saw her at the
time of the accident. Knocked cold, he had been taken to
the hospital before they got her out, only seeing her after
they had knitted her together, months later. Since then he
cherishes her calm, connives for it. If he had seen her at the
worst, would this have been different?

"I don't want to hear," he hears himself say. "I don't
want—"

"I walked, didn't I. I walked, holding the picture. Not an
image. A real canvas, and just carrying. I walked. And then
I stood. Because I had to. What he said was right. Because I
could see he wasn't going to catch me, if I fell."

And you always would. She doesn't say it. It's merely a
fact—the last of them. They have connived as they can.

"August." He says it like a confession.

She gathers up his hands and holds them to her mouth,
pressing deep. "Leeway. I want to. What?"

He might be the one with the pills in him, the answer floats out so easy, past the palisade of jobs he will never get or be dowered with, and the ones he will have to take, if he can get them. Passing it all by. "I want to stay here." Waiting for the horses he wouldn't want to be without, but not following them. Here when his cousins come, but not because of them. "In my own house."

He's never seen her crying. She cries like anybody, blotting at the nose. It occurs to him that with time, passing through the small leeways others allow themselves, he and she may end up like everybody else.

"I'll paint him," she's saying. "I'll paint him three times over. One for each daughter. On that easel. He can buy and buy."

He pats her cheek. "He'll still owe you. But maybe he won't know."

"And the attic—" she says.

"What about the attic?"

Shining like a child giving a present, she snaps her fingers.

She is asleep. "And then I'll paint you—" she says in her sleep. "Over and over. Oh, what a relief it will be. To paint life-size."

On his roof, the warm brick is a poultice at the small of his back. If he could ride again, that ache would disappear. No matter, he's locating himself, and Saratoga too.

It lies between his cousins' big cottages—which should be beleaguered by the times but aren't yet, and all those small, steady merchants of family life television-style, who take over in winter. Northward of it, those Adirondacks lumber away from this shallow-set valley to the Canadian grandeur. On his right hand, a vagueish Vermont, on the best days a cleanly modest mountain line, heavily settled now with what Nola's mother, still sharp-tongued before dinner, calls the young old-timers. College-bred peasants from the decade just before he and Nola were young, some are now selling off the dusty acreage where they grew herbs and handcrafts to the newer dilettante horse farms, which are half tax deductible. Vermont, for all its icicle high-mindedness, is ever a summer state.

Again on his right hand, but back in his own state, are the two river-remains in the vicinity—the Mohawk, with its memories of Jesuits and knitting mills, and the Hudson, a mere stream at Schuylerville. In his Saratoga, these two rivers scarcely bisect the consciousness. No matter, this is his map.

We—are August. To the east and south of him the race-track spreads satisfactorily, coiling its tentacles around Albany and the ship-of-state, bypassing a big city jeweled only with its sister-tracks, from each of which some pure-numbered U.S. highway will lead to Lexington and the Derby, and on to England, Japan, and to all that lesser world which returns here as the yearlings do, every year.

We are in truth our own state. Wars and famines do not enter it, not even for the poor. Childhoods are always big if horses were in them; second childhood flows gently. Chance is a better pursuit than happiness. Where there's only one month to a calendar, all life is in it. Tinsel can pierce with the hurt of steel. And a horse, or a girl, can break a leg at the right time.

Maybe he can get a horse now. No more steps, thousands of them, down and up from porches and long verandahs, struggling across rooms. Down payment might cost no more than a railing. Or he will borrow—a horse only—the kind only Gargiola can afford. He'll pace and canter it, even feed and curry it, until he himself is a character. He will be the cousin who rides.

The heat is still sparkless above the small town he's never had time for. By day two church spires, just yards from each other, dominate. The taller one, in need of repair, deserted by its white congregation for a motel-style sanctuary and rented out now to blacks, may soon go; even the rector of the more prosperous church opposite, hit by a stray shard from that tower, hasn't found himself Christian enough to help. Tot will miss the dawns the two towers make. But Satan can always tempt Saratoga with a new silhouette.

Stretching his arms, he begins to sing from a ditty heard each year in the town's piano bars, ever since he was allowed in. Verses endless, names too. The names come from the old horse nation—Vanderbilt, Phipps, Whitney, or from those late of Hollywood, like "Admiral" Gene Markey, who married three movie stars, and then an heiress, blithely introduced as "Meet forty million dollars," whom he eventually loved the most—or often out of the smellier corners of finance, now grown respectable.

You knock the table, at every owner's name:

> "Oh—
> At the races
> Is still my fav'rite places—
> Though swapping quips with a ——— can be a bore
> And ——— pays up as slow
> As the jitneys she is famous fo-or—"

This year there's even a Watanabe—rhymes with hobby, and the Frenchman Weill, pronounced with gusto as *Veal*. But in order to last, both story and name have to have a certain chime. Meanwhile, with all the tipsters around, no stranger should find it hard to join in.

> "So—
> At the races
> Would surely be God's spot—
> If horses could only talk
> And Wheatleys could trot."

It may take some doing to find Gargiola a rhyme.
Still, who knows? Squint far enough and the whole sky

is a grandstand, spotted with geranium. Stretching wide, he slides down and off, onto the mock-orange bush. He always wanted to.

Pulling himself up, tallying his scratches, he sees Venezuel, just getting out of his Le Car. His jacket glitters with some brand of official epaulet not known to Tot. The track has relented. Or been sweetened.

"Where'd you come from?" he asks Tot.

"Fell off the roof."

"Heh. That's what the women say, when they—you know. Get preg." Venezuel is drunk. His dentures have a foul smell.

"No," Tot says. "When they don't."

"Heh. Been drinking, you, anyway?"

"Some." He thinks of Wheatley and that champagne. "Been up since dawn."

"Heh. Dawn is not yet."

"Yesterday's."

"You seen Gargiola anywhere?"

"Earlier. You working the stables now?"

"Not me. Management."

"Ah good." Low-downs like this poor old boy are everywhere at a track, along with the flies. But in the stables, in that air of liniment and gold dust, the horses are soon to be ministered to. Everything clues in.

"Leaves me a note he's sleeping in town," Venezuel says, "where you suppose?" Hawking up a bit of phlegm, he spits. "That man don't sleep around."

So he's begun his adventure. Long race, Mr. Gargiola, even from where you sleep now. Maybe for luck Venezuel will lend you his antique poker chips.

"Hope he loves horses."

"What the hell does that mean?" Venezuel said.